Prizes

Books by Janet Frame:

The Lagoon and Other Stories (1952) short stories
Owls Do Cry (1957) novel
Faces in the Water (1961) novel
The Edge of the Alphabet (1962) novel
Scented Gardens for the Blind (1963) novel
Snowman Snowman: Fables and Fantasies (1963) short stories
The Reservoir: Stories and Sketches (1963) short stories
The Adaptable Man (1965) novel
A State of Siege (1966) novel
The Reservoir and Other Stories (1966) short stories
The Pocket Mirror (1967) poetry
The Rainbirds (1968) novel (also published as *Yellow
        Flowers in the Antipodean Room*)
Mona Minim and the Smell of the Sun (1969) children's book
Intensive Care (1970) novel
Daughter Buffalo (1972) novel
Living in the Maniototo (1979) novel
To the Is-Land (1982) autobiography
You Are Now Entering the Human Heart (1983) short stories
An Angel at My Table (1984) autobiography
The Envoy from Mirror City (1985) autobiography
The Carpathians (1988) novel
The Goose Bath (2006) poetry
Towards Another Summer (2007) novel

Janet Frame

Prizes

Selected Short Stories

COUNTERPOINT

BERKELEY

Stories in this volume have appeared previously under the imprints of WH Allen, George Braziller, Caxton Press, Pegasus Press, Victoria University Press and The Women's Press, and in the periodicals *Landfall, Mate, New Zealand Listener, New Yorker* and *Vogue*. The previously uncollected stories appeared first as follows: 'Lolly-Legs'— *New Zealand Listener*, 1954; 'Face Downwards in the Grass'—*Mate*, 1957; 'A Boy's Will'—*Landfall*, 1966; 'They Never Looked Back'—*New Zealand Listener*, 1974; 'Two Widowers'—*New Zealand Listener*, 1979.

These stories are fiction and all characters are invented.

© Janet Frame—*The Lagoon and Other Stories*, 1952; *Snowman, Snowman: Fables and Fantasies*, 1963; *The Reservoir: Stories and Sketches*, 1963; *You Are Now Entering the Human Heart*, 1983; previously uncollected stories 1954, 1957, 1966, 1974, 1979.

Library of Congress Cataloging-in-Publication Data

Frame, Janet.
  Prizes : the selected stories of Janet Frame / Janet Frame.
     p. cm.
  ISBN 978-1-58243-515-2
  I. Title.

  PR9639.3.F7P75 2009
  823'.912—dc22

COUNTERPOINT
2117 Fourth Street
Suite D
Berkeley, CA 94710

www.counterpointpress.com

Distributed by Publishers Group West

10 9 8 7 6 5 4 3 2 1

CONTENTS

Foreword

Janet Frame published four volumes of short stories in her lifetime: *The Lagoon and Other Stories* (Caxton 1952), *Snowman Snowman: Fables and Fantasies* (Braziller 1963), *The Reservoir: Stories and Sketches* (Braziller 1963) and *You Are Now Entering the Human Heart* (Victoria University Press 1983). A fifth volume, *The Reservoir and Other Stories* (WH Allen 1966), is sometimes included in the bibliographic count, but this title, which was available only in Commonwealth territories, was actually merely a selection drawn from the two Braziller volumes *The Reservoir* and *Snowman Snowman* that were released only in the United States. Many of Janet Frame's stories first appeared in a variety of publications including the *New Zealand Listener*, *Landfall*, the *New Yorker* and *Harper's Bazaar*. Some of these stories were never included by Frame in a story collection and still await inclusion in a retrospective volume.

The core of the present selection is the choice of 24 short stories Janet Frame herself made for the 1983 anthology *You Are Now Entering the Human Heart*. All of the stories in that volume appear here, with the exception of the 74-page novella 'Snowman Snowman'. The omission of the longer piece has allowed room to incorporate 18 more stories. Most of these are from Frame's earlier collections, but several taken from *Snowman Snowman* and *The Reservoir* will be unknown to most New Zealand readers. We have also added five stories not previously included in books, in order to round out a comprehensive selection from all Frame's published stories.

Any 'best of' selection is by definition a subjective enterprise, and no doubt there will be some disappointment felt by connoisseurs of particular stories that are not reprinted here. However since more than half of the stories in *Prizes* have appeared in numerous literary and educational anthologies around the world, and many have been translated and adapted for radio or live performance, we are confident that this updated and expanded selection of Janet Frame's published stories will be a valued and satisfying resource for new and old admirers of her work.

Pamela Gordon
Chair
Janet Frame Literary Trust

From

The Lagoon and Other Stories

The Lagoon

At low tide the water is sucked back into the harbour and there is no lagoon, only a stretch of dirty grey sand shaded with dark pools of sea-water where you may find a baby octopus if you are lucky, or the spotted orange old house of a crab or the drowned wreckage of a child's toy boat. There is a bridge over the lagoon where you may look down into the little pools and see your image tangled up with sea-water and rushes and bits of cloud. And sometimes at night there is an under-water moon, dim and secret.

All this my grandmother told me, my Picton grandmother who could cut supple-jack and find kidney fern and make a track through the thickest part of the bush. When my grandmother died all the Maoris at the Pa came to her funeral, for she was a friend of the Maoris, and her mother had been a Maori princess, very beautiful they said, with fierce ways of loving and hating.

See the lagoon, my grandmother would say. The dirty lagoon, full of drifting wood and seaweed and crabs' claws. It is dirty and sandy and smelly in summer. I remember we used to skim round white stones over the water, and catch tiddlers in the little creek near by, and make sand castles on the edge, this is my castle we said, you be father I'll be mother and we'll live here and catch crabs and tiddlers for ever.

I liked my grandmother to talk about the lagoon. And when we went for a holiday to Picton where Grandma lived I used to say Grandma tell me a story. About the Maori Pa. About the old man who lived down the Sounds and had a goat and a cow for friends. About the lagoon.

And my grandmother would tell me stories of the Sounds and the Pa and herself when she was young. Being a girl and going out to work in the rich people's houses. But the lagoon never had a proper story, or if it had a proper story my grandmother never told me.

See the water she would say. Full of seaweed and crabs' claws. But I knew that wasn't the real story and I didn't find out the real story till I was grown up and Grandma had died and most of the old Maoris were gone from the Pa, and the old man and the cow and the goat were forgotten.

I went for a holiday in Picton. It was a long journey by train and I was glad at the end of it to see the green and blue town that I remembered from childhood, though it was smaller of course and the trees had shrunk and the hills were tiny.

I stayed with an aunt and uncle. I went for launch rides round the harbour and I went for picnics with summery people in floral frocks and sun hats, and kids in print frocks, or khaki shorts if they were boys, especially if they were boys with fathers in the army. We took baskets with fruit and sandwiches, not tomato for tomato goes damp though some like it damp, and threepences in the pocket for ice-creams. There were races for the kiddies and some for the men and women, and afterwards a man walked round the grounds throwing lollies in the air. They were great days out picnicking in the Sounds with the Maoris singing and playing their ukeleles, but they didn't sing the real Maori songs, they sang You are my sunshine and South of the Border. And then it got dark and the couples came back from the trees and the launches were got ready and everybody went back singing, with the babies crying because they were tired and sunburnt and bitten by sandflies. Sandflies are the devil everybody said, but they were great days for the kiddies.

Perhaps I liked the new Picton, I don't know. If there were things I hadn't noticed before there were also things gone that I thought would be there for ever. The two gum trees that I called the two ladies were gone or if they were there I couldn't find them, and the track over the Domain Hill wasn't there. We used to climb up and watch the steamer coming in from the straits. And there was gorse mixed up with the bush, and the bush itself didn't hold the same fear, even with its secret terrible drippings and rustlings that go on for ever.

There were more people in the town too. The Main Trunk Line brings more tourists, my aunt said. There were people everywhere, lying on the beach being burned or browned by the sun and sea, people whizzing round the harbour in motor-boats like the pop-pop boats we used to whizz round in the bath on Christmas morning. People surf-riding, playing tennis, fishing in the straits, practising in skiffs for the Regatta. People.

But my grandmother wasn't there to show me everything and tell me stories. And the lagoon was dirtier than ever. See the lagoon said my aunt. Full of drifting wood and seaweed and crabs' claws. We could see the lagoon from the kitchen window. We were looking at photographs that day, what silly clothes people wore in those days. There was Grandma sitting on the verandah with her knitting, and there was my great grandmother, the Maori princess with her big brown eyes, and her lace dress on that her husband bought her, handmade lace said my aunt, he loved her till he met that woman from Nelson, men are crazy sometimes, but I suppose women are crazier.

'Is there a story,' I said. I was a child again, Grandma tell me about . . .

My aunt smiled. She guesses things sometimes.

'The sort of story they put in *Truth*,' she said. 'On the morning of the tragedy witness saw defendant etc. etc. Your great grandmother was a murderess. She drowned her husband, pushed him in the lagoon. I suppose the tide was high, I don't know. They would call it The Woman From Nelson . . .' she mused. 'They would have photos. But then nobody knew, only the family. Everybody thought he had had one over the eight and didn't know where he was going.'

My aunt drew aside the curtain and peered out. She reminded me of the women in films who turn to the window in an emotional moment, but the moment wasn't emotional nor was my aunt.

'It's an interesting story,' she said. I prefer Dostoevsky to *Truth*.

The water was brown and shining and to the right lay the dark shadow of the Domain Hill. There were kids playing on the edge, Christopher Robins with sand between the toes, sailing toy warships and paddling with bare feet in the pools.

'Grandmother never told me,' I said.

Again my aunt smiled. 'The reason' (she quoted) 'one talks farthest from the heart is the fear that it may be hurt.'

And then my aunt dropped the curtain across the window and turned to the photographs again.

Was it my aunt speaking or was it my grandmother or my great grandmother who loved a white lace dress?

At low tide there is no lagoon. Only a stretch of dirty grey sand. I remember we used to skim thin white stones over the water and catch tiddlers in the little creek near by and make sand castles, this is my castle we said you be father I'll be mother and we'll live here and catch crabs and tiddlers for ever . . .

Keel and Kool

Father shook the bidi-bids off the big red and grey rug and then he spread it out again in the grass.

'There you are,' he said. 'Mother here, and Winnie here, and Joan you stay beside Winnie. We'll put the biscuit tin out of the way so it won't come into the photo. Now say cheese.'

He stepped back and cupped his hand over the front of the camera, and then he looked over his shoulder — 'to see if the sun's looking too', he told the children who were saying cheese. And then he clicked the shiny thing at the side of the camera.

'There you are,' he said. 'It's taken. A happy family.'

'Oh,' said Mother. 'Were we all right? Because I want to show the photo to Elsie. It's the first we've taken since Eva — went.'

Mother always said went or passed away or passed beyond when she talked of death. As if it were not death really, only pretend.

'We were good weren't we Dad,' said Winnie. 'And now are you going fishing?'

'Yes,' said Father. 'I'm going fishing. I'll put this in a safe place and then I'm off up the river for salmon.'

He carried the camera over to where the coats were piled, and he stowed it in one of the bags carefully, for photos were precious things.

And then he stooped and fastened the top strap of his gumboots to his belt.

'Cheerio,' he said, kissing Mother. He always kissed everyone when he went away anywhere, even for a little while. And then he kissed Winnie and pulled her hair, and he pulled Joan's hair too but he didn't kiss her because she was the girl over the road and no relation.

'I'll come back with a salmon or I'll go butcher's hook.'

They watched him walking towards the river, a funny clumpy walk because he had his gumboots on. He was leaning to one side, with his right shoulder lower than his left, as if he were trying to dodge a blow that might come from the sky or the trees or the air. They watched him going and going, like someone on the films, who grows smaller and smaller and then The End is printed across the screen, and music plays and the lights go up. He was like a man in a story walking away from them. Winnie hoped he wouldn't go too far away because the river was deep and wild and made a roaring noise that could be heard even above the willow trees and pine trees. It was the greyest river Winnie had ever seen. And the sky was grey too with a tiny dot of sun. The grey of the sky seemed to swim into the grey of the river.

Then Father turned and waved.

Winnie and Joan waved back.

'And now we're going to play by the pine tree Mrs Todd, aren't we Winnie,' said Joan.

We'll play ladies,' said Winnie.

Mother sighed. The children were such happy little things. They didn't realise . . .

'All right kiddies,' she said. 'You can run away and play. Don't go near the river and mind the stinging nettle.'

Then she opened her *Woman's Weekly* and put it on her knee. She knew that she would read only as far as Over the Teacups and then she would think all over again about Eva passing away, her first baby. A sad blow, people said, to lose your first, just when she was growing up to be a help to you. But it's all for the best and you have Wonderful Faith Mrs Todd, she's happier in another sphere, you wouldn't have wished it otherwise, and you've got her photo, it's always nice to have their photos. Bear up Mrs Todd.

Mrs Todd shut her eyes and tried to forget and then she started to read Over the Teacups. It was better to forget and not think about it.

Winnie and Joan raced each other through the grass to the pine tree by the fence, Joan's dark hair bobbing up and down and getting in her eyes. 'Bother,' she said. Winnie stared enviously. She wished her own hair was long enough to hang over her eyes and be brushed away. How nice to say bother, and brush your hair out of your eyes. Eva's hair had been long. It was so funny about Eva, and the flowers and telegrams and Auntie May coming and bringing sugar buns and custard squares. It was so funny at home with Eva's dresses hanging up and her shoes under the wardrobe and no Eva to wear them, and the yellow quilt spread unruffled over her bed, and staying unruffled all night. But it was good wearing Eva's blue pyjamas. They had pink round the bottom of the legs and pink round the neck and sleeves. Winnie liked to walk round the bedroom in them and see herself in the mirror and then get into bed and yawn, stretching her arms above her head like a lady. But it would have been better if Eva were there to see.

And what fun if Eva were there at the picnic!

'Come on,' said Joan. 'We'll play ladies in fur coats. I know because my mother's got a fur coat.'

'I'm a lady going to bed,' said Winnie. 'I'm wearing some beautiful blue pyjamas and I'm yawning, and my maid's just brought my coffee to me.' She lay under the pine tree. She could smell the pine and hear the hush-hush of its branches and beyond that the rainy sound of the river, and see the shrivelled-up cones like little brown claws, and the grey sky like a tent with the wind blowing under it and puffing it out. And there was Joan walking up and down in her fur coat, and smiling at all the ladies and gentlemen and saying oh no, I've got heaps of fur coats. Bother, my hair does get in my eyes so.

Joan had been Eva's best friend. She was so beautiful. She was Spanish she said, a little bit anyway. She had secrets with Eva. They used to whisper together and giggle and talk in code.

'I'm tired of wearing my fur coat,' said Joan, suddenly. 'And you can't go on yawning for ever.'

'I can go on yawning for ever if I like,' said Winnie, remembering the giggles and the secrets and the code she couldn't understand. And she yawned and said thank you to the maid for her coffee. And then she yawned again.

'I can do what I like,' she said.

'You can't always,' said Joan. 'Your mother wouldn't let you. Anyway I'm tired of wearing my fur coat, I want to make something.'

She turned her back on Winnie and sat down in the grass away from the pine tree, and began to pick stalks of feathery grass. Winnie stopped yawning. She heard the rainy-wind sound of the river and she wondered where her father was. And what was Mother doing? And what was Joan making with the feathery grass?

'What are you making, Joan?'

'I'm making Christmas trees,' answered Joan graciously. 'Eva showed me. Didn't Eva show you?'

And she held up a Christmas tree.

'Yes,' lied Winnie, 'Eva showed me Christmas trees.'

She stared at the tiny tree in Joan's hand. The grass was wet with last night's dew and the tree sparkled, catching the tiny drop of sunlight that fell from the high grey and white air. It was like a fairy tree or like the song they sang at school — Little fir tree neat and green. Winnie had never seen such a lovely thing to make.

'And Eva showed me some new bits to Tinker Tailor,' said Joan, biting off a piece of grass with her teeth. 'Boots, shoes, slippers, clodhoppers, silk, satin, cotton, rags — it's what you're married in.'

'She showed me too,' lied Winnie. 'Eva showed me lots of things.'

'She showed me things too,' said Joan tenaciously.

Winnie didn't say anything to that. She looked up in the sky and watched a seagull flying over. I'm Keel, I'm Keel it seemed to say. Come home Kool come home Kool. Keel Keel. Winnie felt lonely staring up into the sky. Why was the pine tree so big and dark and old? Why was the seagull crying out I'm Keel I'm Keel as if it were calling for somebody who wouldn't come. Keel Keel, come home Kool, come home Kool it cried.

Winnie wished her mother would call out to them. She wished her father were back from the river, and they were all sitting on the rug, drinking billy tea and eating water biscuits that crackled in your mouth. She wished Joan were away and there were just Father and Mother and Winnie, and no Joan. She wished she had long hair and could make Christmas trees out of feathery grass. She wished she knew more bits to Tinker Tailor. What was it Joan had said? 'Boots shoes slippers clodhoppers.' Why hadn't Eva told her?

'You're going to sleep,' said Joan suddenly. 'I've made three Christmas trees. Look.'

'I'm not going to sleep. I'm hungry,' said Winnie. 'And I think Joan Mason that some people tell lies.'

Joan flushed. 'I *have* made three Christmas trees.'

'It's not that,' said Winnie, taking up a pine needle and making pine-needle writing in the air.

'I just think that some people tell lies.'

'But I'm not a liar, Winnie,' protested Joan anxiously. 'I'm not honestly.'

'Some people,' Winnie murmured, writing with her pine needle.

'You're not fair Winnie Todd,' quivered Joan throwing down her Christmas trees. I know you mean me.'

'Nobody said I did. I just said — some people.'

'Well you looked at me.'

'Did I?'

Winnie crushed her pine needle and smelt it. She wanted to cry. She wished she had never come for a picnic. She was cold too with just her print dress on. She wished she were somewhere far far away from the river and the pine tree and Joan Mason and the Christmas trees, somewhere far far away, she didn't know where.

Perhaps there was no place. Perhaps she would never find anywhere to go. Her mother would die and her father would die and Joan Mason would go on flicking the hair from her eyes and saying bother and wearing her fur coat and not knowing what it was like to have a mother and father dead.

'Yes,' said Winnie. 'You're a liar. Eva told me things about you. Your uncle was eaten by cannibals and your father shot an albatross and had a curse put on him and your hair went green when you went for a swim in Christchurch and you had to be fed on pineapple for three weeks before it turned black again. Eva told me. You're a liar. She didn't believe you either. And take your Christmas trees.' She picked up one of the trees and tore it to pieces.

Joan started to cry.

'Cry baby, liar, so there.'

Winnie reached forward and gave Joan a push, and then she turned to the pine tree and catching hold of the lowest branches, she pulled herself up into the tree. Soon she was over halfway up. The branches rocked up and down, sighing and sighing. Winnie peered down on to the ground and saw Joan running away through the grass, her hair bobbing up and down as she ran. She would be going back to where Winnie's mother was. Perhaps she would tell. Winnie pushed me over and called me names. And then when Winnie got down from the tree and went to join the others her mother would look at her with a hurt expression in her eyes and say blessed are the peacemakers. And her father would be sitting there telling them all about the salmon, but he would stop when she came up, hours and hours later, and say sternly I hoped you would behave yourself. And then he would look at Mother, and Winnie would know they were thinking of Eva and the flowers and telegrams and Auntie May saying bear up, you have Wonderful Faith. And then Mother would say have one of these chocolate biscuits, Joan. And Mother and Father and Joan would be together, sharing things.

Winnie's eyes filled with tears of pity for herself. She wished Eva were there. They would both sit up the pine tree with their hands clutching hold of the sticky branches, and they would ride up and down, like two birds on the waves, and then they would turn into princesses and sleep at night in blue pyjamas with pink round the edges, and in the daytime they would make Christmas trees out of feathery grass and play Tinker Tailor — boots, shoes, slippers, clodhoppers.

'Boots, shoes, slippers, clodhoppers,' whispered Winnie. But there was no one to answer her. Only up in the sky there was a seagull as white as chalk, circling and crying Keel Keel Come home Kool, come home Kool. And Kool would never come, ever.

My Cousins Who Could Eat Cooked Turnips

For a long time I could never understand my cousins in Invercargill. They were good children, Dot and Mavis, they folded up their clothes before they went to bed at night, and they put their garters on the door-knob where they could find them in the morning, and they didn't often poke a face at their father when he wasn't looking.

They had a swing round the back of the house. They let us have turns on it, waiting respectfully at the side, and not saying your turn's over you're only trying to make it last, only one more swing and then it's ours. No. They waited respectfully.

They had a nice trellis-work too, with dunny roses growing up it, you could almost touch the roses if you were swinging high enough. Their mother was our Auntie Dot and their father was Uncle Ted, who was a captain and wore Khaki, and sat at the head of the table, and said sternly eat what you're given, what about the starving children in Europe.

There were always children starving in Europe. Sometimes people came to school, thin women with pamphlets, and told us about Europe, and then after the talk we put our names down for a society where we went and sat on a long form and had a feast once a term.

Actually I didn't think my cousins were of the same family as us, they couldn't have been I thought. They were very clean and quiet and they spoke up when visitors came to their house, aunts and uncles I mean, and they didn't say dirty words or rhymes. They were Cultured.

But for a long time I could never understand them, for instance they could eat cooked turnip.

Now where we lived there were turnips in the garden, some for the cow and some for us. We used to go into the garden, pull up a turnip, wash it under the garden tap and then eat the turnip raw.

But if it came cooked on the table, even at Auntie Dot's, we said no.

At home Dad would say eat your turnip. Nancy eat your turnip. Billy eat your turnip, you too Elsie.

'But we don't like it cooked.'

'Do as I say, eat your turnip.'

Well what could we do in the face of such grim coercion? But we didn't eat it all, and we didn't like it, it didn't seem to have the good earthy taste raw turnip had, and we weren't eating it outside down the garden with the cow looking approval over the fence and the birds singing in the orchard and people hammering and dogs barking and everything being alive and natural uncooked.

It was different inside, the hot room and the chairs drawn up to the table and everybody quiet as if something important and dreadful were about to happen, like a ghost or the end of the world, and my father sitting at the top with his knife and fork held the proper way and his eyes saying elbows off the table.

eat your turnip eat your turnip

No we just couldn't manage to like cooked turnip that way.

And then one week-end we went to Auntie Dot's. We had new fancy garters and new fleecy-lined nighties and we travelled first class on the train because Dad was on the railway and had a free ticket. Auntie Dot met us at the station, and how *are* you all, I got your letter Mona, little Elsie's shooting up isn't she, yes they're so shy at that age, where's Mavis come on Mavis. Auntie Dot was big, with smothering brown eyes and hair. She wore shoes like baskets and a hat with a cherry in front, that bobbed whenever she moved her head, a little for Auntie Dot, here's your cherry Auntie Dot, I've picked the dust off it, I meant to tell you it was loose, thank you child you're a credit to your mother, I hadn't noticed it had fallen.

Uncle Ted drove us home in the car, Mavis and Dot and Elsie and Billy and I in the back and the others in the front. Nobody talked in the back, we didn't ever talk to our cousins. Mavis had on a pink frilly dress with a cape collar and Dot had on a pink frilly dress with a cape collar, and both together the girls looked like lollies, and when they turned to us and smiled shy smiles, they looked like little pink lollies waiting to be licked. Mavis and Dot had lace too. I could see it round their petticoats, and I knew they had fancy garters, and remembered to myself what my mother had said to us

be sure you hang your garters on the door-knob

be sure you fold your nighties

be sure you say can I help with the dishes

and do eat your turnip this time.

When we got to the house with its swing and its clothesline that twirled round and round, and its dunny roses on the trellis-work, we wanted to go home. Each time we came to Auntie Dot's we were visitors to an alien world. Auntie Dot's kitchen smelt like seed-cake and leather. There was a clock with a different kind of ticking on the mantelpiece and when the hour struck, a little bird popped out to say hello, it was all so sad and strange, the seed-cake and the little bird and the teapot with a knitted cosy, and the green gnome sitting on the sideboard, and our mother far away and high up, talking about things we didn't understand. And then going out on to the lawn and standing with our arms hanging as if they didn't belong, staring about us at the swing and the clothesline that twirled round and round, and the different kinds of flowers in the garden. And then coming inside to tea and seeing the table all white and ready, and hearing the grownups talking again, really is that so just fancy they were saying importantly and deliciously, but it seemed sad too, really is that so just fancy, over and over again, and it got sadder when we sat down to tea and saw the turnip.

Cooked turnip. Vitamins said Uncle Ted. Roughage.

(really is that so just fancy)

For a long time I could never understand my cousins. That night they sat there in cold blood, eating cooked turnip. Perhaps it was our new nighties, perhaps it was the swing, perhaps it was the little bird that popped out to say hello, but I looked at Billy and Elsie, and Billy and Elsie looked at me, and that night we sat there too, in cold blood, eating cooked turnip.

And then we understood. And after tea I said to Mavis I've got a new nightie, it's fleecy-lined, we put our fancy garters on the door-knob when we go to bed, we've got a cow at home. Our clothesline isn't like yours it doesn't go round and round. I don't suppose you know what this word means, and I whispered a word in her ear, and Mavis said I do too. I know lots of words.

Mavis and I were very good friends. In the morning we got up and played on the swing, and my mother looked out of the window and laughed and waved to me, and she didn't seem far away any more, and everything was all right again. And we played house together, Mavis and I, and we drank tea out of little china cups, and we said really is that so just fancy, and we swung, all day we swung as high as the dunny roses.

Dossy

Only on the shadows, sang out Dossy, and the little girls with straight fair hair sang out answering, only on the shadows, and the two of them went hopping and skipping very carefully for three blocks, and then they got tired, and they forgot, and they stopped to pick marigolds through the crack in the corner fence, but only Dossy could reach them because she was bigger. Pick me a marigold, Dossy, to put in my hair, said the little girl and Dossy picked a big yellow flower and she had to bend down to stick it in the little girl's hair.

'Race you to the convent gate,' she said, and together the two of them tore along the footpath and Dossy won, Dossy won easily.

'I'm bigger,' she said.

And the little girl looked up at Dossy's bigness and supposed that Dossy must live in a big house to match. Everything matched thought the little girl. Mother and Father. Mother singing and Father singing. Mother washing the dishes and Father drying. Mother in her blue dress and Father in his black suit.

And when you were small you did things that small people did, Grandma said, and when you were big like Dossy you did things the grownup way. And the little girl thought that Dossy must live in a big house to match her bigness. A big house at the end of a long long street. With a garden. And a plum tree. And a piano in the front room. And a piano-stool to go round and round on. And lollies in a blue tin on the mantelpiece for Father to reach up to and say have a striped one, chicken, they last longer.

The little girl put her hand in Dossy's and said Can I come to live with you, Dossy. Can I live in your house.

And Dossy looked down at the little girl with her shiny new shoes on and her neat blue dress and her thick hair-ribbon, and then she looked down at her own dirty shoes and turned up dress from her aunties, and she drew away her hand that was dirty and sticky with marigolds and said nothing, but went over to the fence to peep through at the nuns. The little girl followed her and together they looked through at the nuns. They watched them walking up and down with their hands folded in front and their eyes staring straight ahead, and the little girl thought I'll be a nun some day and wear black and white and have a black and white nightie, and I'll pray all day and sit under the plum tree and perhaps God won't mind if I get hungry and eat two or three plums, and every night I'll comb out my mother's long golden hair with a gold comb and I'll have a black and white bed.

Dossy, said the little girl, will you be a nun with me?

Dossy giggled and giggled. I don't think, she said.

The nuns heard someone laughing and they stopped at the gate to see who it was. They saw a little girl playing ball by herself on the footpath.

It's little Dossy Park, they said. With no mother and living in that poky little house in Hart Street and playing by herself all the time, goodness knows what she'll turn out to be.

Swans

They were ready to go. Mother and Fay and Totty, standing by the gate in their next best to Sunday best, Mother with her straw hat on with shells on it and Fay with her check dress that Mother had made and Totty, well where was Totty a moment ago she was here?

'Totty,' Mother called. 'If you don't hurry we'll miss the train, it leaves in ten minutes. And we're not to forget to get off at Beach Street. At least I think Dad said Beach Street. But hurry Totty.'

Totty came running from the wash-house round the back.

'Mum quick I've found Gypsy and her head's down like all the other cats and she's dying I think. She's in the wash-house. Mum quick,' she cried urgently.

Mother looked flurried. 'Hurry up, Totty and come back Fay, pussy will be all right. We'll give her some milk now there's some in the pot and we'll wrap her in a piece of blanket and she'll be all right till we get home.'

The three of them hurried back to the wash-house. It was dark with no light except what came through the small square window which had been cracked and pasted over with brown paper. The cat lay on a pile of sacks in a corner near the copper. Her head was down and her eyes were bright with a fever or poison or something but she was alive. They found an old clean tin lid and poured warm milk in it and from one of the shelves they pulled a dusty piece of blanket. The folds stuck to one another all green and hairy and a slater with hills and valleys on his back fell to the floor and moved slowly along the cracked concrete floor to a little secret place by the wall. Totty even forgot to collect him. She collected things, slaters and earwigs and spiders though you had to be careful with earwigs for when you were lying in the grass asleep they crept into your ear and built their nest there and you had to go to the doctor and have your ear lanced.

They covered Gypsy and each one patted her. Don't worry Gypsy they said. We'll be back to look after you tonight. We're going to the Beach now. Goodbye Gypsy.

And there was Mother waiting impatiently again at the gate.

'Do hurry. Pussy'll be all right now.'

Mother always said things would be all right, cats and birds and people even as if she knew and she did know too, Mother knew always.

But Fay crept back once more to look inside the wash-house.

'I promise,' she called to the cat. 'We'll be back, just you see.'

And the next moment the three Mother and Fay and Totty were outside the gate and Mother with a broom-like motion of her arms was sweeping the two little girls before her.

O the train and the coloured pictures on the station, South America and Australia, and the bottle of fizzy drink that you could only half finish because you were too full, and the ham sandwiches that curled up at the edges, because they were stale, Dad said, and he *knew*, and the rabbits and cows and bulls outside in the paddocks, and the sheep running away from the noise and the houses that came and went like a dream, clackety-clack, Kaitangata, Kaitangata, and the train stopping and panting and the man with the stick tapping the wheels and the huge rubber hose to give the engine a drink, and the voices of the people in the carriage on and on and waiting.

'Don't forget Beach Street, Mum,' Dad had said. Dad was away at work up at six o'clock early and couldn't come. It was strange without him for he always managed. He got the tea and the fizzy drinks and the sandwiches and he knew which station was which and where and why and how, but Mother didn't. Mother was often too late for the fizzy drinks and she coughed before she spoke to the children and then in a whisper in case the people in the carriage should hear and think things, and she said I'm sure I don't know kiddies when they asked about the station, but she was big and warm and knew about cats and little ring-eyes, and Father was hard and bony and his face prickled when he kissed you.

O look the beach coming it must be coming.

The train stopped with a jerk and a cloud of smoke as if it had died and finished and would never go anywhere else just stay by the sea though you couldn't see the water from here, and the carriages would be empty and slowly rusting as if the people in them had come to an end and could never go back as if they had found what they were looking for after years and years of travelling on and on. But they were disturbed and peeved at being forced to move. The taste of smoke lingered in their mouths, they had to reach up for hat and coat and case, and comb their hair and make up their face again, certainly they had arrived but you have to be neat arriving with your shoes brushed and your hair in place and the shine off your nose. Fay and Totty watched the little cases being snipped open and shut and the two little girls knew for sure that never would they grow up and be people in bulgy dresses, people knitting purl and plain with the ball of wool hanging safe and clean from a neat brown bag with hollyhocks and poppies on it. Hollyhocks and poppies and a big red initial, to show that you were you and not the somebody else you feared you might be, but Fay and Totty didn't worry they were going to the Beach.

The Beach. Why wasn't everyone going to the Beach? It seemed they were the only ones for when they set off down the fir-bordered road that led to the sound the sea kept making forever now in their ears, there was no one else going. Where had the others gone? Why weren't there other people?

'Why Mum?'

'It's a week-day chicken,' said Mum smiling and fat now the rushing was over. 'The others have gone to work I suppose. I don't know. But here we are. Tired?' She looked at them both in the way they loved, the way she looked at them at night at other people's places when they were weary of cousins and hide the thimble and wanted to go home to bed. Tired? she would say. And Fay and Totty would yawn as if nothing in the world would keep them awake and Mother would say knowingly and fondly The dustman's coming to someone. But no they weren't tired now for it was day and the sun though a watery sad sun was up and the birds, the day was for waking in and the night was for sleeping in.

They raced on ahead of Mother eager to turn the desolate crying sound of sea to the more comforting and near sight of long green and white waves coming and going forever on the sand. They had never been here before, not to this sea. They had been to other seas, near merry-go-rounds and swings and slides, among people, other girls and boys and mothers, mine are so fond of the water the mothers would say, talking about mine and yours and he, that meant Father, or the old man if they did not much care but Mother cared always.

The road was stony and the little girls carrying the

basket had skiffed toes by the time they came to the
end, but it was all fun and yet strange for they were by
themselves no other families and Fay thought for a moment
what if there is no sea either and no nothing?

But the sea roared in their ears it was true sea, look it
was breaking white on the sand and the seagulls crying
and skimming and the bits of white flying and look at all
of the coloured shells, look a little pink one like a fan, and
a cat's eye. Gypsy. And look at the seaweed look I've found
a round piece that plops, you tread on it and it plops, you
plop this one, see it plops, and the little girls running up
and down plopping and plopping and picking and prying
and touching and listening, and Mother plopping the
seaweed too, look Mum's doing it and Mum's got a crab.

But it cannot go on for ever.

'Where is the place to put our things and the merry-
go-rounds and the place to undress and that, and the place
to get ice-creams?'

There's no place, only a little shed with forms that have
bird-dirt on them and old pieces of newspapers stuffed in
the corner and writing on the walls, rude writing.

'Mum, have we come to the wrong sea?'

Mother looked bewildered. 'I don't know kiddies, I'm
sure.'

'Is it the wrong sea?' Totty took up the cry.

It was the wrong sea. 'Yes kiddies,' Mother said, 'now
that's strange I'm sure I remembered what your father told
me but I couldn't have but I'm sure I remembered. Isn't
it funny. I didn't know it would be like this. Oh things
are never like you think they're different and sad. I don't
know.'

'Look, I've found the biggest plop of all,' cried Fay who
had wandered away intent on plopping. 'The biggest plop
of all,' she repeated, justifying things. 'Come on.'

So it was all right really it was a good sea, you could pick up the foam before it turned yellow and take off your shoes and sink your feet down in the wet sand almost until you might disappear and come up in Spain, that was where you came up if you sank. And there was the little shed to eat in and behind the rushes to undress but you couldn't go in swimming.

'Not in this sea,' Mother said firmly.

They felt proud. It was a distinguished sea oh and a lovely one noisy in your ears and green and blue and brown where the seaweed floated. Whales? Sharks? Seals? It was the right kind of sea.

All day on the sand, racing and jumping and turning head over heels and finding shells galore and making castles and getting buried and unburied, going dead and coming alive like the people in the Bible. And eating in the little shed for the sky had clouded over and a cold wind had come shaking the heads of the fir trees as if to say I'll teach you, springing them backwards and forwards in a devilish exercise.

Tomatoes, and a fire blowing in your face. The smoke burst out and you wished. Aladdin and the genie. What did you wish?

I wish today is always but Father too jumping us up and down on his knee. This is the maiden all forlorn that milked the cow.

'Totty, it's my turn, isn't it Dad?'

'It's both of your turns. Come on, sacks on the mill and *more on still.*' Not Father away at work but Father here making the fire and breaking sticks, quickly and surely, and Father showing this and that and telling why. Why? Did anyone in the world ever know why? Or did they just pretend to know because they didn't like anyone else to know that they didn't know? Why?

They were going home when they saw the swans. 'We'll go this quicker way,' said Mother, who had been exploring. 'We'll walk across the lagoon over this strip of land and soon we'll be at the station and then home to bed.' She smiled and put her arms round them both. Everything was warm and secure and near, and the darker the world outside got the safer you felt for there were Mother and Father always, for ever.

They began to walk across the lagoon. It was growing dark now quickly and dark sneaks in. Oh home in the train with the guard lighting the lamps and the shiny slippery seat growing hard and your eyes scarcely able to keep open, the sea in your ears, and your little bagful of shells dropped somewhere down the back of the seat, crushed and sandy and wet, and your baby crab dead and salty and stiff fallen on the floor.

'We'll soon be home,' Mother said, and was silent.

It was dark black water, secret, and the air was filled with murmurings and rustlings, it was as if they were walking into another world that had been kept secret from everyone and now they had found it. The darkness lay massed across the water and over to the east, thick as if you could touch it, soon it would swell and fill the earth.

The children didn't speak now, they were tired with the dustman really coming, and Mother was sad and quiet, the wrong sea troubled her, what had she done, she had been sure she would find things different, as she had said they would be, merry-go-rounds and swings and slides for the kiddies, and other mothers to show the kiddies off to, they were quite bright for their age, what had she done?

They looked across the lagoon then and saw the swans, black and shining, as if the visiting dark tiring of its form, had changed to birds, hundreds of them resting and moving softly about on the water. Why, the lagoon was filled with swans, like secret sad ships, secret and quiet. Hush-sh the water said; rush-hush, the wind passed over the top of the water; no other sound but the shaking of rushes and far away now it seemed the roar of the sea like a secret sea that had crept inside your head for ever. And the swans, they were there too, inside you, peaceful and quiet watching and sleeping and watching, there was nothing but peace and warmth and calm, everything found, train and sea and mother and father and earwig and slater and spider.

And Gypsy?

But when they got home Gypsy was dead.

The Day of the Sheep

It should not have rained. The clothes should have been slapped warm and dry with wind and sun and the day not have been a leafless cloudy secret hard to understand. It is always nice to understand the coming and going of a day. Tell her, blackbird that pirrup-pirruped and rainwater that trickled down the kitchen window-pane and dirty backyard that oozed mud and housed puddles, tell her though the language be something she cannot construe having no grammar of journeys.

Why is the backyard so small and suffocating and untidy? On the rope clothesline the washing hangs limp and wet, Tom's underpants and the sheets and my best tablecloth. We'll go away from here, Tom and me, we'll go some other place, the country perhaps, he likes the country but he's going on and on to a prize in Tatts and a new home, flat-roofed with blinds down in the front room and a piano with curved legs, though Tom's in the Dye Works just now, bringing home handkerchiefs at the end of each week, from the coats with no names on.

'Isn't it stealing Tom?'

'Stealing my foot, I tell you I've worked two years without a holiday.' You see? Tom striving for his rights and getting them even if they turn out to be only a small anonymous pile of men's handkerchiefs, but life is funny and people are funny, laugh and the world laughs with you.

She opens the wash-house door to let the blue water out of the tubs, she forgot all about the blue water, and then of all the surprises in the world there's a sheep in the wash-house, a poor sheep not knowing which way to turn, fat and blundering with the shy anxious look sheep have.

'Shoo Shoo.'

Sheep are silly animals they're so scared and stupid, they either stand still and do nothing or else go round and round getting nowhere, when they're in they want out and when they're out they sneak in, they don't stay in places, they get lost in bogs and creeks and down cliffs, if only they stayed where they're put.

'Shoo Shoo.'

Scared muddy and heavy the sheep lumbers from the wash-house and then bolts up the path, out the half-open gate on to the street and then round the corner out of sight, with the people stopping to stare and say well I declare for you never see sheep in the street, only people.

It should not have rained, the washing should have been dry and why did the sheep come and where did it come from to here in the middle of the city?

A long time ago there were sheep (she remembers, pulling out the plug so the dirty blue water can gurgle away, what slime I must wash more often why is everything always dirty) sheep, and I walked behind them with bare feet on a hot dusty road, with the warm steamy nobbles of sheep dirt getting crushed between my toes and my father close by me powerful and careless, and the dogs padding along the spit dribbling from the loose corners of their mouths, Mac and Jock and Rover waiting for my father to cry Way Back Out, Way Back Out. Tom and me will go some other place I think. Tom and me will get out of here.

She dries her hands on the corner of her sack apron. That's that. A flat-roofed house and beds with shiny covers, and polished fire-tongs, and a picture of moonlight on a lake.

She crosses the backyard, brushing aside the wet

clothes to pass. My best tablecloth. If visitors come tonight I am sunk.

But no visitors only Tom bringing cousin Nora, while the rain goes off, she has to catch the six o'clock bus at the end of the road. I must hurry I must be quick it is terrible to miss something. Cousin Nora widowed remarried separated and anxious to tell. Cousin Nora living everywhere and nowhere chained to number fifty Toon Street it is somewhere you must have somewhere even if you know you haven't got anywhere. And what about Tom tied up to a little pile of handkerchiefs and the prize that happens tomorrow, and Nance, look at her, the washing's still out and wet, she is tired and flurried, bound by the fearful chain of time and the burning sun and sheep and day that are nowhere.

'But of course Nance I won't have any dinner, you go on dishing up for Tom while I sit here on the sofa.'

'Wait, I'll move those newspapers, excuse the muddle, we seem to be in a fearful muddle.'

'Oh is that today's paper, no it's Tuesday's, just think on Tuesday Peter and I were up in the North Island. He wanted me to sell my house you know, just fancy, he demanded that I sell it and I said not on your life did you marry me for myself or for my house and he said of course he married me for myself but would I sell the house, why I said, well you don't need it now he said, we can live up north, but I do need it I've lived in it nearly all of my life, it's my home, I live there.'

Cousin Nora, dressed in navy, her fleecy dark hair and long soft wobbly face like a horse.

'Yes I've lived there all my life, so of course I said quite definitely no. Is that boiled bacon, there's nothing I like better, well if you insist, just the tiniest bit on a plate, over here will do, no no fuss, thank you. Don't you think I was right about the house? I live there.'

What does Tom think? His mouth busies itself with boiled bacon while his fingers search an envelope for the pink sheet that means Tatts results, ten thousand pounds first prize, a flat-roofed house and statues in the garden. No prize but first prize will do, Tom is clever and earnest, the other fellows have tickets in Tatts, why not I the other fellows take handkerchiefs home and stray coats sometimes why not I and Bill Tent has a modern house one of those new ones you can never be too interested in where you live. Tom is go-ahead. In the front bedroom there's an orange coloured bed-lamp, it's scorched a bit now but it was lovely when it came, he won it with a question for a radio quiz, his name over the air and all —

Name the planets and their distance from the sun.

Name the planets.

Oh the sun is terribly far away but of course there's only been rain today, pirrup-pirruping blackbirds, how it rains and the sheep why I must tell them about the sheep.

Nora leans forward, 'Nance you are dreaming, what *do* you think about the house?'

'Oh, always let your conscience be your guide.'

(Wear wise saws and modern instances like a false skin a Jiminy Cricket overcoat.)

'That's what I say too, your conscience, and that's why we separated, you heard of course?'

Yes Nance knows, from Nora herself as soon as it happened Dear Nance and Tom you'll hardly believe it but Peter and I have decided to go our own ways, you and Tom are lucky you get on so well together no fuss about where to live you don't know how lucky you are.

No fuss but lost, look at the house look at the kitchen, and me going backwards and forwards carrying dishes and picking up newspapers and dirty clothes, muddling backwards and forwards in little irrelevant journeys, but going backwards always, to the time of the sun and the hot dusty road and a powerful father crying Way Back Out Way Back Out.

'Oh, Oh I must tell you, there was a sheep today in the wash-house.'

'A what?'

'A sheep. I don't know where he lived but I chased him away.'

'Oh I say, really, ha ha, it's a good job we've got somewhere to live, I in my house (even though I had to break with Peter) and you and Tom in yours.

'We *have* got somewhere to live haven't we, not like a lost sheep ha ha. What's the matter Tom?'

'74898, not a win.'

The pink ticket thrust back quickly into the envelope and put on the stand beside the wireless, beside the half-open packet of matches and the sheaf of bills and the pile of race-books.

'Well, I'm damned, let's turn on the news, it's almost six.'

'Oh it's almost six and my bus!'

'So it is Nora.'

Quick it is terrible to lose something for the something you miss may be something you have looked for all your life, in the North Island and the South Island and number fifty Toon Street.

'Goodbye and thank you for the little eat and you must come and see me sometime and for goodness sake Nance get a perm or one of those cold waves, your hair's at the end of its tether.'

Here is the news.

Quick goodbye then.

Why am I small and cramped and helpless why are

there newspapers on the floor and why didn't I remember to gather up the dirt, where am I living that I'm not neat and tidy with a perm. Oh if only the whole of being were blued and washed and hung out in the far away sun. Nora has travelled she knows about things, it would be nice to travel if you knew where you were going and where you would live at the end or do we ever know, do we ever live where we live, we're always in other places, lost, like sheep, and I cannot understand the leafless cloudy secret and the sun of any day.

Child

Breathe in slowly and quietly, Miss Richardson said. The class breathed in slowly and quietly all except Ivan Calcott who made a noise breathing in. On purpose.

Miss Richardson strapped him. She was tall with a fair square head like the top of a clothes-peg, and she smelt like the inside of our front wardrobe. She took us for poems in the morning, O Young Lochinvar has come out of the West, and songs in the afternoon, O Shenandoah I long to hear you and Speed Bonny Boat like a Bird on the Wing.

She snapped her lips open and shut, quickly.

'Breathe in, class, slowly and quietly and breathe out, counting up to ten.'

The class breathed in slowly and quietly and breathed out counting up to ten except Minnie Passmore and me who got as far as fifteen.

We didn't mean it, it just happened we had more breath left and it was more interesting being let out by numbers than just by ordinary blowing, but Miss Richardson didn't understand at all.

She strapped us both and we went back to our places while the rest of the class stared to see if we would cry but we didn't cry, and then as a further punishment we had to sing together O Shenandoah I long to hear you far away you rolling river, and soon the bell went and it was after school.

And very suddenly Minnie Passmore was my best friend.

'Eleven twelve thirteen fourteen fifteen,' she whispered to me on the way home.

'Eleven twelve thirteen fourteen fifteen,' I whispered back. O Shenandoah I long to hear you.

We laughed. We lived up the same road only her house was further up and her hedge was macrocarpa and ours was African Thorn. And she didn't have a mother and father, she lived with her grandma and grandad.

Oh how lovely to have no mother and father and live with your grandma and grandad, to have a macrocarpa hedge instead of African Thorn, to have button-up shoes instead of lace-ups, to have a fringe and a dress with a cape collar and a skipping rope with shiny blue handles!

'You're my best friend,' I said to Minnie Passmore.

'And you're my best friend,' Minnie Passmore said to me. 'Come up to our place and see the kite Grandad's making.'

'I have to tell Mum first,' I said, 'in case I've been kidnapped and she doesn't know.'

I told Mum and she said, 'Who picked the bread at dinner-time?'

'I didn't,' I said. 'There was a hole in it when I got it, as if a mouse had been sleeping there.'

'No more pennies for you,' said Mum. 'Now run away before I change my mind.'

She shook her pinny at me. Sometimes she put wheat in her pinny and shook the wheat out to the fowls, calling Chook Chook Chook.

I felt ashamed of having her. Minnie didn't have a mother. Minnie was standing at the corner of the house, watching, and not saying anything, as if she were thinking Oh how sad to have a big mother with a blue pinny to shake at you as if it were wheat for a little fowl!

Minnie's house was high on the side of a hill, up a long long path with grannie's bonnets on both sides and an apple tree in the middle of the lawn. And the macrocarpa hedge was dark and mysterious and unknown. If I'd climbed it I wouldn't have known where to put my feet or which branches were safe or which were the best hiding places. This is the Way the World goes round and somebody must touch, I'd say, and then I'd hide after they had guessed who had touched, and macrocarpa is best for hiding though it gets in your hair and stains your hands.

But Minnie's macrocarpa was unknown and terrifying, even Minnie didn't know it, nor Minnie's grandfather and grandmother.

And the apples from the little apple tree were eaten by birds and fallen in the grass and lost.

'Why, Minnie?' I said.

'Grandma and Grandad are old,' Minnie said. 'Come on Jan. Grandad,' she called. 'Grandad.'

Grandma came out of the back door. 'Hello, Minnie, you've brought a playmate.'

'My best friend,' Minnie said.

I glowed inside myself. Minnie Passmore's best friend. Sometimes visitors came at home, swarming into the dining room and seeming to fill every corner, and when I handed them a cup of tea and a piece of fruit cake they'd take my hand and ask

'What are you coming out as?'

I was usually coming out as a bandit because of Tom Mix and Tim McCoy.

'Who's your best friend?'

I didn't ever know that one, I don't think I had a best friend, though there was Poppy whose father drank beer and we used the bottles for playing school, we got them to breathe in and breathe out up to ten, and sing Shenandoah.

No I didn't have a best friend.

But now there was Minnie Passmore. O Minnie Passmore with the button-up shoes and the fringe and the cape collar.

And the grandma and grandad.

'Yes, she's my best friend,' I said to Grandma Passmore.

'Eleven twelve thirteen fourteen fifteen,' said Minnie.

'Eleven twelve thirteen fourteen fifteen,' I said back.

We laughed and Grandma Passmore laughed. She had a little dog brooch made out of wood. It looked like a real dog but it was only wood.

'Where's Grandad,' Minnie asked.

'He's up the back by the clothesline. Change your dress first Minnie and Jan'll wait for you up there.'

Minnie's grandfather was sitting on a tree stump outside the wash-house. He had a bag of lollies in his hand and the first thing he did was to throw me a peppermint.

'Catch.'

I caught.

'I've made a kite for Minnie to fly on the hill.'

I didn't say anything. I just watched him pick up the kite from behind the tree stump. We had a grandfather once, we had two grandfathers. The first grandfather lived with us, he slept in the room beside the cellar. He put on glasses for reading and his mouth opened when he slept and he put his hands behind his back when he walked. He smelt like peanut butter.

He got sick, this grandfather, and our mother gave us wooden knitting needles to knit with and keep us quiet. Sh-Sh Grandad's sick.

That grandfather died and we went next door when the funeral was on and the lady next door made us drink tea and eat scrambled egg.

I watched Grandad Passmore, and I sucked my peppermint, sliding it just behind my top teeth and pressing my tongue against it till the edges of the lolly wore away and the breath of it came out when I opened my mouth.

'Ja-a-n,' Minnie called. 'I'm com-ing.'

'I'm by the wash-house,' I called back. Minnie was my very best friend. O Shenandoah I long to hear you, away you rolling river. Speed Bonny boat like a bird on the wing.

I think it was the most wonderful kite in the world. The tail was made out of newspaper, *Otago Daily Times*, only you wouldn't have guessed it with the little bits of paper twisted and pointed like white fins, and when you held the brown paper body up in the air you could see the light through it. It was like a new kind of fish and you were standing under the sea with Minnie and Grandfather Passmore.

Grandfather Passmore didn't speak much except to say Catch whenever it was time for a new peppermint. And when the string was got ready and he gave us the kite all he said was There you are Minnie Mouse, go up the hill and fly your kite.

He didn't smile. He just sat there on the tree stump with the bag of peppermints in his hand. There were no other people in the garden, no dogs, no cats, no sparrows swinging on the clothesline, only Grandad Passmore.

Minnie and I climbed through the barbed wire fence at the top of the garden and followed the sheep track to the top of the hill.

'I'm having first go,' Minnie said.

'But I haven't even had a carry of it,' I protested.

Minnie settled the argument. 'It's mine,' she said. 'It belongs to me, it's mine.'

'All right,' I said. 'But you'll hurry up with my turn won't you, it's such a corker kite.'

Minnie agreed. 'Yes it's a corker kite.'

She clutched hold of it, as if it might escape, as if it were a live thing like me and Minnie and Grandad and Grandma Passmore.

We left the sheep track and walked on through the cocksfoot, picking off the heads and scattering the seeds as we walked, while the seeds sneaked down inside our shoes and tickled, only I didn't take my shoes off to empty them for mine were lace-ups and I couldn't be bothered. O for button-ups! O for a dress with a cape collar.

We reached the top of the hill and before you could say Jack Robinson Minnie had loosed the string of the kite and was racing along the top of the hill with the kite flopping and falling at first like a bird with a broken wing, and then being lifted up on the back of the wind, riding up and down, and then struggling to free itself so it could go yet higher up and up and disappear. Where? But Minnie wouldn't let it disappear. She held on tight, again as if the kite were a real live thing, like Grandad or Grandma Passmore or my own mother and father. Then Minnie came back and I knew it was going to be my turn. Minnie was my best friend. O Shenandoah I long to hear you far away you rolling river. Minnie had everything a kite and a skipping rope and button-up shoes and a dress with a cape collar.

It was time for my go.

'Oh Oh,' I said because I wanted to say something and there was nothing else to say. Oh, Oh. The world was good, like something to eat. There was a wind rushing over the top of the hill, and sometimes ducks flew over, dark and diamond-shaped, their wings whirring, their heads craned forward eagerly. Away on the other hill there were other birds cradled in the heaving tops of the pine trees. And down from the other hill was the place where I lived, with the African Thorn hedge, and the dahlias in the garden, and my big mother with a blue pinny to shake at me as if it were wheat for a little chook.

Spirit

'Spirit 350?'

'Yes.'

'You died yesterday?'

'Yes. Sunning myself in the garden.'

'Quite so. Now if you'll rest from hovering I'll ask you a few questions, just a matter of form you know, we are crowded here and like to find suitable eternal places for our clients. Now. What about your life? A brief outline perhaps.'

'There's nothing much to say. The usual thing. Born in the South Island went to some kind of school learned writing and spelling and profit and loss and compositions My Holidays What I would most like to be when I grow up —'

'What did you most want to be?'

'Oh an inventor or explorer or sea captain.'

'And were you?'

'Oh no no of course not, these are just fancies we get when we are little kids running round the garden playing at being grownups. To tell the truth I married early, Emily Barker.'

'Emily Barker? Do you have names?'

'Of course. I was Harry and there was my brother Dick and my sister Molly. Does that seem strange to you?'

'A little out of the ordinary perhaps. Go on.'

'There's nothing much to say, as I told you before. We are creatures of habit. Lived in a little house, had four kids, worked at gardening, each day a round of eating and sleeping and other pleasures, pictures on the weekend, the bar on Friday nights at five for bar lunch cold fish and dead potatoes, footy in the weekend, footy's a kind of game, every day mostly just going backwards and forwards doing this and that.'

'I see, quite a simple existence. Any enemies?'

'Yes we all have enemies. A big black death swoops down from the skies at any moment to carry us away. A kind of death got me yesterday while I was sunning myself in the garden. It's funny, and next year there will be a notice in the paper Sacred to the memory of, Gone but not forgotten.'

'You have newspapers?'

'Of course. And radio for the wrestling and the serials, and books too. And there's some sort of music and some of the folks paint and dance but give me three feeds a day and a comfortable place to live.'

'You say there's music and dancing?'

'Not for me. They're always trying to leave their mark on the world some sort of a trail but it's like the wind and the sand ha ha.'

'Well Spirit 350, I think that's all I want to know, if you just wait a moment I'll get you your eternal home. A nice permanently juicy leaf, quite small but comfortable.'

'A leaf. A leaf. But I was a man. Men can't live on leaves.'

'I'm sorry, I'll get your leaf. Nothing can be done now.'

'But I tell you I was a human being, a man, "in form and moving how like an angel" (they say). I've wept and laughed and fallen in love, I can remember and think, look at me thinking, I can think.'

'Here is your leaf Spirit 350. Aeons and aeons of juice here. You'll be alone of course but there'll be no swooping blackbirds to bother you. You may eat and sleep and slide up and down even making a little permanent silver patch of your own and remember no blackbirds to bother you.'

My Father's Best Suit

My father's best suit was light grey and somehow it had got a tear in one of the coat sleeves, and anyhow the pants were threadbare and shiny so my father sent my sister and I down town to get a reel of grey mending cotton, the right grey because it was my father's best suit. So my sister and I went down town to get the cotton. We went to the drapery shop where we got our school things, the one on the corner with the sign up saying The Friendly Shop, and we said to the man a reel of cotton please, this grey for Dad's suit. But the man didn't have the grey, and we went to other shops, ones down little side streets where they sold fancy-work and aprons and babies' bonnets and magazines for women, and in there we said a reel of cotton please, this grey for Dad's suit, but they didn't have any there either, and we went to lots of other shops but we couldn't get the right grey, so we came home.

'It's my best suit,' said Dad. 'I've had it ever since we left Wyndham.'

'Are you sure you couldn't get the right grey?' asked Mum.

We told her no.

And Dad was so particular about his clothes, but he had to make do with a different grey for the tear in the coat sleeve and the threadbare parts in the pants.

Of course it was in the days of the depression, and that's why my father cared so much. That's why we had footnotes on our bill too, from the draper's shop at the corner, and that's why we had mince for dinner nearly every day, and specked fruit from the Chinaman's and stale cakes from

Dent's whenever visitors came, and I suppose that's why we wore our aunt's old clothes, dark reds and browns and purples, marocain and voile mostly. The dresses dipped at the back, you could feel the hem touching away below the back of your knee, but when you looked down in front it was up near your knees, so you bent down and smoothed the hem out and then stood quickly so it would stay in the right place, but it moved further and further up the more you stretched yourself. The proportion was all wrong. Not that we minded. We had our interests. We got shouted to the pictures, the Jungle Mystery and the Ghost City where we cheered the goodies and booed the baddies, and we collected a piece of birthday cake every time Mickey Mouse had a birthday, and we saved up serial tickets for a bicycle and a watch and a camera and other ethereal gadgets. Of course we never saved up enough. Sometimes we'd miss a serial or get two of the same kind of card and nobody would swap with us, and other times we'd get tired of saving and throw the card away, and then go looking for it afterwards and getting wild because we couldn't find it and then we'd fight about whose fault it was.

We did plenty of fighting. We had Wars. We wrote in invisible ink with lemon, and we wrote spidery writing with green feathers, and we wrote with the blood of dahlias.

And still my father wore his light grey suit on Sundays to the Union meetings.

Miss Gibson
and the Lumber-room

Dear Miss Gibson, I'll tell you the truth now I'm twenty-one and independent and not having to write a composition once a week the glory of the bush the rata on fire the last rays of the setting sun touching the hill-tops with gold the beauty of nature the gentle zephyr caressing the meadow, dear Miss Gibson I was an awful liar.

It's about the lumber-room. Do you remember? It was partly your fault you know. You took out a little blue book intermediate composition hints and suggestions for the pupil and teacher, and you read us a sort of essay about the man who opened the door of the lumber-room and spent a long afternoon over the treasures of the past. Tears came to his eyes I remember, and the more fragile girls in the class took out their handkerchiefs when you read that bit. His voice broke with emotion too, he stared into space, here was the first book, now thumbed and torn with childish hands, here was the tennis racket his first one that his grandmother gave him, how his heart leapt with the soft white ball that he tossed into the air, oh Miss Gibson it was a sad sad essay thoughts on entering the old lumber-room.

And when you had finished reading it you said girls that is your subject for next week, and mind your ands and buts and your paragraphing, and J. mind your writing because no examiner would ever etc.

Well I went home and wrote my essay. We lived in a large house at the time. We had a few servants to help with the housework because with a large house you can't manage on your own, and we had a cook too, a French woman called Marie-Suzanne whose coiffure was Parisian, and who said oui-oui madame, mais oui, cela m'est égal, and other idiomatic phrases.

Of course we had a gardener too, an old man who lived in a hut somewhere on the estate. He played the violin at night sometimes, and if we were happening to have a party we always invited Charles to play for us on the terrace, he was of gipsy descent it was said, dark and romantic with a beard and flashing eyes, and his past was Bohemian.

I didn't put him in my essay. I didn't put Marie-Suzanne in either. I saved them up for *The Cook and the Gardener*, a curious romance in dramatic form performed by the F. family in the summer-house, admission sixpence and George will provide refreshments at half-time, wine-gums and blackballs.

There will be a solo by Valmai from Dunedin, Jesus bids us shine, and a Scottish dance also by Valmai, but I'm forgetting that it's the lumber-room I'm writing about, I'll tell you the story of the concert another time, and how we did *Honest Jacob* on the same programme, he found gold in the bread and took it straight back to the baker, showing that Honesty is the Best Policy, and that's why I'm writing to you about the lumber-room.

Because, Miss Gibson, I was an awful liar.

You don't remember what I put of course. I walked into our lumber-room, it was on the third floor of our home, the windows were stained glass with angels blowing trumpets, hand-painted probably by an artistic relative. The room was crowded with memories. I mused there all afternoon and the tears very properly came to my eyes.

I found my first gown my christening frock all in silver and I thought there was a time when meadow grove and stream, we had done that poem quite recently, I quoted some and said O childhood, and I put in thou and thee and hast.

I found my first reading-book, with the dear sad red and gold pictures, and I yearned for the days that were no more. I put in Tennyson here, tears idle tears I know not what they mean, O Miss Gibson you couldn't have understood how moved I was just standing there by the stained glass window, with the sun throwing a warm lingering light over the book, O Miss Gibson this was the saddest part of my essay.

And then I found other things of the past. I found my sleeping doll with big blue eyes, and my bicycle and my old watch that I had long ago out-grown with the three opals in it, given on my third birthday by Great Aunt Mildred who used to come and see us from London, and tell us about the days when she was little and how she used to look through Buckingham Palace fence at the King, and how when she grew older she had supper with him, she was dressed in white with pearls.

And I found the copy of Shakespeare that I read when I was six years old, right through *Othello* even and *Measure for Measure* I read, and I found the violin that my father gave me, a Stradivari, I used to play Bach at an early age, I played at parties and everybody clapped afterwards . . .

Miss Gibson, I got fourteen out of twenty for my essay of course you don't remember that, and you put highly improbable underneath it.

Fourteen out of twenty highly improbable watch your writing.

Well as I say I'm twenty-one now and a sort of student

at a University.

I was an awful liar all right. It didn't happen as I said it did. I didn't ever have a sleeping doll, only a rag one that I pulled the stuffing out of and then the arms came off quite by accident, and I didn't have a watch of course, and all I read at six years old was *My Favourite Comic*, *Terry and Trixie of the Circus*, *Rin-Tin-Tin the Wonder Dog*, I don't even think I read them when I was five, I can't remember, and even later all I read was *Bunch of the Boarding School the Sneak of the Fourth*, *The Princess Prefect*, anyway it wasn't Shakespeare, and I didn't have a violin to play Bach on at parties, they would have coughed and wriggled if I'd played Bach, even the loveliest bits.

And I didn't have a house with a hundred rooms, and a French cook and a gardener with a beard, I had a little place to live in. I had a mother who cooked for us, and she cooked nicely too, and my father dug the garden in the weekends, and he planted pansies, and we had cats and dogs and rabbits and a mouse in the scullery, and we had visitors sometimes who swore, and I liked being alive and I didn't care twopence about the past it was the present that mattered, and Miss Gibson, if you really want to know, we didn't even have a lumber-room.

A Note on the Russian War

The sunflowers got us, the black seeds stuck in our hair, my mother went about saying in a high voice like the wind sunflowers kiddies, ah sunflowers.

We lived on the Steppes, my mother and the rest of my family and I, but mostly my mother because she was bigger than the rest. She stood outside in the sun. She held a sunflower in her hand. It was the biggest blackest sunflower in Russia, and my mother said over and over again ah sunflowers.

I shall never forget being in Russia. We wore big high boots in the winter, and in the summer we went barefoot and wriggled our toes in the mud whenever it rained, and when there was snow on the ground we went outside under the trees to sing a Russian song, it went like this, I'm singing it to myself so you can't hear, tra-tra-tra, something about sunflowers and a tall sky and the war rolling through the grass, tra-tra—tra, it was a very nice song that we sang.

In space and time.

There are no lands outside, they are fenced inside us, a fence of being and we are the world my mother told us we are Russian because we have this sunflower in our garden.

It grew in those days near the cow-byre and the potato patch. It was a little plant with a few little black seeds sometimes, and a scraggy flower with a black heart, like a big daisy only yellow and black, but it was too tall for us to see properly, the daisies were nearer our size.

All day on the lawn we made daisy chains and buttercup chains, sticking our teeth through the bitter stems.

All day on the lawn, don't you remember the smell of them, the new white daisies, you stuff your face amongst them and you put the buttercups under your chin to see if you love butter, and you do love butter anyway so what's the use, but the yellow shadow is Real Proof, O you love early, sitting amongst the wet painted buttercups.

And then out of the spring and summer days the War came. An ordinary war like the Hundred Years or the Wars of the Roses or the Great War where my father went and sang Tipperary. All of the soldiers on my father's side sang Tipperary, it was to show they were getting somewhere, and the louder they sang it the more sure they felt about getting there.

And the louder they sang it the more scared they felt inside.

Well in the Russian War we didn't sing Tipperary or Pack up Your Troubles or There's a Long Long Trail A-Winding.

We had sunflowers by the fence near where the fat white cow got milked. We had big high boots in winter.

We were just Russian children on the Steppes, singing tra-tra-tra, quietly with our mother and father, but war comes whatever you sing.

The Birds Began to Sing

The birds began to sing. There were four and twenty of them singing, and they were blackbirds.

And I said what are you singing all day and night, in the sun and the dark and the rain, and in the wind that turns the tops of the trees silver?

We are singing they said. We are singing and we have just begun, and we've a long way to sing, and we can't stop, we've got to go on and on. Singing.

The birds began to sing.

I put on my coat and I walked in the rain over the hills. I walked through swamps full of red water, and down gullies covered in snow-berries, and then up gullies again, with snow-grass growing there, and speargrass, and over creeks near flax and tussock and manuka.

I saw a pine tree on top of a hill.

I saw a skylark dipping and rising.

I saw it was snowing somewhere over the hills, but not where I was.

I stood on a hill and looked and looked.

I wasn't singing. I tried to sing but I couldn't think of the song.

So I went back home to the boarding-house where I live, and I sat on the stairs in the front and I listened. I listened with my head and my eyes and my brain and my hands. With my body.

The birds began to sing.

They were blackbirds sitting on the telegraph wires and hopping on the apple trees. There were four and twenty of them singing.

What is the song I said. Tell me the name of the song.

I am a human being and I read books and I hear music and I like to see things in print. I like to see vivace andante words by music by performed by written for. So I said what is the name of the song, tell me and I will write it and you can listen at my window when I get the finest musicians in the country to play it, and you will feel so nice to hear your song so tell me the name.

They stopped singing. It was dark outside although the sun was shining. It was dark and there was no more singing.

The Pictures

She took her little girl to the pictures. She dressed her in a red pixie-cap and a woolly grey coat, and then she put on her own black coat that it was so hard to get the fluff off, and they got a number four tram to the pictures.

They stood outside the theatre, the woman in the black coat and the little girl in the red pixie-cap and they looked at the advertisements.

It was a wonderful picture. It was the greatest love story ever told. It was Life and Love and Laughter, and Tenderness and Tears.

They walked into the vestibule and over to the box where the ticket-girl waited.

'One and a half in the stalls, please,' said the woman.

The ticket-girl reached up to the hanging roll of blue tickets and pulled off one and a half, and then looked in the money-box for sixpence change.

'Thank you,' said the woman in the black coat.

And very soon they were sitting in the dark of the theatre, with people all around them, and they could hear the sound of lollies being unwrapped and papers being screwed up, and people half-standing in their seats for other people to pass them, and voices saying can you see are you quite sure.

And then the lights went down further and they stood up for God Save the King. The woman would have liked to sing it, she would have liked to be singing instead of being quiet and just watching the screen with the photo of the King's face and the Union Jack waving through his face.

She had been in a concert once and sung God Save the

King and How'd you like to be a baby girl. She had worn a long white nightie that Auntie Kit had run up for her on the machine, and she carried a lighted candle in her hand. Mother and Father were in the audience, and although she had been told not to look, she couldn't help seeing Mother and Father.

But she didn't sing this time. And soon everybody was sitting down and getting comfortable and the Pictures had begun.

The lion growling and then looking over his left shoulder, the kangaroo leaping from a height. That was Australian. The man winding the camera after it was all over. The Eyes and Ears of the World, The End.

There was a cartoon, too, about a cat and a mouse. The little girl laughed. She clapped her hands and giggled and the woman laughed with her. They were the happiest people in the world. They were at the pictures seeing a mouse being shot out of a cannon by a cat, away up the sky the mouse went and then landed whizz-thump behind the cat. And then it was the cat's turn to be shot into the sky whizz-thump and down again.

It was certainly a good picture. Everybody was laughing, and the children down the front were clapping their hands.

There was a fat man quite close to the woman and the little girl. The fat man was laughing haw-haw-haw.

And when the end came and the cat and mouse were both sitting on a cloud, the lights were turned up for Interval, and the lolly and ice-cream boys were walking up to the front of the theatre, ready to be signalled to, well then they were all wiping their eyes and saying how funny how funny.

The woman and the little girl had sixpence worth of paper lollies to eat then. There were pretty colours on the screen, and pictures of how you ought to furnish your home and where to spend your winter holiday, and the best salon to have your hair curled at, and the clothes you ought to wear if you were a discriminating woman, everything was planned for you.

The woman leaned back in her seat and sighed a long sigh.

She remembered that it was such a nice day outside with all the spring flowers coming into the shops, and the blue sky over the city. Spring was the nicest of all. And in the boarding-house where the woman and little girl lived there was a daffodil in the window-box.

It was awful living alone with the little girl in a boarding-house. But there was the daffodil in the window-box, and there were the pictures to go to with the little girl.

And now the pictures had started again. It was the big picture, Errol Flynn and Olivia de Havilland.

Seven thousand feet, the woman said to herself. She liked to remember the length of the picture, it was something to be sure of.

She knew she could see the greatest love story in the world till after four o'clock. It was nice to come to the pictures like that and know how long the story would last.

And to know that in the end he would take her out in the moonlight and a band would play and he would kiss her and everything would be all right again.

So it didn't really matter if he left her, no it didn't matter a bit, even if she cried and then went into a convent and scrubbed stone cells all day and nearly all night . . .

It was sad here. Some of the people took out their handkerchiefs and sniffed in them. And the woman in the black coat hoped it wasn't too near the end for the lights to go up and everybody to see.

But it was all right again because she escaped from the convent and he was waiting for her in the shelter of the trees and they crossed the border into France.

Everything is so exciting and nice thought the woman with the little girl. She wanted the story to last for ever.

And it was the most wonderful love story in the world. You could tell that. He kissed her so many times. He called her beloved and angel, and he said he would lay down his life for her, and in the end they kissed again, and they sailed on the lake, the beautiful lake with the foreign name. It was midnight and in the background you could see their home that had a white telephone in every room, and ferns in pots and marble pillars against the sky, it was lovely.

And on the lake there was music playing, and moonlight, and the water lapping very softly.

It is a wonderful ending, thought the woman. The full moon up there and the lights and music, it is a wonderful ending.

So the woman and the little girl got up from their seats because they knew it was the end, and they walked into the vestibule, and they blinked their eyes in the hard yellow daylight. There was a big crowd. Some had shiny noses where the tears had rolled.

The woman looked again at the advertisement. The world's greatest love story. Love and Laughter, Tenderness and Tears. It's true, thought the woman, with a happy feeling of remembering.

Together they walked to the tram-stop, the little girl in the red pixie-cap and the woman in the black coat. They stood waiting for a number three car. They would be home just in time for tea at the boarding-house. There were lots of other people waiting for a number three car. Some had gone to the pictures too, and they were talking about it, I liked the bit where he, where she.

And although it was long after four o'clock the sun seemed still to be shining hard and bright. The light from it was clean and yellow and warm. The woman looked about her at the sun and the people and the tram-cars, and the sun, the sun sending a warm glow over everything.

There was a little pomeranian being taken along on a lead, and a man with a bunch of spring flowers done up in pink paper from the Floriana at the corner, and an old man standing smoking a pipe and a schoolboy yelling Sta-a-r, Sta-a-r.

The world was full of people and little dogs and sun.

The woman stood looking, and thinking about going for tea, and the landlady saying, with one hand resting on the table and the other over her face Bless those in need and feed the hungry, and the fat boarder with his soup-spoon half-way up to his mouth, The Government will go out, and the other boarder who was a tram-conductor answering as he reached for the bread, The Government will Stay In. And the woman thought of going upstairs and putting the little girl to bed and then touching and looking at the daffodil in the window-box, it was a lovely daffodil. And looking about her and thinking the woman felt sad.

But the little girl in the pixie-cap didn't feel sad, she was eating a paper lolly, it was greeny-blue and it tasted like peppermints.

My Last Story

I'm never going to write another story.

I don't like writing stories. I don't like putting he said she said he did she did, and telling about people, the small dark woman who coughs into a silk handkerchief and says excuse me would you like another soda cracker Mary, and the men with grease all over their clothes and lunch tins in their hands, the Hillside men who get into the tram at four forty-five, and hang on to the straps so the ladies can sit down comfortably, and stare out of the window and you never know what they're thinking, perhaps about their sons in Standard two, who are going to work at Hillside when it's time for them to leave school, and that's called work and earning a living, well I'm not going to write any more stories like that. I'm not going to write about the snow and the curly chrysanthemums peeping out of the snow and the women saying how lovely every cloud has a silver lining, and I'm not going to write about my grandmother sitting in a black dress at the back door and having her photo taken with Dad because he loved her best and Uncle Charlie broke her heart because he drank beer. I'm never going to write another story after this one. This is my last story.

I'm not going to write about the woman upstairs and the little girl who bangs her head against the wall and can't talk yet though she's five you would think she'd have started by now, and I'm not going to write about Harry who's got a copy of *We Were the Rats* under his pillow and I suppose that's called experience of Life.

And about George Street and Princes Street and the

trams up to twelve. I'm not going to write about my family and the house where I live when I'm in Oamaru, the queerest little house I've ever seen, with trees all round it oaks and willows and silver birches and apple trees that are like a fairy-tale in October, and ducks waggling their legs in the air, and swamp hens in evening dress, navy blue with red at the neck, nice and boogie-woogie, and cats that have kittens without being ethical.

And my sister who's in the sixth form at school and talks about a Brave New World and Aldous Huxley and DH Lawrence, and asks me is it love it must be love because when we were standing on the bridge he said. He said, she said, I'm not going to write any more stories about that. I'm not going to write any more about the rest of my family, my other sister who teaches and doesn't like teaching though why on earth if you don't like it they say.

That's Isabel, and when it's raining hard outside and I think of forty days and forty nights and an ark being built, when it's dark outside and the rain is tangled up in the trees, Isabel comes up to me, and her eyes are so sad what about the fowls, the fowls I can see them with their feathers dripping wet and perches are such cold places to sleep. My sister has a heart of gold, that's how they express things like that.

Well I'm not going to do any more expressing.

This is my last story.

And I'm going to put three dots with my typewriter, impressively, and then I'm going to begin . . .

I think I must be frozen inside with no heart to speak of. I think I've got the wrong way of looking at Life.

From

Snowman Snowman:
Fables and Fantasies

A Windy Day

When the wind blows in this way the cars bedded in the streets struggle to get free of their green-and-grey canvas or plastic nightshirts; the planes, the new type with their wings down over their hips, rock in the sky. The wind lifts the lids of the dustbins, breaks milk bottles, turns newspapers over and over, around corners, and buffets city sparrows perched in the pruned grey trees.

Spring enters on every gust of wind.

Look at the pearl-coloured sky, the satin clouds ruffled this way and that above the chimney tops! The sun is fresh, never left standing or sour, poured out clean on the stones for the dusty-throated wind to lick.

Trains rattle under dark sagging bridges. People talk from pavement to pavement. Children unwind hair ribbons. The black-and-white tomcat slinks along the crumbling wall.

The motorcyclist, his knees tight against his mount, surges through the tidal streets, riding a seahorse to the lonely shore.

The wind moans near the eaves of the house, Why-do-you? Why-do-you?

Settled pigeons call with folded grey voices, Tear up the eviction order.

Homeless birds, intruders, cry for the sea and the marshland.

The sun burns a transfer of spring on the city.

Do not be afraid of spring.

The Terrible Screaming

One night a terrible screaming sounded through the city. It sounded so loudly and piercingly that there was not a soul who did not hear it. Yet when people turned to one another in fear and were about to remark, Did you hear it, that terrible screaming? they changed their minds, thinking, Perhaps it was my imagination, perhaps I have been working too hard or letting my thoughts get the upper hand (one must never work too hard or be dominated by one's thoughts), perhaps if I confess that I heard this terrible screaming others will label me insane, I shall be hidden behind locked doors and sit for the remaining years of my life in a small corner, gazing at the senseless writing on the wall.

Therefore no one confessed to having heard the screaming. Work and play, love and death, continued as usual. Yet the screaming persisted. It sounded day and night in the ears of the people of the city, yet all remained silent concerning it, and talked of other things. Until one day a stranger arrived from a foreign shore. As soon as he arrived in the city he gave a start of horror and exclaimed to the Head of the Welcoming Committee, 'What was that? Why, it has not yet ceased! What is it, that terrible screaming? How can you possibly live with it? Does it continue day and night? Oh what sympathy I have for you in this otherwise fair untroubled city!'

The Head of the Welcoming Committee was at a loss. On the one hand the stranger was a Distinguished Person whom it would be impolite to contradict; on the other hand, it would be equally unwise for the Head of the Welcoming Committee to acknowledge the terrible screaming. He decided to risk being thought impolite.

'I hear nothing unusual,' he said lightly, trying to suggest that perhaps his thoughts had been elsewhere, and at the same time trying to convey his undivided attention to the concern of the Distinguished Stranger. His task was difficult. The packaging of words with varied intentions is like writing a letter to someone in a foreign land and addressing it to oneself; it never reaches its destination.

The Distinguished Stranger looked confused. 'You hear no terrible screaming?'

The Head of the Welcoming Committee turned to his assistant. 'Do you perhaps hear some unusual sound?'

The Assistant who had been disturbed by the screaming and had decided that very day to speak out, to refuse to ignore it, now became afraid that perhaps he would lose his job if he mentioned it. He shook his head.

'I hear nothing unusual,' he replied firmly.

The Distinguished Stranger looked embarrassed. 'Perhaps it is my imagination,' he said apologetically. 'It is just as well that I have come for a holiday to your beautiful city. I have been working very hard lately.'

Then aware once again of the terrible screaming he covered his ears with his hands.

'I fear I am unwell,' he said. 'I apologise if I am unable to attend the banquet, in honour of my arrival.'

'We understand completely,' said the Head of the Welcoming Committee.

So there was no banquet. The Distinguished Stranger consulted a specialist who admitted him to a private rest home where he could recover from his disturbed state of mind and the persistence in his ears of the terrible screaming.

The Specialist finished examining the Distinguished

Stranger. He washed his hands with a slab of hard soap, took off his white coat, and was preparing to go home to his wife when he thought suddenly, Suppose the screaming does exist?

He dismissed the thought. The Rest Home was full, and the fees were high. He enjoyed the comforts of civilisation. Yet supposing, just supposing that all the patients united against him, that all the people of the city began to acknowledge the terrible screaming? What would be the result? Would there be complete panic? Was there really safety in numbers where ideas were concerned?

He stopped thinking about the terrible screaming. He climbed into his Jaguar and drove home.

The Head of the Welcoming Committee, disappointed that he could not attend another banquet, yet relieved because he would not be forced to justify another item of public expenditure, also went home to his wife. They dined on a boiled egg, bread and butter and a cup of tea, for they both approved of simple living.

Then he went to their bedroom, took off his striped suit, switched out the light, got into bed with his wife, and enjoyed the illusion of making uncomplicated love.

And outside in the city the terrible screaming continued its separate existence, unacknowledged. For you see its name was Silence. Silence had found its voice.

The Mythmaker's Office

'The sun,' they said, 'is unmentionable. You must never refer to it.' But that ruse did not work. People referred to the sun, wrote poems about it, suffered under it, lying beneath the chariot wheels, and their eyes were pierced by the sapphire needles jabbing in the groove of light. The sun lolled in the sky. The sun twitched like an extra nerve in the mind. And the sunflowers turned their heads, watching the ceremony, like patient ladies at a tennis match.

So that ruse did not work.

But the people in charge persisted, especially the Minister of Mythmaking who sat all day in his empty office beating his head with a gold-mounted stick in order to send up a cloud of ideas from underneath his wall-to-wall carpet of skin. Alas, when the ideas flew up they arrived like motes in other people's eyes and the Minister of Mythmaking as an habitually polite occupier of his ceiling-to-floor glass ministry did not care to remove ideas from the eyes of other people.

Instead, he went outside and threw coloured stones against the Office of Mythmaking.

'What are you doing, my good chap?' the Prime Minister asked, on his way to a conference.

'Playing fictional fives,' the Minister of Mythmaking replied, after searching for an explanation.

'You would be better occupied,' the Prime Minister told him, 'in performing the correct duties of your office.'

Dazed, shoulders drooping with care, the Minister of Mythmaking returned to his office where once again he sat alone, staring at the big empty room and seeing his face four times in the glass walls. Once more he took his gold-mounted stick and, beating his head, he sent up another cloud of ideas which had a stored musty smell for they had been swept under the carpet years ago and had never been removed or disturbed until now. One idea pierced the Minister in the eye.

'Ah,' he said. 'Death. Death is unmentionable. Surely that will please all concerned. Death is obscene, unpublishable. We must ban all reference to it, delete the death notices from the newspapers, make it an indecent offence to be seen congregating at funerals, drive Death underground.

'Yes,' the Minister of Mythmaking said to himself. 'This will surely please the public, the majority, and prove the ultimate value of Democracy. All will cooperate in the denial of Death.' Accordingly he drafted an appropriate bill which passed swiftly with averted eyes through the House of Parliament and joined its forebears in the worm-eaten paper territories in panelled rooms.

Death notices disappeared from the newspapers. Periodical raids were carried out by the police upon undertakers' premises and crematoria to ensure that no indecent activities were in progress. Death became relegated to a Resistance Movement, a Black Market, and furtive shovellings on the outskirts of the city.

For people did not stop dying. Although it was now against the law, obscene, subversive, Death remained an intense part of the lives of every inhabitant of the kingdom. In the pubs and clubs after work the citizens gathered to exchange stories which began, 'Do you know the one about . . . ?' and which were punctuated with whispered references to Death, the Dead, Cemeteries, Mortuaries. Often you could hear smothered laughter and observe expressions of shame and guilt as ribaldry placed its fear-releasing hand simultaneously upon Death and Conscience. At other times arguments broke out, fights began, the police were called in, and the next day people were summoned to court on charges relating to indecent behaviour and language, with the witness for the prosecution exclaiming, 'He openly uttered the word . . . the word . . . well I shall write it upon a piece of paper and show it to the learned judge . . .' And when the judge read the words 'Death', 'the dead' upon the paper his expression would become severe, he would pronounce the need for a heavy penalty, citizens must learn to behave as normal citizens, and not flout the laws of common decency by referring to Death and the practices of burial . . .

In books the offending five-letter word was no longer written in full; letters other than the first and last were replaced by dots or a dash. When one writer boldly used the word Death several times, and gave detailed descriptions of the ceremonies attending death and burial, there followed such an outcry that his publishers were prosecuted for issuing an indecent work.

But the prosecutors did not win their case, for witnesses convinced the jury that the references to death and its ceremonies were of unusual beauty and power, and should be read by all citizens.

'In the end,' a witness reminded the court, 'each one of us is involved in dying, and though we are forbidden by law to acknowledge this, surely it is necessary for us to learn the facts of death and burial?'

'What!' the public in court said. 'And corrupt the rising generation!' You should have seen the letters to the paper after the court's decision was made known!

The book in question sold many millions of copies; its relevant passages were marked and thumbed; but people placed it on their bookshelves with its title facing the wall.

Soon, however, the outcry and publicity which attended the case were forgotten and the city of the kingdom reverted to its former habits of secrecy. People died in secret, were buried in secret. At one time there was a wave of righteous public anger (which is a dangerous form of anger) against the existence of buildings such as hospitals which in some ways cater to the indecencies of death and are thus an insult to the pure-minded. So effective had been the work of the Mythmaker's Office that the presence of a hospital, its evil suggestiveness, made one close one's eyes in disgust. Many of the buildings were deliberately burned to the ground, during occasions of night-long uninhibited feasting and revelry where people rejoiced, naked, dancing, making love while the Watch Committee, also naked, but with pencils and notebooks, maintained their vigilance by recording instances of behaviour which stated or implied reference to the indecencies of Death.

People found dying in a public place were buried in secrecy and shame. Furtive obscene songs were sung about road accidents, immodesties such as influenza, bronchitis, and the gross facts of the sickroom. Doctors, in spite of their vowed alliance with the living, became unmentionable evils, and were forced to advertise in glass cabinets outside tobacconists and night clubs in the seedier districts of the kingdom.

The avoidance of Death, like the avoidance of all inevitability, overflowed into the surrounding areas of living, like a river laying waste the land which it had formerly nourished and made fertile.

The denial of Death became also a denial of life and growth.

'Well,' said the Prime Minister surrounded by last week's wrapped, sliced, crumbling policies, 'Well,' he said proudly to the Minister of Mythmaking, 'you have accomplished your purpose. You have done good work. You may either retire on a substantial pension or take a holiday in the South of France, at the kingdom's expense. We have abolished Death. We are now immortal. Prepare the country for thousands of years of green happiness.'

And leaning forward he took a bite of a new policy which had just been delivered to him. It was warm and doughy, with bubbles of air inside to give it lightness.

'New policies, eaten quickly, are indigestible,' the Minister of Mythmaking advised, wishing to be of service before he retired to the South of France.

The Prime Minister frowned. 'I have remedies,' he said coldly. Then he smiled. 'Thousands of years of green happiness!'

Yet by the end of that year the whole kingdom except for one man and one woman had committed suicide. Death, birth, life had been abolished. People arrived from the moon, rubbing their hands with glee and sucking lozenges which were laid in rows, in tins, and dusted with sugar.

In a hollow upon dead grass and dead leaves the one human couple left alive on earth said, 'Let's make Death.'

And the invalid sun opened in the sky, erupting its contagious boils of light, pouring down the golden matter upon the waste places of the earth.

The Pleasures of Arithmetic

From my window I look upon the windows of at least ten living rooms in each of which there is a television set which grips light in black-and-white body-hold, which fires people in evening suits at a small target behind the eyes where thoughts also land from time to time unharmed cushioning their fall through darkness. Each night in each of these ten living rooms there are ten times how many people watching the same programme, receiving news bulletins (the diminutive of bullets), listening to the same music, and in the end thinking the same thoughts, in the end hosts only at the point of a gun to thoughts donated to them by courtesy of the television company.

Each night in ten rooms ten times how many people.

Thoughts moulded on the same last bind the wayward feet, encourage hard dead growths of nothingness, cause bewildering obstinate pain whose only remedy is resection of the mind.

Thoughts in identical clothes — disguised fox wolf mother enemy husband crowd the frontiers, dull suspicion, criticism, my house is yours, I hold no weapons, I sleep in the belly of the fox before I wake in darkness.

Stamped approved thoughts of equal value, interchangeable, serving as passport, reply coupon, income tax return, pension deposit, life insurance.

I dispense myself red-hot behind the grille, POSITION CLOSED.

PLEASE DO NOT ASK FOR CREDIT AS A REFUSAL

CAUSES OFFENCE.

But who would offend, who would dare to offend?

Two million times ten rooms, three million times, fifty million times how many people . . .

The sky swipes with the back of its hand, the sun overtakes in the lane of outer darkness . . .

Multiply replenish the earth with thoughts while the deepfreeze control kills quietly.

Arithmetic is a fascinating pleasure.

'So in the end,' said the parson, 'the Many became One.'

'What we need,' said the politician, 'is Unity.'

'Our aim,' said the poet, 'is like-mindedness.'

How wonderful that all have accomplished their aim, that the wilderness has blossomed with plastic lily of the valley, that the sensitive eye, out-trembling dragonfly, cat's whisker, petals exposed to frost, has made its home in how many million times how many living rooms!

I am glad that I learned arithmetic at school — how else could I experience its perils and pleasures?

Take heed. The sky will not turn the other cheek, the strength of the sun is a single strength, do we raid the monastic thought of the moon?

Of course.

Arithmetic takes no account of Progress. We are still walking to and fro emptying the sea with a sieve while Love sleeps at the Pole, his measurements carved from ice.

The Daylight and the Dust

The Daylight and the Dust were on holiday together with nowhere to go.

'I might swoop and bury,' the Dust said.

'I might lie between sheets of morning,' the Daylight said. But they packed a little gold bag and a little grey bag and went on tour to blind and smother.

The faithless Daylight betrayed the Dust. The Dust was pursued by his enemies and driven into exile, and to this day the bones of the dead may or may not lie uncovered in the city.

The Daylight continued his journey alone with his little gold bag. He walked up and down the sky, upside down, like a fly, and if you look in the sky you will see him. His little gold bag is the sun.

The sun is a portmanteau of furnaces, boiling remorse, hot scones, tourist equipment and change of history.

And still the Dust blows homeless, in exile, in hiding, cowers in crevices and shaded hollows, on ledges and stone faces, and in anger tears the privacy from impersonal bones and skulls threaded like identical beads in the jewel case of the dead.

The Dust is Breath. Is not Breath the true and only refugee?

Solutions

This is a story which belongs in the very room in which I am typing. I am not haunted by it, but I shall tell it to you. It happened once — twice, thrice? — upon a time.

A young man was so bedevilled by the demands of his body that he decided to rid himself of it completely. Now this worry was not a simple matter of occasional annoyance. As soon as the man sat down to work in the morning — he was a private student working all day at this very table with its green plastic cover, drop ends, two protective cork mats — he would be conscious perhaps of an itch in his back which he would be forced to scratch, or he would feel a pain in his arm or shoulder and be unable to rest until he had shaken himself free of the pain which would then drop to the carpet and lie there powerless and be sucked into the vacuum cleaner on a Thursday morning when the woman came to clean the house.

Sometimes as the pain lay upon the carpet the man would engage it in conversation; there would be a lively exchange of bitterness and wit, with the man assuring his pain that he felt no ill-will towards it but he wished that its family would cease inhabiting his body just as he was beginning work for the day. But the pain was cunning. It gave no message to its family which returned again and again, and when it was successfully disposed of by the vacuum cleaner and the County Council Dustmen and transported to a County Council grave, another family of pain took its place.

'I must get rid of my body,' the man thought. 'What use is it to me? It interferes with my work, and since my work is concentrated in my head I think I shall get rid of my body and retain only my head.'

Ah, what freedom then!

There was another difficulty. As soon as the young man wanted to begin his work in the morning, all the feelings which he preferred to inhabit his head to nourish and revive his thoughts, would decide to pack their picnic lunches for the day, and without asking permission, they would set out on the forbidden route to the shady spot between the man's legs where his penis lived in a little house with a red roof, a knocker on the front door, and two gothic columns at the front gate. And there, in the little house in the woods, with the penis as a sometimes thoughtful, sometimes turbulent host, the man's feelings would unwrap their picnic lunch and enjoy a pleasant feast, often sitting outside in the shade of the two gothic columns. And how ardently the sun shone through the trees, through the leaves, in a red haze of burning!

Now you understand that the man became more and more distressed at the way his body demanded so much attention. It had also to be washed, clothed, warmed, cooled, scratched, rubbed, exercised, rested; and should it suffer the slightest harm, pain, like a dragonfly, would alight at the spot with its valise full of instruments of torture which dragonflies used to carry (once, twice, thrice upon a time) when they were the envoys of genuine dragons.

The man grew more and more depressed. He felt himself becoming bankrupt — with his feelings engaged hour after hour in extravagant parties which took no account of the cost, so that bills mounted and could not be paid, and strange authorities intruded to give orders and confuse the situation. And with so little work being done the man did not know where he would find money for rent and food. Sometimes he was so depressed and alone that he wept. His feelings did not seem to care. Whenever he glanced at the little house in the woods he could see at once that all the lights in the house were blazing; he could hear the boisterous singing at night, and witness the riotous carousing during the day under the melting indiarubber sun.

'What shall I do?' the man cried when he woke one morning feeling tired and discouraged. 'Shall I rid myself of my body?'

He decided to rid himself of his body, to keep only his head which, he was convinced, would work faithfully for him once it was set free.

Therefore, the same morning, feeling lighthearted and singing a gay song, the man sharpened his kitchen knife which he had bought at Woolworths for two and eleven and which had grown blunt from much use as a peeler of vegetables, spreader of marmalade on toast, cutter of string on mysterious packages from foreign countries, whittler of wood on pencils; and, unfolding a copy of the *Guardian*, the man laid it on the kitchen floor, leaned forward, applied the knife to his throat, and in a moment his head had been cut off and the blood was seeping through the Editorial, Letters to the Editor, and the centre news page.

The problem which confronted the man's head now was to get rid of the body, and to clean the blood from the kitchen floor. The head had rolled, its face rather pale with the excitement of its new freedom, as far as the fireplace. Now the man knew of three little mice who lived behind the screen which covered the disused fireplace, and who emerged on expeditions during the night and during the day when they supposed that all the people in the house were at work. The three mice had survived many attempts to kill them. One of the lodgers from upstairs had shaken three little heaps of poisoned cereal on a strip of hardboard in front of the fireplace and had waited in vain for any sign that the mice had been tempted. She did not know that the young man had warned them. He had been in the kitchen one evening making himself a cup of tea, and he was just about to take a slice of bread from his wrapped sliced white loaf when he saw one of the mice sniffing at the poisoned cereal.

'I wouldn't eat it, if I were you,' the young man said. 'Appearances are deceptive you know. Even I have to be careful with every slice of my wrapped sliced white loaf.'

'Why are you warning me?' the little mouse asked. 'Don't you want to poison me? I thought everybody wanted to poison little mice like me.'

'Don't touch that heap of cereal,' the young man said melodramatically.

The mouse was formal. 'I am grateful sir,' he said, and disappeared.

But naturally the mice were grateful, following the tradition of all rescued animals in fairy stories, and as the young man had indeed been living in a fairy story of despair he had no difficulty now, when he had freed himself from his body, in asking and receiving help from the three mice. They were willing to dispose of the body and to clean the kitchen until the floor was without a trace of blood. In their turn, the mice asked the help of the dustbin downstairs, and because the dustbin had often acted as a gay restaurateur serving delectable suppers to the three mice, and because he did not wish to lose his reputation — for reputations are valuable property and must be stored in a safe place (the dustbin kept his just inside the rim of his grey tin hat), he agreed to come into the house, climb the stairs, remove the body, help to clean away the mess, and put all the refuse and the information concerning it, beneath his tin hat. And all this he accomplished with swiftness and agility which won praise and applause from the three mice. Also, with a kindly impulse, the dustbin carried the man's head to his room and even gave it lessons in flying, for the dustbin lid was a relative of the flying carpet and knew the secrets of flight, and that was why he had been so agile in climbing the stairs and moving in and out of the kitchen.

How patiently he taught the head to fly! He waited so courteously and sympathetically until the art was mastered, and then bidding the head goodbye returned downstairs (conscious of his new reputation as a hero), out the back door, to his home in the tiny backyard where he lived in the company of a shelf of plant pots and a string bag of clothes pegs which continually quarrelled amongst themselves about who were superior, the plastic clothes pegs or the wooden clothes pegs. These quarrels were all the more bitter because they took place among the older generation of clothes pegs; the younger had forgotten or did not know how to quarrel; they were intermarrying and shared shirt flats on the same clothesline; together they topped the country spaces of blankets, and holidayed near the ski slopes of sheets and pillowcases . . .

Meanwhile, upstairs, the head was flying rapturously to and fro in the bed-sitting-room, and it continued thus in wild freedom all morning and afternoon.

Once it stopped flying and looked thoughtful. 'Am I a man?' it asked itself.

'Or am I a head? I shall call myself a man, for the most important part of me remains.'

'I'll have one day free,' the man said, 'to think things over, and then I'll start my intellectual work with no dictation or interference ever again from my presumptuous imperious body. Oh I feel as if I could fly to the sky and circle the moon; thoughts race through me, eager to be set down upon paper and studied by those who have never had the insight or strategy to rid themselves of their cumbersome bodies. My act has made my brain supreme. I shall work day and night without interruption . . .'

And on and on the man flew, round and round the room in his dizzy delight. Once he flew to the window and looked out, but fortunately no one in the street saw him or there might have been inquiries. Then in the evening, to his surprise, he began to feel tired.

'It seems that sleep is necessary after all,' he said. 'But only a wink or two of sleep, and then I daresay I shall wake refreshed.'

So he lay down beneath the top blanket of his bed, closed his eyes, and slept a deep sleep, and when he woke next morning his first thought almost set him shouting with exhilaration,

'How wonderful to be free!'

That morning the landlady remarked to her husband, 'The man in the upstairs room seems to have gone away. I'm sure he did not come home last night. The room is so quiet. His rent is due this morning, and we need the money. I'll give him a few days' grace, and then if we are not paid we shall have to see about finding a new lodger — for this one doesn't seem to do any work really, does he? I mean any real work where you catch the bus in the morning and come home tired at night with your *Evening News* under your arm, and you are too tired to read it.'

Also that morning the woman lodger remarked to the other lodger who lived in the small room upstairs, 'The man who shares the kitchen with us has not used his milk — see it's still in the bottle. I was curious and peeped in the door this morning (I was only wondering about the milk, it might go sour, in this heat) and his bed is unruffled, it's not been slept in. Perhaps I should tell the landlady. She likes to know what goes on. He seems to have vanished. There's no sign of him.'

'Ah,' the man was saying at that very moment as he flew about the room, 'I don't need to eat now, yet I am full of vigour and excitement. My former despair has vanished. I will start work as soon as I hear the two lodgers and the landlady and landlord bang the front door as they go out on their way to work.'

He heard the two lodgers in the kitchen, washing up their breakfast dishes. He heard the landlady putting her clothes through the spin-drier. He heard the landlord go out and start the car.

Then he heard the front door bang, once, twice, three, four times. The house was quiet at last. The man gave a long sigh of content, and prepared to work.

The house was indeed quiet. In the kitchen the three mice emerged from their hiding place to explore and examine the turn of events, for events are like tiny revolving wheels, and mice like to play with them and bowl them along alleyways of yellow light where dustbins glitter and the hats of dustbins shine with pride in their distant relation, the Magic Carpet . . .

The three mice pattered around the kitchen, and then curious about their friend who had rid himself of his body, they came — one, two, three — into the man's room where they were surprised to observe, on the green plain of the table, the man resting in an attitude of despair.

'Alas,' he was murmuring. 'Where are my fingers to grasp my pen or tap my typewriter, and my hand to reach books from the shelf? And who will comb my hair and rub the hair tonic into my scalp? Besides, my head itches, there is wax in my ears, I need to keep clearing my throat; how can I blow my nose with dignity? And as for shaving every morning, why, my beard will grow and grow like clematis upon a rotten tree.' Tears trickled from the man's eyes.

The three mice felt very sad. 'We could help you,' they suggested, 'by bringing books to you; but that is all. You need arms, hands, fingers.'

'I need much more,' the man replied. 'Who will listen to my words and love me? And who will want to warm an absent skin or picnic in a deserted house, in darkness, or drink from rivers that have run dry?

'Still,' the man continued, 'my thoughts are free. I have sacrificed these comforts for my thoughts. Yet although I am no longer a slave to my body I am even now subject to irritations. My vanity demands that I rub hair tonic into my scalp to postpone my baldness, for baldness comes early to our family. My need for relief demands that I scratch a spot just above my right ear. My training in hygiene insists that I blow my nose with a square white handkerchief which has my name — MAN — embroidered in one corner! Oh if only I could escape from the petty distractions of my head! Then I would indeed do great work, think noble thoughts. Even my head offends me now. If only I did not possess my head, if I could rid myself of it, if I could just keep my brain and the protective shell enclosing it, then surely I could pursue my work in real freedom!'

Then the idea came to him. Why not ask the mice to fetch the knife from the kitchen (they could carry it easily, one taking the blade, the second the handle, the third acting as guide) and remove all parts of my head except the little walnut which is my brain? It could easily be done. If the mice hurry, the man thought, and set my brain free, no one knows what great work I might accomplish even today before the sun goes down!

So the mice offered to help. They performed the cutting

operations and once again the dustbin and the dustbin lid agreed to collect and conceal the remains. Then, when the task was finished the mice laid what was left of the head, upon the table, and silently (for the man could not communicate with them any more) they and the dustbin and the dustbin lid went from the room, the mice to their corner by the fireplace, the dustbin to his place beneath the shelf where the pot plants lived and the older generation of plastic clothes pegs and wooden clothes pegs continued their quarrels in the string bag where they lived.

Blind, speechless, deaf, the man lay upon the table beside his blank writing paper, his books, his typewriter. He did not move. No one could have divined his thoughts; he himself could no longer communicate them.

That night when the lodger returned from work she peered into the room, and seeing no one there, she reported the fact to the landlady who only that afternoon had replied to inquiries for a rented room.

'The man must have flitted,' the landlady said, opening the door and gazing around the room. 'The bed has not been slept in. His luggage is still here. But I think he has flitted because he could not pay his rent. I think he was the type. No regular work. No getting up in the morning to catch the bus and coming home at night with the *Evening News* in his pocket and being too tired to read it.'

Then the landlady gave a slight shiver of anticipation. 'Now I can come into the room and scour it out, wash the curtains, clean the linoleum and the chair covers, redecorate. I'll move the furniture, too, repair the damages he is sure to have done — look, no casters on the chairs, and the spring of that armchair broken, and the cord hanging from the window, and look at the soot on the window sill!'

Then the landlady glanced at the table and noticed the

shrivelled remains of the man.

'Just look!' she exclaimed to the lodger. 'An old prune left lying around. Eating prunes no doubt while he worked; or pretended to work. Such habits only encourage the mice. No wonder they haven't been tempted by the poison I left out for them if they have been living on titbits from this man!' And with an expression of disgust the landlady removed the deaf, blind, speechless, wrinkled man, took him downstairs and threw him into the dustbin, and not even the dustbin recognised him, for he could never any more proclaim his identity — Man; nor could he see that he was lying in a dustbin; nor could he feel anything except a roaring, like the sound in an empty shell which houses only the memory of the tide with its walls.

And the next morning when the three mice were up early and down to the dustbin for breakfast, one saw the shrivelled man, and not recognising him, exclaimed, 'A prune! I've never tasted prunes, but I can always try.' And so the three mice shared the prune, spitting out the hard bits.

'It wasn't bad,' they said. 'It will do for breakfast.'

Then they hurried downstairs to hide while the landlady who was not going to work that day prepared the man's empty room for its new tenant, a clean businessman who would work from nine till five and bring inconvenience upon no one, least of all upon himself.

One Must Give Up

There comes a time when one must give up.

So I have given up.

I have cancelled delivery of my newspaper. I have removed the connection from my radio, permanently disabling it. The bailiffs in a journey of blessed misunderstanding have taken away my seventeen-inch Portadyne television set where I could switch to both channels and watch interviewers in swivelling chairs driving discussions like cranes through the studio, panellists cut off in the prime of dissension, ladies embracing meat extract and gas ovens, weathermen playing snakes and ladders (throw the dice, up a ladder, down a green-and-yellow-headed snake) with areas of high and low pressure, clicking pop singers cradled inside their own giant candy initial, biting a slice in their self-hunger when out of sight of the camera — after all, one must consume oneself, in the end — timid newsmen introducing a smoky hiccup of old film, women interviewers with pearls at the throat in the manner of doubts in the mind, wax in the ear, stitch in the side, or wolves at the door.

I have given up.

I am now a maker of my own news and distributor of my own time. I receive news which no one thought to broadcast on radio or film for television or report in the newspapers. I choose for myself once again. It is so long since I knew such freedom. Tight-lipped runners arrive bearing word from far countries — from friends two streets away. The cherry tree is in flower. The crocuses are out. The woman in the opposite house washes away the sins committed upon the crazy pavement where dogs have danced, human feet have shed their burden of dust, soot, guilt collected from pacing up and down at midnight upon selected graves.

The pavement is clean once more. The woman empties her blue polythene bucket, sluicing the waste down the County Council gutter while small boys at the end of the street stop and watch the mesmeric flow of water running downhill, hopefully, to the Great Bight occupied by the fabled sea.

Cars pass: minicars, sports cars with the canvas drawn away from their folded ribs, lorries bearing the titles of their load — Military Pickle, Plastic Toilet Seats, Wonderloaf. In the chemist's, around the corner, people read old bound copies of *Time* and *Life* as they wait for their Lotion, Mixture, Linctus.

The butcher arranges the white trays, pooled with blood, in rows in his window, while the cashier in her question box, puppet theatre or cave tries to find the reason for the stains on her white overall, since she never handles the meat and steps quickly through the wilderness of sawdust to reach her sanctuary. The thought occurs, Does money cause bloodstains? Have I been knifed in secret by weapons disguised as coins?

In the grocer's the icing on the twopenny-halfpenny torpedo buns slowly melts with the warmth of the oilstove burning in the corner. Stacked upon the top shelf the rusting tins of unpopular food lean, like aged acrobats, their punched-in bellies turned to the light, their proclamations faded to torn wrinkled banners circling their bodies. Some, marked down in price, wonderful value, wear no labels, no news.

The jet unwinds its cotton in the sky where the old-women clouds thread their needles of light, facing the sun, and sew by hand the new bridal dresses for their daughters who are marrying the brothers Rain. Wearing dark suits, with rainbow rosettes in their buttonholes, the grooms will lead their brides to earth, honeymooning in puddles and lakes, making mirrors of each other, returning by sunbeam to the sky where the old-women clouds sit at the door, rumbling their pearly gossip.

The crippled sun chain smokes in a wheel chair striped red and gold . . .

Fact or fancy. There comes a time when one must rely upon one's own news, images, interpretations, when one must resist the pressure upon one's house of conforming, orthodox, shared seasons, and, using the panel in the secret room, make one's escape to fluid, individual weather; stand alone in the dark listening to the worm knocking three times, the rose resisting, and the inhabited forest of the heart accomplishing its own private moments of growth.

Two Sheep

Two sheep were travelling to the saleyards. The first sheep knew that after they had been sold their destination was the slaughterhouse at the freezing works. The second sheep did not know of their fate. They were being driven with the rest of the flock along a hot dusty valley road where the surrounding hills leaned in a sun-scorched wilderness of rock, tussock and old rabbit warrens. They moved slowly, for the drover in his trap was in no hurry, and had even taken one of the dogs to sit beside him while the other scrambled from side to side of the flock, guiding them.

'I think,' said the first sheep who was aware of their approaching death, 'that the sun has never shone so warm on my fleece, nor, from what I see with my small sheep's eye, has the sky seemed so flawless, without seams or tucks or cracks or blemishes.'

'You are crazy,' said the second sheep who did not know of their approaching death. 'The sun is warm, yes, but how hot and dusty and heavy my wool feels! It is a burden to go trotting along this oven shelf. It seems our journey will never end.'

'How fresh and juicy the grass appears on the hill!' the first sheep exclaimed. 'And not a hawk in the sky!'

'I think,' replied the second sheep, 'that something has blinded you. Just look up in the sky and see those three hawks waiting to swoop and attack us!'

They trotted on further through the valley road. Now and again the second sheep stumbled.

'I feel so tired,' he said. 'I wonder how much longer we

must walk on and on through this hot dusty valley?'

But the first sheep walked nimbly and his wool felt light upon him as if he had just been shorn. He could have gambolled like a lamb in August.

'I still think,' he said, 'that today is the most wonderful day I have known. I do not feel that the road is hot and dusty. I do not notice the stones and grit that you complain of. To me the hills have never seemed so green and enticing, the sun has never seemed so warm and comforting. I believe that I could walk through this valley for ever, and never feel tired or hungry or thirsty.'

'Whatever has come over you?' the second sheep asked crossly. 'Here we are, trotting along hour after hour, and soon we shall stand in our pens in the saleyards while the sun leans over us with its branding irons and our overcoats are such a burden that they drag us to the floor of our pen where we are almost trampled to death by the so dainty feet of our fellow sheep. A fine life that is. It would not surprise me if after we are sold we are taken in trucks to the freezing works and killed in cold blood. But,' he added, comforting himself, 'that is not likely to happen. Oh no, that could never happen! I have it on authority that even when they are trampled by their fellows, sheep do not die. The tales we hear from time to time are but malicious rumours, and those vivid dreams which strike us in the night as we sleep on the sheltered hills, they are but illusions. Do you not agree?' he asked the first sheep.

They were turning now from the valley road, and the saleyards were in sight, while drawn up in the siding on the rusty railway lines, the red trucks stood waiting, spattered inside with sheep and cattle dirt and with white chalk marks, in cipher, on the outside. And still the first sheep did not reveal to his companion that they were being driven to certain death.

When they were jostled inside their pen the first sheep gave an exclamation of delight.

'What a pleasant little house they have let to us! I have never seen such smart red-painted bars, and such four-square corners. And look at the elegant stairway which we will climb to enter those red caravans for our seaside holiday!'

'You make me tired,' the second sheep said. 'We are standing inside a dirty pen, nothing more, and I cannot move my feet in their nicely polished black shoes but I tread upon the dirt left by sheep which have been imprisoned here before us. In fact I have never been so badly treated in all my life!' And the second sheep began to cry. Just then a kind elderly sheep jostled through the flock and began to comfort him.

'You have been frightening your companion, I suppose,' she said angrily to the first sheep. 'You have been telling horrible tales of our fate. Some sheep never know when to keep things to themselves. There was no need to tell your companion the truth, that we are being led to certain death!'

But the first sheep did not answer. He was thinking that the sun had never blessed him with so much warmth, that no crowded pen had ever seemed so comfortable and luxurious. Then suddenly he was taken by surprise and hustled out a little gate and up the ramp into the waiting truck, and suddenly too the sun shone in its true colours, battering him about the head with gigantic burning bars, while the hawks congregated above, sizzling the sky with their wings, and a pall of dust clung to the barren used-up hills, and everywhere was commotion, pushing, struggling, bleating, trampling.

'This must be death,' he thought, and he began to struggle and cry out.

The second sheep, having at last learned that he would meet his fate at the freezing works, stood unperturbed now in the truck with his nose against the wall and his eyes looking through the slits.

'You are right,' he said to the first sheep. 'The hill has never seemed so green, the sun has never been warmer, and this truck with its neat red walls is a mansion where I would happily spend the rest of my days.'

But the first sheep did not answer. He had seen the approach of death. He could hide from it no longer. He had given up the struggle and was lying exhausted in a corner of the truck. And when the truck arrived at its destination, the freezing works, the man whose duty it was to unload the sheep noticed the first lying so still in the corner that he believed it was dead.

'We can't have dead sheep,' he said. 'How can you kill a dead sheep?'

So he heaved the first sheep out of the door of the truck onto the rusty railway line.

'I'll move it away later,' he said to himself. 'Meanwhile here goes with this lot.'

And while he was so busy moving the flock, the first sheep, recovering, sprang up and trotted away along the line, out the gate of the freezing works, up the road, along another road, until he saw a flock being driven before him.

'I will join the flock,' he said. 'No one will notice, and I shall be safe.'

While the drover was not looking, the first sheep hurried in among the flock and was soon trotting along with them until they came to a hot dusty road through a valley where the hills leaned in a sun-scorched wilderness of rock, tussock, and old rabbit warrens.

By now he was feeling very tired. He spoke for the first

time to his new companions.

'What a hot dusty road,' he said. 'How uncomfortable the heat is, and the sun seems to be striking me for its own burning purposes.'

The sheep walking beside him looked surprised.

'It is a wonderful day,' he exclaimed. 'The sun is warmer than I have ever known it, the hills glow green with luscious grass, and there is not a hawk in the sky to threaten us!'

'You mean,' the first sheep replied slyly, 'that you are on your way to the saleyards, and then to the freezing works to be killed.'

The other sheep gave a bleat of surprise.

'How did you guess?' he asked.

'Oh,' said the first sheep wisely, 'I know the code. And because I know the code I shall go around in circles all my life, not knowing whether to think that the hills are bare or whether they are green, whether the hawks are scarce or plentiful, whether the sun is friend or foe. For the rest of my life I shall not speak another word. I shall trot along the hot dusty valleys where the hills are both barren and lush with spring grass.

'What shall I do but keep silent?'

And so it happened, and over and over again the first sheep escaped death, and rejoined the flock of sheep who were travelling to the freezing works. He is still alive today. If you notice him in a flock, being driven along a hot dusty road, you will be able to distinguish him by his timidity, his uncertainty, the frenzied expression in his eyes when he tries, in his condemned silence, to discover whether the sky is at last free from hawks, or whether they circle in twos and threes above him, waiting to kill him.

From

The Reservoir:
Stories and Sketches

The Reservoir

It was said to be four or five miles along the gully, past orchards and farms, paddocks filled with cattle, sheep, wheat, gorse, and the squatters of the land who were the rabbits eating like modern sculpture into the hills, though how could we know anything of modern sculpture, we knew nothing but the Warrior in the main street with his wreaths of poppies on Anzac Day, the gnomes weeping in the Gardens because the seagulls perched on their green caps and showed no respect, and how important it was for birds, animals and people, especially children, to show respect!

And that is why for so long we obeyed the command of the grownups and never walked as far as the forbidden Reservoir, but were content to return 'tired but happy' (as we wrote in our school compositions), answering the question, Where did you walk today? with a suspicion of blackmail, 'Oh, nearly, nearly to the Reservoir!'

The Reservoir was the end of the world; beyond it, you fell; beyond it were paddocks of thorns, strange cattle, strange farms, legendary people whom we would never know or recognise even if they walked among us on a Friday night downtown when we went to follow the boys and listen to the Salvation Army Band and buy a milk shake in the milk bar and then return home to find that everything was all right and safe, that our mother had not run away and caught the night train to the North Island, that our father had not shot himself with worrying over the bills, but had in fact been downtown himself and had bought the usual Friday night treat, a bag of liquorice allsorts and a bag of chocolate roughs, from Woolworths.

The Reservoir haunted our lives. We never knew one until we came to this town; we had used pump water. But here, in our new house, the water ran from the taps as soon as we turned them on, and if we were careless and left them on, our father would shout, as if the affair were his personal concern, 'Do you want the Reservoir to run dry?'

That frightened us. What should we do if the Reservoir ran dry? Would we die of thirst like Burke and Wills in the desert?

'The Reservoir,' our mother said, 'gives pure water, water safe to drink without boiling it.'

The water was in a different class, then, from the creek which flowed through the gully; yet the creek had its source in the Reservoir. Why had it not received the pampering attention of officialdom which strained weed and earth, cockabullies and trout and eels, from our tap water? Surely the Reservoir was not entirely pure?

'Oh no,' they said, when we inquired. We learned that the water from the Reservoir had been 'treated'. We supposed this to mean that during the night men in light-blue uniforms with sacks over their shoulders crept beyond the circle of pine trees which enclosed the Reservoir, and emptied the contents of the sacks into the water, to dissolve dead bodies and prevent the decay of teeth.

Then, at times, there would be news in the paper, discussed by my mother with the neighbours over the back fence. Children had been drowned in the Reservoir.

'No child,' the neighbour would say, 'ought to be allowed near the Reservoir.'

'I tell mine to keep strictly away,' my mother would reply.

And for so long we obeyed our mother's command, on

our favourite walks along the gully simply following the untreated cast-off creek which we loved and which flowed day and night in our heads in all its detail — the wild sweet peas, boiled-lolly pink, and the mint growing along the banks; the exact spot in the water where the latest dead sheep could be found, and the stink of its bloated flesh and floating wool, an allowable earthy stink which we accepted with pleasant revulsion and which did not prompt the 'inky-pinky I smell Stinkie' rhyme which referred to offensive human beings only. We knew where the water was shallow and could be paddled in, where forts could be made from the rocks; we knew the frightening deep places where the eels lurked and the weeds were tangled in gruesome shapes; we knew the jumping places, the mossy stones with their dangers, limitations, and advantages; the sparkling places where the sun trickled beside the water, upon the stones; the bogs made by roaming cattle, trapping some of them to death; their gaunt telltale bones; the little valleys with their new growth of lush grass where the creek had 'changed its course', and no longer flowed.

'The creek has changed its course,' our mother would say, in a tone which implied terror and a sense of strangeness, as if a tragedy had been enacted.

We knew the moods of the creek, its levels of low-flow, half-high-flow, high-flow which all seemed to relate to interference at its source — the Reservoir. If one morning the water turned the colour of clay and crowds of bubbles were passengers on every suddenly swift wave hurrying by, we would look at one another and remark with the fatality and reverence which attends a visitation or prophecy,

'The creek's going on high-flow. They must be doing something at the Reservoir.'

By afternoon the creek would be on high-flow, turbulent, muddy, unable to be jumped across or paddled in or fished in, concealing beneath a swelling fluid darkness whatever evil which 'they', the authorities, had decided to purge so swiftly and secretly from the Reservoir.

For so long, then, we obeyed our parents, and never walked as far as the Reservoir. Other things concerned us, other curiosities, fears, challenges. The school year ended. I got a prize, a large yellow book the colour of cat's mess. Inside it were editions of newspapers, *The Worms' Weekly*, supposedly written by worms, snails, spiders. For the first part of the holidays we spent the time sitting in the long grass of our front lawn nibbling the stalks of shamrock and reading insect newspapers and relating their items to the lives of those living on our front lawn down among the summer-dry roots of the couch, tinkertailor, daisy, dandelion, shamrock, clover, and ordinary 'grass'. High summer came. The blowsy old red roses shed their petals to the regretful refrain uttered by our mother year after year at the same time, 'I should have made potpourri, I have a wonderful recipe for potpourri in Dr Chase's Book.'

Our mother never made the potpourri. She merely quarrelled with our father over how to pronounce it.

The days became unbearably long and hot. Our Christmas presents were broken or too boring to care about. Celluloid dolls had loose arms and legs and rifts in their bright pink bodies; the invisible ink had poured itself out in secret messages; diaries frustrating in their smallness (two lines to a day) had been filled in for the whole of the coming year . . . Days at the beach were tedious, with no room in the bathing sheds so that we were forced to undress in the common room downstairs with its floor patched with wet and trailed with footmarks and sand and its tiny barred window (which made me believe that I was living in the French Revolution).

Rumours circled the burning world. The sea was drying

up, soon you could paddle or walk to Australia. Sharks had been seen swimming inside the breakwater; one shark attacked a little boy and bit off his you-know-what.

We swam. We wore bathing togs all day. We gave up cowboys and ranches; and baseball and sledding; and 'those games' where we mimicked grownup life, loving and divorcing each other, kissing and slapping, taking secret paramours when our husband was working out of town. Everything exhausted us. Cracks appeared in the earth; the grass was bled yellow; the ground was littered with beetle shells and snail shells; flies came in from the unofficial rubbish-dump at the back of the house; the twisting flypapers hung from the ceiling; a frantic buzzing filled the room as the flypapers became crowded. Even the cat put out her tiny tongue, panting in the heat.

We realised, and were glad, that school would soon reopen. What was school like? It seemed so long ago, it seemed as if we had never been to school, surely we had forgotten everything we had learned, how frightening, thrilling and strange it would all seem!

Where would we go on the first day, who would teach us, what were the names on the new books?

Who would sit beside us, who would be our best friend?

The earth crackled in early-autumn haze and still the February sun dried the world; even at night the rusty sheet of roofing-iron outside by the cellar stayed warm, but with rows of sweat-marks on it; the days were still long, with night face to face with morning and almost nothing in-between but a snatch of turning sleep with the blankets on the floor and the windows wide open to moths with their bulging lamplit eyes moving through the dark and their grandfather bodies knocking, knocking upon the walls.

Day after day the sun still waited to pounce. We were tired, our skin itched, our sunburn had peeled and peeled again, the skin on our feet was hard, there was dust in our hair, our bodies clung with the salt of sea-bathing and sweat, the towels were harsh with salt.

School soon, we said again, and were glad; for lessons gave shade to rooms and corridors; cloakrooms were cold and sunless. Then, swiftly, suddenly, disease came to the town. Infantile Paralysis. Black headlines in the paper, listing the number of cases, the number of deaths. Children everywhere, out in the country, up north, down south, two streets away.

The schools did not reopen. Our lessons came by post, in smudged print on rough white paper; they seemed makeshift and false, they inspired distrust, they could not compete with the lure of the sun still shining, swelling, the world would go up in cinders, the days were too long, there was nothing to do, there was nothing to do; the lessons were dull; in the front room with the navy-blue blind half down the window and the tiny splits of light showing through, and the lesson papers sometimes covered with unexplained blots of ink as if the machine which had printed them had broken down or rebelled, the lessons were even more dull.

Ancient Egypt and the flooding of the Nile!

The Nile, when we possessed a creek of our own with individual flooding!

'Well let's go along the gully, along by the creek,' we would say, tired with all these.

Then one day when our restlessness was at its height, when the flies buzzed like bees in the flypapers, and the warped wood of the house cracked its knuckles out of boredom, the need for something to do in the heat, we found once again the only solution to our unrest.

Someone said, 'What's the creek on?'

'Half-high flow.'

'Good.'

So we set out, in our bathing suits, and carrying switches of willow.

'Keep your sun hats on!' our mother called.

All right. We knew. Sunstroke when the sun clipped you over the back of the head, striking you flat on the ground. Sunstroke. Lightning. Even tidal waves were threatening us on this southern coast. The world was full of alarm.

'And don't go as far as the Reservoir!'

We dismissed the warning. There was enough to occupy us along the gully without our visiting the Reservoir. First, the couples. We liked to find a courting couple and follow them and when, as we knew they must do because they were tired or for other reasons, they found a place in the grass and lay down together, we liked to make jokes about them, amongst ourselves. 'Just wait for him to kiss her,' we would say. 'Watch. There. A beaut. Smack.'

Often we giggled and lingered even after the couple had observed us. We were waiting for them to do it. Every man and woman did it, we knew that for a fact. We speculated about technical details. Would he wear a frenchie? If he didn't wear a frenchie then she would start having a baby and be forced to get rid of it by drinking gin. Frenchies, by the way, were for sale in Woolworths. Some said they were fingerstalls, but we knew they were frenchies and sometimes we would go downtown and into Woolworths just to look at the frenchies for sale. We hung around the counter, sniggering. Sometimes we nearly died laughing, it was so funny.

After we tired of spying on the couples we would shout after them as we went our way.

Pound, shillings and pence,
a man fell over the fence,
he fell on a lady,
and squashed out a baby,
pound, shillings and pence!

Sometimes a slight fear struck us — what if a man fell on us like that and squashed out a chain of babies?

Our other pastime along the gully was robbing the orchards, but this summer day the apples were small green hard and hidden by leaves. There were no couples either. We had the gully to ourselves. We followed the creek, whacking our sticks, gossiping and singing, but we stopped, immediately silent, when someone — sister or brother — said, 'Let's go to the Reservoir!'

A feeling of dread seized us. We knew, as surely as we knew our names and our address Thirty-three Stour Street Ohau Otago South Island New Zealand Southern Hemisphere The World, that we would some day visit the Reservoir, but the time seemed almost as far away as leaving school, getting a job, marrying.

And then there was the agony of deciding the right time — how did one decide these things?

'We've been told not to, you know,' one of us said timidly.

That was me. Eating bread and syrup for tea had made my hair red, my skin too, so that I blushed easily, and the grownups guessed if I told a lie.

'It's a long way,' said my little sister.

'Coward!'

But it *was* a long way, and perhaps it would take all day and night, perhaps we would have to sleep there among the pine trees with the owls hooting and the old needle-filled warrens which now reached to the centre of the earth where pools of molten lead bubbled, waiting to seize us if we tripped and then there was the crying sound made by the trees, a sound of speech at its loneliest level where the meaning is felt but never explained, and it goes on and on in a kind of despair, trying to reach a point of understanding.

We knew that pine trees spoke in this way. We were lonely listening to them because we knew we could never help them to say it, whatever they were trying to say, for if the wind who was so close to them could not help them, how could we?

Oh no, we could not spend the night at the Reservoir among the pine trees.

'Billy Whittaker and his gang have been to the Reservoir, Billy Whittaker and the Green Feather gang, one afternoon.'

'Did he say what it was like?'

'No, he never said.'

'He's been in an iron lung.'

That was true. Only a day or two ago our mother had been reminding us in an ominous voice of the fact which roused our envy just as much as our dread, 'Billy Whittaker was in an iron lung two years ago. Infantile paralysis.'

Some people were lucky. None of us dared to hope that we would ever be surrounded by the glamour of an iron lung; we would have to be content all our lives with paltry flesh lungs.

'Well are we going to the Reservoir or not?'

That was someone trying to sound bossy like our father, 'Well am I to have salmon sandwiches or not, am I to have lunch at all today or not?'

We struck our sticks in the air. They made a whistling sound. They were supple and young. We had tried to make musical instruments out of them, time after time we hacked at the willow and the elder to make pipes to blow our music, but no sound came but our own voices. And why did two sticks rubbed together not make fire? Why couldn't we ever *make* anything out of the bits of the world lying about us?

An aeroplane passed in the sky. We craned our necks to read the writing on the underwing, for we collected aeroplane numbers.

The plane was gone, in a glint of sun.

'Are we?' someone said.

'If there's an eclipse you can't see at all. The birds stop singing and go to bed.'

'Well are we?'

Certainly we were. We had not quelled all our misgiving, but we set out to follow the creek to the Reservoir.

What is it? I wondered. They said it was a lake. I thought it was a bundle of darkness and great wheels which peeled and sliced you like an apple and drew you towards them with demonic force, in the same way that you were drawn beneath the wheels of a train if you stood too near the edge of the platform. That was the terrible danger when the Limited came rushing in and you had to approach to kiss arriving aunts.

We walked on and on, past wild sweet peas, clumps of cutty grass, horse mushrooms, ragwort, gorse, cabbage trees; and then, at the end of the gully, we came to strange territory, fences we did not know, with the barbed wire tearing at our skin and at our skirts put on over our bathing suits because we felt cold though the sun stayed in the sky.

We passed huge trees that lived with their heads in the sky, with their great arms and joints creaking with age and the burden of being trees, and their mazed and linked roots rubbed bare of earth, like bones with the flesh cleaned from them. There were strange gates to be opened or climbed over, new directions to be argued and plotted, notices which said TRESPASSERS WILL BE PROSECUTED BY ORDER. And there was the remote immovable sun shedding without gentleness its influence of burning upon us and upon the town, looking down from its heavens and considering our infantile-paralysis epidemic, and the children tired of holidays and wanting to go back to school with the new stiff books with their crackling pages, the scrubbed ruler with the sun rising on one side amidst the twelfths, tenths, millimetres, the new pencils to be sharpened with the pencil shavings flying in long pickets and light-brown curls scalloped with red or blue; the brown school, the bare floors, the clump clump in the corridors on wet days!

We came to a strange paddock, a bull-paddock with its occupant planted deep in the long grass, near the gate, a jersey bull polished like a wardrobe, burnished like copper, heavy beams creaking in the wave and flow of the grass.

'Has it got a ring through its nose? Is it a real bull or a steer?' Its nose was ringed which meant that its savagery was tamed, or so we thought; it could be tethered and led; even so, it had once been savage and it kept its pride, unlike the steers who pranced and huddled together and ran like water through the paddocks, made no impression, quarried no massive shape against the sky.

The bull stood alone.

Had not Mr Bennet been gored by a bull, his own tame bull, and been rushed to Glenham Hospital for thirty-three stitches? Remembering Mr Bennet we crept cautiously close to the paddock fence, ready to escape.

Someone said, 'Look, it's pawing the ground!'

A bull which pawed the ground was preparing for a charge. We escaped quickly through the fence. Then, plucking courage, we skirted the bushes on the far side of the paddock, climbed through the fence, and continued our walk to the Reservoir.

We had lost the creek between deep banks. We saw it now before us, and hailed it with more relief than we felt, for in its hidden course through the bull-paddock it had undergone change, it had adopted the shape, depth, mood of foreign water, foaming in a way we did not recognise as belonging to our special creek, giving no hint of its depth. It seemed to flow close to its concealed bed, not wishing any more to communicate with us. We realised with dismay that we had suddenly lost possession of our creek. Who had taken it? Why did it not belong to us any more? We hit our sticks in the air and forgot our dismay. We grew cheerful.

Till someone said that it was getting late, and we reminded one another that during the day the sun doesn't seem to move, it just remains pinned with a drawing pin against the sky, and then, while you are not looking, it suddenly slides down quick as the chopped-off head of a golden eel, into the sea, making everything in the world go dark.

'That's only in the tropics!'

We were not in the tropics. The divisions of the world in the atlas, the different coloured cubicles of latitude and longitude fascinated us.

'The sand freezes in the desert at night. Ladies wear bits of sand . . .'

'grains . . .'

'grains or bits of sand as necklaces, and the camels . . .'

'with necks like snails . . .'

'with horns, do they have horns?'

'Minnie Stocks goes with boys . . .'
'I know who your boy is, I know who your boy is . . .'

> Waiting by the garden gate,
> Waiting by the garden gate . . .

'We'll never get to the Reservoir!'
'Whose idea was it?'
'I've strained my ankle!'
Someone began to cry. We stopped walking.
'I've strained my ankle!'
There was an argument.
'It's not strained, it's sprained.'
'strained.'
'sprained.'
'All right sprained then. I'll have to wear a bandage, I'll have to walk on crutches . . .'
'I had crutches once. Look. I've got a scar where I fell off my stilts. It's a white scar, like a centipede. It's on my shins.'
'Shins! Isn't it a funny word? Shins. Have you ever been kicked in the shins?'
'shins, funnybone . . .'
'It's humerus . . .'
'knuckles . . .'
'a sprained ankle . . .'
'a strained ankle . . .'
'a whitlow, an ingrown toenail the roots of my hair warts spinal meningitis infantile paralysis . . .'
'Infantile paralysis, Infantile paralysis you have to be wheeled in a chair and wear irons on your legs and your knees knock together . . .'
'Once you're in an iron lung you can't get out, they lock it, like a cage . . .'

'You go in the amberlance . . .'

'*ambulance* . . .'

'amberlance . . .'

'ambulance to the hostible . . .'

'the *hospital*, an *amberlance to the hospital* . . .'

'Infantile Paralysis . . .'

'Friar's Balsam! Friar's Balsam!'

'Baxter's Lung Preserver, Baxter's Lung Preserver!'

'Syrup of Figs, California Syrup of Figs!'

'The creek's going on high-flow!'

Yes, there were bubbles on the surface, and the water was turning muddy. Our doubts were dispelled. It was the same old creek, and there, suddenly, just ahead, was a plantation of pine trees, and already the sighing sound of it reached our ears and troubled us. We approached it, staying close to the banks of our newly claimed creek, until once again the creek deserted us, flowing its own private course where we could not follow, and we found ourselves among the pine trees, a narrow strip of them, and beyond lay a vast surface of sparkling water, dazzling our eyes, its centre chopped by tiny grey waves. Not a lake, nor a river, nor a sea.

'The Reservoir!'

The damp smell of the pine needles caught in our breath. There were no birds, only the constant sighing of the trees. We could see the water clearly now; it lay, except for the waves beyond the shore, in an almost perfect calm which we knew to be deceptive — else why were people so afraid of the Reservoir? The fringe of young pines on the edge, like toy trees, subjected to the wind, sighed and told us their sad secrets. In the Reservoir there was an appearance of neatness which concealed a disarray too frightening to be acknowledged except, without any defence, in moments of deep sleep and dreaming. The little sparkling innocent waves shone now green, now grey, petticoats, lettuce leaves; the trees sighed, and told us to be quiet, hush-sh, as if something were sleeping and should not be disturbed — perhaps that was what the trees were always telling us, to hush-sh in case we disturbed something which must never ever be awakened?

What was it? Was it sleeping in the Reservoir? Was that why people were afraid of the Reservoir?

Well we were not afraid of it, oh no, it was only the Reservoir, it was nothing to be afraid of, it was just a flat Reservoir with a fence around it, and trees, and on the far side a little house (with wheels inside?) and nothing to be afraid of.

'The Reservoir, The Reservoir!'

A noticeboard said DANGER, RESERVOIR.

Overcome with sudden glee we climbed through the fence and swung on the lower branches of the trees, shouting at intervals, gazing possessively and delightedly at the sheet of water with its wonderful calm and menace,

'The Reservoir! The Reservoir! The Reservoir!'

We quarrelled again about how to pronounce and spell the word.

Then it seemed to be getting dark — or was it that the trees were stealing the sunlight and keeping it above their heads? One of us began to run. We all ran, suddenly, wildly, not caring about our strained or sprained ankles, through the trees out into the sun where the creek, but it was our creek no longer, waited for us. We wished it were our creek, how we wished it were our creek! We had lost all account of time. Was it nearly night? Would darkness overtake us, would we have to sleep on the banks of the creek that did not belong to us any more, among the wild sweet peas and the tussocks and the dead sheep? And would the eels come up out of the creek, as people said they did, and on their travels through the paddocks would they change into people who would threaten us and bar our way, TRESPASSERS WILL BE PROSECUTED, standing arm in arm in their black glossy coats, swaying, their mouths open, ready to swallow us? Would they ever let us go home, past the orchards, along the gully? Perhaps they would give us Infantile Paralysis, perhaps we would never be able to walk home, and no one would know where we were, to bring us an iron lung with its own special key!

We arrived home, panting and scratched. How strange! The sun was still in the same place in the sky!

The question troubled us, 'Should we tell?'

The answer was decided for us. Our mother greeted us as we went in the door with, 'You haven't been long away, kiddies. Where have you been? I hope you didn't go anywhere near the Reservoir.'

Our father looked up from reading his newspapers.

'Don't let me catch you going near the Reservoir!'

We said nothing. How out-of-date they were! They were actually afraid!

Prizes

Life is hell, but at least there are prizes. Or so one thought. One knew of the pit ahead, of the grownups lying there rewarded, arranged, and faded, who were so long ago bright as poppies. One learned to take one's own deserved place on the edge, ready to leap, not to hang back in a status-free huddle where bodies were warm together and the future darkness seemed less frightening. Therefore, one learned to win prizes, to be surrounded in sleep by a dream of ordinal numbers, to stand in best clothes upon platforms in order to receive medals threaded upon black-and-gold ribbons, books 'bound in calf', scrolled certificates. One's face became, from habit, incandescent with achievement.

I had my share of prizes, and of resentment when nobody recognised my efforts; for instance, year after year, when the New Zealand Agricultural and Pastoral Society held its show in the Onui Drill Hall, I made a buttonhole of a rose and a sprig of maidenhair fern tied together with raffia, which I entered for the Flower Display, Gentleman's Buttonhole. It was never displayed, and it never won a prize. One morning, a militant woman in a white coat made a speech to the whole school from the front steps, before Bertie Dowling played the kettledrum for us to march inside, and in her speech the woman accused too many people of entering for the Buttonhole Section, and advised us not to try to make buttonholes, as they were an art beyond our years that even grownups found difficult to master. 'It has never been explained,' the woman said, 'why so many children enter buttonholes in the Flower Show.' (Bertie Dowling had the sticks raised, ready to play the drum. He was very clever at it; he was a small, sunburned, wiry boy with long feet like a rabbit.)

I felt antagonistic towards the woman visitor. Who was she to order me not to make buttonholes for the Flower Show? I persisted, as I say, year after year, yet always, once I had surrendered my exhibit, neat in its little box cadged from the jeweller's, I never heard of it again. I had so much determination and so little wisdom that I never grasped the futility of my struggle, although I realised that when talents were being devised and distributed my name was not included in the short list of those blessed with the power to make gentlemen's buttonholes that would reach the display table at the Flower Show in the Drill Hall and win First, Second, or Third Prize.

I won six and fourpence for handwriting. At that time, I was in love with my parents, therefore, I decided to buy my mother a best-china cup, saucer, and plate with the entire six and fourpence, even though at that time I also had a fondness for Sante Chocolate Bars, jelly beans, and chocolate fish whose insides were a splurge of pink rubbery substance with tiny air holes in it. When I gave my mother the best-china cup, saucer, and plate she said, 'You shouldn't have,' and, wrapping the set carefully in tissue paper, she placed it in the sideboard cupboard with the other dishes that we never used — not even for the banquet to see the New Year in — like the gravy boat, the tiny cream jug with the picture of a Dutch girl, the vegetable dishes with the picture of a rooster crowing on each one. Then my mother locked the door. I never saw her using the cup, saucer, and plate. It was best china, too, the man in Peak's told me. My mother always said she was keeping the set for when she could *really* use it, drinking out of the cup, resting a silver spoon in the saucer, tasting (with a cake fork) a slice of marble cake upon the plate. Although I could not then discern the difference between using something and *really* using it, there was evidently a distinction so important that when my mother died she had still not been able to use, really to use, my six-and-fourpenny gift to her.

My next prize was for a poem that revealed both my lack of scientific knowledge and my touching disbelief in change by concluding with the lines

> And till the sky falls from above,
> These things of nature I shall love.

Uncle Ted, of my favourite wireless station in Christchurch, read my poem over the air, between a recording of The Nutcracker, Waltz of the Flowers, and the fifth episode of David and Dawn in Fairyland, and two days later I received through the post an order for ten shillings, with part of which I bought for myself an unsatisfactory diary and a John Bull Printing Set, which I used, printing my name, and rude rhymes, and insults to the rest of the family, until the ink dried on the navy-blue pad; the remainder of the ten shillings I saved in a Post Office Bank, which could not be opened unless it was taken to the Post Office. I broke into it with a kitchen knife when my bathing cap perished and the weather was warm enough for swimming.

Prizes. They arrived unexpectedly, or I waited greedily for them at the end of every school year, when I received one or two, sometimes three, books with the school motto, 'Pleasure from Work', inscribed on the flyleaf beneath the cramped, detailed writing of the form mistress setting out the reasons for my prize. Reasons were necessary, for no school had yet learned to distribute prizes at random, first come, first served, in the manner that my mother had adopted, in exasperation, when she was pestered for raisins, dates, or the last of the chocolate biscuits. I collected so many books: *Treasure Island*; *Silas Marner*; *Emma*; *Poems of Longfellow*, with a heart-throbbing picture of Hiawatha bearing Minnehaha across the river:

> Over wide and rushing rivers
> In his arms he bore the maiden;

India, with illustrations coloured as if with cochineal; *Boys and Girls Who Became Famous*; and — during the war, when books were scarce — a musty old rained-on and stained volume of poems about blossoms, barns, and wine presses, printed in tall, dark type, where snakes lurked in every capital letter.

Prizes. Some did not get prizes. Dotty Baker with the greasy hair never got a prize. Maud Gray, who found it hard to read even simple sentences aloud, never got a prize. Maud Gray! She was the stodgiest girl in the class; all the teachers made fun of her, and most of the pupils, including myself, followed their example. Her eyes were brittle and brown, like cracked acorn shells; her face was pale and blotched, like milk on the turn.

Years later, I was visiting Onui. I was walking desolately in the rain along the main street, wearing my dirty old gabardine and my dowdy clothes and feeling fifteen instead of twenty-five, when, just beyond the bed of poppies in the centre of the street, I saw two beautiful women wheeling prams, and their proud gait was so noticeable I tried to recall when and where I had seen before that superior parading of the victorious. And then I realised that I had walked onto the platform in the same way, year after year, to receive my prizes. Dotty Baker, Maud Gray! As they passed with their cocooned, quilted, embroidered treasure, I could not even assert my superiority by whispering, 'You cheated in history, you couldn't learn poetry by heart, you never had your name in the paper . . . First in geometry, French, English, history . . .'

They smiled at me and I smiled at them. We shared the pit, each in her place. The rain poured upon the bed of crushed poppies between us. Yet the delicacy and distance of the two women were unmistakable; I grudged their proud cloaks as they trooped, clients of love, on their specially reserved side of the world. But — prizes. They never won prizes. My only retaliation was prizes — listing them, remembering.

I wrote to a children's newspaper, sending poems that were awarded ten or five or three marks. When I had earned one hundred marks, I received the usual prize of two guineas. For one guinea my father bought me a tennis racket, as he said, 'on the cheap', but when he showed it to me I was alarmed to discover that the strings were black instead of white, and the name was unfamiliar — Double Duke. I was the loneliest person in the world with my black-stringed Double Duke. Why had my father not realised that every other girl at school possessed a white-stringed Vantage? Ah, it was sad enough to have an old wireless at home with a name no one had heard of and with tubes so few in number compared with the tubes in other sets. The conversations in class went: 'Have you got a wireless at home? How many tubes?' The prestige of owning things mattered so much, and to have a tennis racket with a strange name and grotesque strings was punishment indeed. I was so ashamed of my tennis racket that I seldom used it.

With my other guinea from the newspaper I had the

unexpected fortune to be chosen by Hessie Sutton, a woman up the road, as her pupil for music lessons — the piano — at a reduced rate, and every Tuesday and Friday after school I claimed an hour of Hessie Sutton's time in the front room of the house where she lived with her mother and a white parrot whose perpetual screaming inspired complaining letters to the evening paper.

The front room was large and carpeted, with sparkling, bubble-shaped windows. The piano made wonderfully clean sounds as the keys sank into and sprang from their green bedding; the sounds filled me with a polished sense of opulence and cleanliness, and each note emerged bravely and milkily alone and poured into me, up to my neck. I swallowed. I liked Hessie Sutton's piano. We had none at home. At my aunt's house, where I went to practise once a week, there was an old piano with soapy yellow keys that stuck halfway, and the lower or upper half of each sound had been weathered down so that each note came forth deprived, diseased, with an invalid petulance and stricture.

'But you must not bite your nails,' Hessie Sutton warned me. 'You will never be able to play the piano if you bite your nails!' That was my first intimation that Hessie Sutton was a spy. I clenched my fists, hiding my fingernails.

At school, I said, 'I learn music, do you?' Dolly Baker, Maud Gray, and others learned music, but mostly they were like uncooked pastry at it; they suffered a dearth of warmth, expansion, gold finish. On the cold June days, when the Music Festival was held, we sat miserably in the hall, our coats over our knees, listening to a 'Marche Militaire' being played by schoolgirl dentists and carpenters.

My first piece was named 'Puck'. I went down to the

stationer's to buy it on tick, and the ginger-haired boy served me, and his face had a rust-coloured blush, like a dock leaf in autumn, because he had to go to the small room at the back of the shop and ask his parents if it would be all right to serve me, as our bill had not been paid. On my way home with 'Puck', I met Hessie Sutton and smiled at her, shyly and excitedly, but when she glanced at the parcel under my arm and the music half wrapped, and gave an understanding smile, my face clouded in a fierce frown. How dare she see me and divine my excitement! How dare she! How I hated her!

That afternoon, when I went for my lesson, she heightened my sense of shame. 'I saw you.' She pounced as soon as I entered the room. 'I saw you,' she said, like a detective giving evidence, 'coming home with your new piece of music. I guessed how excited you were!'

'I wasn't caring at all,' I said sullenly.

'Yes, you were,' Hessie Sutton insisted. 'I saw it in your face! I *knew*!'

I did not understand why she should appear so triumphant, as if by seizing on a momentary aspect of my behaviour she had uncovered a life of deceit in me. Why, she honked with triumph like the soldier who brought back the golden horn from the underworld as proof of the secret activities of the twelve dancing princesses! I did not realise that people's actions are mysteries that are so seldom solved.

'I knew, I knew!' Hessie Sutton kept saying as I sat down to try out 'Puck'.

From that day, I no longer enjoyed my music lessons. I was weary of being spied upon. People were saying, observing me closely, 'She's filling out, she's growing tall, look at her hair, isn't that Grace's chin she's got, and there's no doubting where her smile comes from!'

You see how derivative I was made out to be? Nothing belonged to me, not even my body, and now with Hessie Sutton and her spying ways I could not call my feelings my own. Why did people have so much need to stake their claim in other people? Were they scared of the bailiffs' arriving in their own house? I stopped learning music. I was in despair. I could no longer use prizes as a fortress. In spite of my books bound in calf, my scrolled certificates, the prize essay on the Visit to the Flour Mill, and my marks of merit in the children's newspaper, I was being invaded by people who wanted *their* prizes from *me*.

And now I lie in the pit, finally arranged, faded, robbed of all prizes, while still under every human sky the crows wheel and swoop, dividing, dividing the spoils of the dead.

A Sense of Proportion

The sun's hair stood on end. The sky accommodated all visiting darkness and light. Leaves were glossy green, gold, brown, dried, dead and bleached in drifts beneath the trees. Snow fell in all seasons, white hyphens dropping evenly, linking syllables of sky and earth. Flowers bloomed forever, spinning their petal-spokes like golden wheels, sucking the sun like whirlpools. Black-polished, brick-dusted, spotted ladybirds big as aeroplanes with pleated wings like sky-wide curtains parting, flew home to flame and cinders.

Houses had painted roofs of red and yellow with tall chimneys emitting scribbles of pale blue smoke. All houses had gardens around them, paths with parallel sides enclosing pebbles; gates were five-barred, with children swinging from them. The children wore red stockings. They had ribbons tied in their hair. Their eyes were round and blue, their eyebrows were arched, their lips were rosy. Their hands displayed five fingers for all to see, their feet pointed the same way, left or right, in gaudy shoes with high heels. The ocean was filled with sailing boats, the sky was filled with rainbows, suns, scalloped clouds.

Coats had many buttons, intricate collars with lace edges. The bricks of houses were carefully outlined. Front doors had four panels and a knocker in its exact position.

Winds were visible, fat men or witches with puffed cheeks in the four corners of the sky. The trees leaned with their skirts up over their heads.

The streets were full of painted rubber balls divided carefully into bright colours.

Men wore hats placed firmly upon their heads.

Dogs walked, their tails like masts in the air.

Cats had mile-long whiskers like rays of the sun. They sat, their tails curled about them, containing them. Their ears were pricked, forever listening.

The moon, like the sun, had a face, a smile, eyes, teeth. The moon journeyed on a cloud convoyed by elaborately five-pointed stars.

There was no distance or shade in our infant drawing. Everything loomed close to the eye; rainbows in the heavens could be clutched as securely as the few blades of bright green grass (the colour of strong lemonade) growing symmetrically in the lower right-hand corner of the picture.

Some years passed during which we learned to draw and paint from a small tin of Reeve's Water Colours: Chinese White, Gamboge Tint, Indigo, Yellow Ochre (which I pronounced and believed to be *Yellow Ogre*), Burnt Sienna: the names gave excitement, pain, wonder. We were shown how to paint a sunset in the exact gradations of colour, to make blue water-colour sky, a scientific rainbow (Read Over Your Greek Book In Verse) receding into the distance. The teacher placed an apple and a pear in a glass bowl upon the table. We drew them, making careful shading, painstakingly colouring the autumn tints of the apple.

We did not paint the worm inside it.

We drew vases of flowers, autumn scenes, furniture which existed merely to cast a perfect shadow to be portrayed by a BB pencil. The Art lessons were long and tedious. I could never get my shadow or my distance correct. My rainbows and paths would not recede, and my furniture, my boats at anchor, my buildings stood flat upon the page, all in a total clamour of foreground.

'You must draw things,' said Miss Collins the Art

Teacher, 'as they seem. Notice the way the path narrows as it approaches the foothills.'

'But it is the same breadth all the way!'

'No,' Miss Collins insisted. 'You must learn to draw these tricks of the eye. You must learn to think in terms of them.'

I never learned to draw tricks of the eye. My paint refused to wash in the correct proportion when I was trying to fill the paper sky with sunrises, sunsets, and rainbows. My garden spades were without strength or shape; their shadows stayed unowned, apart, incredible, more like stray tatters shed from a profusion of dark remnants of objects. My vases had no depth, and their flowers withered in their laborious journey from the table to the page of my scholastic Drawing Book Number Three.

The classroom was dusty and hot and there was the soft buzz of talking, and people walking to and fro getting fresh water and washing brushes; and Miss Collins touring the aisles, giving gentle but insistent advice about colours and shadows. Her hair was in plaits, wound close to her head. In moments of calm or boredom the fact or fancy rippled about the classroom, lapping at our curiosity, Miss Collins wears a wig. Once, long ago, in the days of the Spartans and Athenians, someone had observed Miss Collins in the act of removing her wig.

'She is quite bald,' the rumour went.

Like so many of the other teachers Miss Collins lived with her mother in a little house, a woven spider's nest with the leaves and rain closing in, just at the edge of town. She cherished a reputation as a local painter and at most exhibitions you could see her poplar trees, tussock scenes, mountains, lakes, all in faded colours, with sometimes in the corner, or looking out of the window of a decayed farmhouse, the tiny fierce black lines that were the shape of people.

Every term she gave us examinations which were days of flurry and anxiety when we filed into the Art Room and took our places at the bare desks and gazed with respectful awe at the incongruous display on the table — fruit, a vase of flowers, perhaps a kettle or similar utensil whose shape would strain our ability to 'match sides'. And for the next forty minutes our attention would be fixed upon the clutter of objects, the submissive Still Life which yet huddled powerfully before us, preying upon us with its overlapping corners and sides and deceptive shadows.

How I envied Leila Smith! Leila Smith could draw perfect kettles, rainbows, cupboards. Her pictures always showed the exact number of strokes of rain, when rain fell, and snowflakes when the scene required them. By instinct Leila Smith *knew*. On those days when the gods attended the classroom, penetrating the dust-layered windows hung with knotted cords so complicated that a special Window Monitor was needed to operate them, and the window sills ranged with dead flowers and beans in water — when the gods walked up and down the aisles at our Art Examination they showed extra care for Leila Smith, they guided her hand across the page. When they passed my desk, alas, they vindictively jogged my elbow. Miss Collins despaired of ever teaching me.

'How's your drawing?' my father would say, who had spent the winter evenings painting in oils from a tiny cigarette card the ship that carried him to the First World War. His sisters painted as well; their work hung in the passage — roses, dogs, clouded ladies, and one storm at sea.

'I can't draw,' I said. 'I can't paint.'

Miss Collins readily agreed with me. 'Your perspective and proportion are well below average. Your shading is poor.'

The obsession with shading fascinated me. All things, even kettles and fire shovels, stood under the sun complete and unique with their shadows, fighting to preserve them. It was an act of charity for us to draw the shadow with as much love (frustration, despair) as we gave to drawing the shape itself. In the world of Miss Collins, morning and evening were perpetual, with the shadows spread beautifully alongside each object, their contours matching perfectly, a mirror image of the body. Why was it that in my world the sun stood everlastingly at noon; objects were stripped of their shadows, forced to stand in brilliant light, alone?

In the end Miss Collins gave up trying to teach me to draw and paint. She spent her time giving hints to Leila Smith. Oh how wonderful were Leila's flowers and fire shovels, garden spades and kettles!

Sometimes Miss Collins would ask us to paint things 'out of our head'.

It showed, she said, whether we had any imagination.

I had no imagination. My poverty could not even provide shadows or proportionate rainbows. The paths in my head stayed the same width right to the foothills and over the mountains which were no obstacles to vision, as mountains are agreed to be; they were transparent mountains, and there was the path, the same width as before, annihilating distance, at last disappearing only at the boundary of the picture.

Distance did not cloud the outline of objects; trees were not blurred; you could count the leaves upon the trees, even on the slopes of the mountain you could count the pine needles hanging in their green brushes.

Yes, it was true; I had no sense of proportion.

When I last saw Miss Collins she had been taken to the

hospital after a stroke, and was lying quietly in the hospital bed. She was dying. The torment of the unshaded world lay before her, the sun in her sky stood resolutely at noon, her life was out of proportion, there was no distance, the foreground blazed with looming and light.

She closed her eyes and died.

Her life, in its spider's web, had absorbed her. She had been aided, comforted, made less lonely, by acknowledging and yielding to a trick of the eye. How does one learn to accept that trick and its blessings before it is too late, before the shadows are razed and the sun stands pitiless at perpetual noon?

The Bull Calf

'Why do I always have to milk the cows?' Olive said. 'Couldn't the others do it for a change? But no, it is always me. Up early and over the hills to find Scrapers. At night home from school and over the hills again to find Scrapers, to bring her down across the creek (here it is difficult; I tie a rope over her horns and make my leap first; she follows, if she is willing) through the gate that hangs on one hinge, into the cow byre with its cracked concrete floor. Pinning her in the bail. Putting on the leg rope. Day after day rain shine or snow.

'I'm tired of milking the cows,' Olive said. 'Beauty, Pansy, and now Scrapers who is bony like bare rafters and scaffolding. One day I will refuse.'

Sometimes she did refuse, in the early morning with sleep gumming her eyes, her body sticky with night, her hair tangled.

'Milk your own cows!' she cried then, retreating to the bedroom and sitting obstinately on the bed, chanting rhymes and French verbs which her mother could not understand because she had left school at sixteen to go to service . . .

But the thought of Scrapers waiting haunted Olive, and soon she would get up from the bed, clatter to the scullery, bumping furniture on the way to show her resentment of everything in the world including corners and walls and doors, take the bucket with a swill of warm water in the bottom for washing the teats, and climb the hill in search of Scrapers who, if her bag was full, would be waiting mercifully not far away.

Olive went to High School. In the morning she worried about being late. And every morning when the teacher called suddenly, 'Form Twos, Form Twos,' Olive worried in case no one formed twos with her. Very often she found herself standing alone. Is it because I stink? she thought. Then she would press the back and front of her uniform, down below, to smooth away the bulge of the homemade sanitary towel, layers of torn sheet sewn together with the blood always leaking through. The other girls used bought towels which were safe and came in packets with tiny blue-edged notices inside the packet, WEAR BLUE LINE AWAY FROM THE BODY. The other girls did not seem to mind when in Drill, which was later called Physical Education to keep up with the times, the teacher would command sharply, 'Uniforms Off, Come on Everybody, Uniforms Off!' Why should they mind when they were using towels which did not show, or even the new type where the advertisement had a picture of a woman in a bathing suit, shouting with rapture from the edge of a high-diving board, 'No Belts, No Pins, No Pads!' But on the days when Olive wore her homemade towel she would ask, blushing, 'Please can I keep my uniform on?'

'Oh,' Miss Copeland said. 'Yes.'

And Olive and one or two other girls with their uniforms on would huddle miserably on the end seat, by the bar stools, out of everybody's way.

Olive and her sisters had hickies on their chins and foreheads. The advertisements warned them never to wear 'off-the-face' hats. Whole pages of the newspapers were devoted to the picture-story of the disasters which befell Lorna, Mary or Marion who continued to wear off-the-face hats in spite of having hickies on their chins and foreheads. Lorna, Mary, Marion were lonely and unwanted until they used Velona Ointment. Olive and her sisters used

Velona Ointment. It had a smell like the oil of a motorcar engine and it came off in a sticky grass-green stain on the pillowcase.

But mostly Olive was tired. She stayed up late working on mathematical problems, writing French translations and essays, and in the morning she was up so early to go over the hill and find Scrapers. There were so many trees and hollows on the hill, and often it was in these hollows where the grass was juiciest, nourished by the pools of yesterday's rain or the secret underground streams, that Scrapers would be hiding. Sometimes Olive had to walk to the last Reserve before she found Scrapers. Then there was the problem of tying the rope across her horns and leading her home.

Sometimes Scrapers refused to cooperate. Olive would find her dancing up and down, tossing her horns and bellowing.

'Scrapers, Scrapers, come on, be a good cow!'

Still Scrapers refused, Olive could not understand why. I'll be late for school, she thought, after struggling with and trying to chase the entranced cow. But it was no use. Olive would hurry down the hill, across the creek, through the broken-hinged gate and up the path to the house where the family, waiting for breakfast, would ask, 'Where's the milk?' while Olive in turn confronted them with her question, 'What's the matter with Scrapers? She's dancing and tossing her horns and refusing to be milked.'

Her mother received the news calmly. 'Leave the cow. She'll be all right in a few days.'

Nobody explained. Olive could not understand. She would pour stale milk on her Weet-Bix, finish her breakfast, brush the mud from her shoes, persuade the pleats into her uniform, and hurry away to school.

It was always the same. She stood alone in Assembly,

concealing herself behind the girl in front who was taller, Captain of the 'A' Basketball Team, Holder of a Drill Shield. Olive did not want the teachers on the platform to see her standing alone, hiding behind the girl in front of her.

> Peace perfect peace in this dark world of sin
> the cross of Jesus whispers Peace within

she sang, sensing the mystery. Her heart felt heavy and lonely.

When she climbed the hill in search of the cow she always stopped in the paddock next door to pat the neighbour's bull calf which was growing plumper and stronger every day. Everyone knew what happened to bull calves. They were taken to the slaughterhouse while they were still young, or they became steers journeying from saleyard to saleyard until they grew old and tough and despised, without the pride and ferocity of bulls and the gentleness and patience of cows. If you were caught in a paddock with them and they attacked you it was in bursts of irritation which left them standing as if bewildered, half-afraid at their own daring. They did not seem able to decide; they panicked readily; they had no home, they were forever lost in strange surroundings, closed in by new fences and gates with unfamiliar smells, trees, earth; with dogs snapping at their heels, herding them this way and that, in and out, up and down . . .

Olive knew that one day Ormandy's bull calf would be a steer. 'Calfie, calfie,' she would whisper, putting her flattened palm inside the calf's mouth and letting it suck.

Night came. The spotted grey cockabullies in the creek wriggled under the stones to sleep, and soon the birds were hushed in the willow trees and the hedge and the sighing pines. This evening Olive was late in fetching Scrapers. She was late and tired. Her best black stockings, cobbled at the back of the leg, were splashed with mud, there were no clean ones for tomorrow; her stockings never lasted, all the other girls bought their stockings at Morton's, and theirs were cashmere, with a purple rim around the top, a sign of quality, while Olive's were made of coarse rayon. She was ashamed of them, she was ashamed of everything and everyone. She kicked her shoes against a clump of grass. Toe and heel plates! Why must she always have toe and heel plates on her shoes? Why must they always be lace-ups? She yawned. Her skin felt itchy. The pressure of her tight uniform upon her breasts was uncomfortable. Why hadn't Auntie Polly realised, and made the seams deeper, to be let out when necessary? Olive's sisters wore uniforms made by real dressmakers. Her sisters were lucky. How they teased her, pointing to the pictures in the *True Confession* magazines, digging their elbows slyly at each other and murmuring, 'Marylin's breasts were heavy and pendulous.'

'That means you,' they said to Olive. 'You'll be like Mum with two full moons bobbing up and down, moons and balloons and motor tyres.'

Yes, her sisters were lucky.

'Why don't they help with the cow?' Olive asked. 'Why don't they milk the cow for a change?'

She walked slowly up the hill, keeping to the path worn by herself and Scrapers; it was rucked with dry, muddy hoofprints and followed along the edge of the pine plantation. When she reached the top of the hill and there was still no sign of Scrapers she went to the fence bordering the native plant reserve and looked out over the town and the sea and the spilled dregs of light draining beyond the horizon. The silver-bellied sea turned and heaved in the slowly brightening moon-track, and the red and green roofs of the town were brushed with rising mist and moon. She identified objects and places: the Town Clock; the main street; the houseboat down at the wharf; the High School, and just behind the trees at the corner, next to the bicycle sheds, the little shop that sold hot mince pies and fish and chips at lunchtime. Then she gazed once more at the sea, waiting for the Sea-Foam-Youth-Grown-Old to appear. It was her secret dream. She knew he would never reach her. She knew that his bright glistening body became old, shrivelled, yellow, as soon as he touched the sand; it was the penalty. She sighed. The grieving hush-hush of the trees disturbed her. Their heads were bowed, banded with night. The wind moved among them, sighing, only increasing their sorrow. It came to her, too, with its moaning that she could not understand; it filled the world with its loneliness and darkness.

Olive sighed again. What was the use of waiting for the Sea-Foam-Youth-Grown-Old? What was the use of anything? Would the trees never stop saying Why, Why?

She was Olive Blakely going to milk Scrapers. She was Olive Blakely standing on the hill alone at night. The cutty grass and the tinkertailor were brushing against her black stockings; there was bird dirt on the fence post; the barbed wire had snapped and sagged.

That evening she milked Scrapers on the hill. What a miracle! The cow stood motionless for her and did not give those sudden sly kicks which she practised from time to time. Scrapers was an expert at putting her foot in the bucket.

Olive patted the velvety flank. Scrapers was standing so calmly. Why was she so calm when a few days ago she had danced, tossed, bellowed, jumping fences and running with her tail high in the air? Now she stood peacefully chewing, seeming to count the chews before each swallow, introducing a slight syncopation before returning the cud to her mouth which she opened slowly once or twice in a lazy yawn releasing her warm grassy-smelling breath on the cool air. Her teeth were stained and green, her eyes swam and glistened like goldfish. She let down her milk without protest.

Leaning to one side to balance the full bucket with its froth of creamy milk, Olive walked carefully down the hill. Damn, she thought. I will have to iron my uniform tonight, and sponge it to remove the grass stains. And damn again, I have trodden in cow muck. Cow muck, pancakes, cowpad . . .

She mused on the words. The Welsh children up the road said *cowpad*. They were a compact, aloof, mysterious family with the two girls going to High School. They had a cousin called Myfanwy. Olive wished that she were called Myfanwy. Or Eitne. Or anything except plain pickled Olive.

She crossed the creek. The milk slopped against her legs, dampening her stockings and staining the hem of her uniform.

'Damn again,' she said. She would have to look in Pear's *Dictionary*, 'Household Hints', to find how to remove milk stains; she never remembered.

Then just as she was approaching the gate she noticed two men leaning over the bull calf in the corner of the paddock, near the hedge. 'Mr Ormandy, Mr Lewis,' Olive said to herself. 'Old Ormandy.'

He had been named *Old Ormandy* when he stopped people from picking his plums but there was no law against picking them, was there, when the tree hung over the fence into the road, inviting anyone to take the dusty plums split and dark blue with pearls of jelly on their stalk and a bitter, blighted taste at the centre, near the stone.

Old Ormandy. The girl Ormandy picked her nose and ate it. Their uncle had been in court for sly-grogging.

Olive watched the two men. What were they doing to the bull calf? It was so dark. What were they doing in the dark? She waited until they had left the bull calf before she went over to say good night to it.

'Calfie, calfie,' she whispered. It was lying outstretched. She bent over it, seeking to pat its face and neck. Its nose felt hot and dry, its eyes were bright, and between its back legs there was blood, and a patch of blood on the grass. The calf had been hurt. Old Ormandy and Lewis were responsible. Why hadn't they noticed the calf was ill? Or perhaps they had deliberately been cruel to it?

'I wouldn't put it past them,' Olive said aloud, feeling strangely satisfied that she was expressing her indignation in the very words her father used when he became suspicious. 'I wouldn't put it past them.'

She trembled and patted the calf.

'Calfie, calfie,' she whispered again. 'Sook sook. Never mind, calfie, I'll get someone to help you.'

But her heart was thudding with apprehension. Supposing the calf were to die? She had seen many animals die. They were not pampered and flattered in death, like human beings; they became immediate encumbrances, threats to public health, with neighbours and councillors quarrelling over the tedious responsibility of their burial. Or were dead human beings — in secret of course — regarded in this way also, and was their funeral procession a concealment, with flowers, of feelings which the living were afraid to admit? Olive's thoughts frightened her. She knew that all things dead were in the way; you tripped over them, they did not move, they were obstacles, they were no use, even if they were people they were no use, they did not complain or cry out, like sisters, if you pinched them or thumped them on the back, they were simply no use at all.

She did not want the bull calf to die. She could see its eyes glistening, pleading for help. She picked up the milk bucket and hurried through the gate to the house and even before she reached the garden tap (she had to be careful here for the tap leaked, the earth was bogged with moss and onion flower) she heard her Father's loud voice talking.

His friends, the Chinese people, had come to visit him, and he was telling the old old story. His operation. He had been ill with appendicitis and while he was in hospital he had made friends with the Chinese family who came often now to visit him, filling the house with unfamiliar voices and excitements, creating an atmosphere that inspired him to add new dimensions of peril to his details of the operation.

'Going gangrene . . . they wheeled me in . . .'

Almost running up to the house, fearing for the life of the bull calf, Olive had time only to hear her father's loud voice .talking to the visitors before she opened the kitchen door. She was almost crying now. She was ashamed of her tears in front of the visitors. She tried to calm herself. Everyone looked up, startled.

'It's calfie, Ormandy's bull calf, it's been hurt, there's all blood between its legs and its nose is hot!'

Olive's mother glanced without speaking at her father who returned the glance, with a slight smile at the corner of his mouth. The Chinese visitors stared. One of them, a young man, was holding a bowl with a flower growing in it, a most beautiful water narcissus whose frail white transparent petals made everything else in the room — the cumbersome furniture, the heavy-browed bookcase, the chocolate-coloured panelled ceiling, the solid black-leaded stove — seem like unnecessary ballast stored beyond, and at the same time within, people to prevent their lives from springing up joyfully, like the narcissus growing out of water into the clear sky.

'The bull calf, what will we do about it?' Olive urged, breaking the silence, and staring at the flower because she could not take her eyes from its loveliness and frailty.

Her mother spoke. 'It's all right,' she said. 'There's nothing the matter with the calf.'

Olive stopped looking at the flower. She turned to her mother. She felt betrayed. Her mother, who took inside the little frozen birds to try to warm them back to life, who mended the rabbit's leg when it was caught in the trap, who fed warm bran to the sick horse that was lying on its side, stretched out!

'But it's bleeding! The calf might die! I saw Mr Ormandy with it, Old Ormandy and another man!'

She knew the man had been Mr Lewis, yet she said 'another man' because it seemed to convey the terrible anonymity which had suddenly spread over every person and every deed. Nobody was responsible; nobody would own up; nobody would even say.

'The bull calf's all right, I tell you,' her father said, impatient to return to his story of the operation. 'Forget it. Go and do your homework.'

Olive sensed embarrassment. They seemed ashamed of her. They were ashamed of something. Why didn't they tell her? She wished she had not mentioned the bull calf.

'But I saw it with my own eyes,' she insisted, in final proof that the calf was hurt and needed help.

Again everybody was silent. She could not understand. Why were they so secretive? What was the mystery?

Then her father swiftly changed the subject.

'Yes, they wheeled me in . . . going gangrene . . . I said to Lottie, I said, on the night . . .'

Olive was about to go from the room when the young man in the corner beckoned to her. He smiled. He seemed to understand. He held out the bowl with the narcissus in it, and said, 'You have it. It is for you.'

Gratefully she took the bowl, and making no further mention of the sick calf she went to her bedroom. She put the narcissus on her dressing table. She touched the petals gently, stroking them, marvelling again at the transparency of the whole flower and the clear water where every fibre of the bulb seemed visible and in motion as if brushed by secret currents and tides. She leaned suddenly and put her cheek against the flower.

Then she lay down on her bed and with her face pressed to the pillow, she began to cry.

The Teacup

When he came to live in the same house she hoped that he would be friendlier, take a deeper interest in her, invite her to the pictures or to go dancing with him or in the summer walking arm in arm in the park. They might even go for a day to the seaside, she thought, or on one of those bus tours visiting Windsor Castle, London Airport, or the Kentish Hopfields. How exciting it would be!

He had been working at the factory for over two years now, since he came out of the Army, and they had often spoken to each other during the day, shared football coupons and bets in the Grand National, lunched together at the staff canteen where you could get a decent meal for two and ten, extra for tea, coffee, and bread and butter. He had talked to her of his family, how they were all dead except his brother and himself; of his life in the Army, travelling the world, a good life, India, Japan, Germany. Once or twice he had mentioned (this was certain and had made her heart flurry) that he would like to 'find someone and settle down'.

He needs someone, she thought. He is quite alone and needs someone.

She told him of her own life, how she had thought of emigrating to Australia and had gone to Australia House where an official asked her age and when she told him he said sharply, 'We are looking for younger people; the young and the skilled.'

She was forty-four. They did not want people of forty-four in Australia. Not single women.

'They wouldn't take me either,' he had said, and, quick with sympathy she had exclaimed, 'Oh, Bill!'

She had never called him by his first name before. He had always been Mr Forest. He addressed her as Miss Rogers, but she knew that if they became closer friends he would call her Edith, that is, Edie. She told him that she was staying in South London, living in a room in a house belonging to this family; that she knitted jerseys for the little girl, helped the landlady with the washing and sewing, and looked after the bird and the cat when the family went on holiday. She told how regularly every second weekend she stayed with her sister at Blackheath, for a change; how her other sister had emigrated years ago to Australia and now was married with three children and a house of her own, she sent photos of the family, you could see them outside in the garden in the sun and how brown the children looked and the garden was bright with flowers, tropical blooms that you never see in England except in Kew Gardens, and wasn't it hot there under glass among the rubber plants? But the photos never showed her sister's husband, for they were separated, he had left her; her other sister's husband had gone too, packed up and vanished, even while his daughter still suffered from back trouble and now she was grown up and crippled, lying on the sofa all day, but managing wonderfully with the district nurse coming on Wednesday afternoons, no, Tuesdays, Wednesday was early closing. And her sister's son had a grant to study accountancy, he would qualify, there was a future ahead of him . . .

So they talked together, and soon it was commonplace for him to call her Edith (not Edie, not yet) and her to say Bill, though in front of the others at work they still said Miss Rogers and Mr Forest. Then one night she invited him home for tea, and he accepted the invitation. How happy she was that evening! How she wished it had been her own home with her own furniture and curtains and not just one room and the small shared kitchen but two or three or four rooms to walk in and out of, opening and closing the doors, each room serving its purpose, one for visitors, another . . .

She bought extra food that evening, far too much, and it turned out that he didn't care for what she had bought, and he didn't mind saying so, politely of course, but he had been in the Army and was used to speaking his mind.

'There's no fuss in the Army. You say what you think.'

'Of course it's best,' she said, trying not to sound disappointed because he did care for golden sponge pudding and had preferred not to sample the peeled shrimps, cocktail brand.

But on the whole they spent a pleasant evening. She knitted, and showed him photographs of her family. They went for a short walk in the park and while they were walking she linked her arm with his, as she had seen other women do, and her eyes were bright with happiness. She mentioned to him that a small room was vacant on the top floor where she stayed, and that if ever he decided to change his lodging wouldn't it be a good idea if he took the room?

She could manage things for him; she could arrange meals, see to shopping and washing; he would be independent of course . . .

A few weeks later when he had been on holiday at his brother's and had arrived back at his lodgings only to find that the two women of the house, having decided after waiting long enough that he was definitely not going to ask one of them to marry him, had given him notice to leave, he remembered the vacancy that Miss Rogers — Edith — had mentioned, and one week later he had come to live in the house, half a flight of stairs up from her own room.

She helped to prepare his room. She cleaned the windows and drew the curtains wide to give him full advantage of the view — the back gardens of the two or three adjacent houses, the road beyond, with the Pink Paraffin lorries parked outside their store; the garden of the large house belonging to the County Councillor.

She made the bed, draping the candlewick bedspread, shelving it at the top beneath the pillows, shifting the small table from the corner near the door to a more convenient position near the head of the bed.

A reading lamp? Would he need a reading lamp?

With a tremble of excitement she realised that she knew nothing about him, that from now on, each day would be filled to the brim with discovery. Either he read in bed or he didn't read in bed. Did he like a cup of tea in the early morning? What did he do in the evenings? What did he sound like when he coughed in the middle of the night when all was quiet?

Downstairs in the small kitchen which she shared with Jean, another lodger in the house, an unmarried woman a few years younger than herself, she segregated on a special shelf covered by half a yard of green plastic which hung, scalloped at the edge, the utensils he would need for his meals; his own special spoon, knife, fork. On the top shelf there. were two large cups, one with the handle broken. Jean had broken it. She had confessed long ago but the subject still came up between her and Edith and always served to discharge irritation between them.

As Edith was choosing the special teacup to be used solely by Bill, she picked up the handleless one, and remarked to Jean, 'These are nice cups, they hold plenty of tea, but that woman from Australia who used to stay in the room before you came, she broke the handle off this cup.'

'No, I broke it,' Jean confessed again.

'No. It was that woman from Australia who stayed here in the room before you came. I was going to emigrate to Australia once. I went as far as getting the papers and filling them in.'

The woman from Australia had also been responsible for other breakages and inconveniences. She had never cleaned the gas stove, she had blocked the sink with vegetables, she hadn't fitted in with arrangements for bathing and washing, and the steam from her baths had peeled the wallpaper off the bathroom wall, newly decorated too. She had left behind a miscellany of objects which were labelled as 'belonging to the woman from Australia' and which Edith carefully preserved and replaced when the cupboards were cleaned out, as if the woman from Australia were still a needful presence in the house.

Attached to the special shelf prepared for Bill there was a row of golden cuphooks; upon one of them Edith hung the teacup she had chosen for him; a large deep cup with a gold, green and dark-blue pattern around the rim and the words ARKLOW POTTERY EIRE DONEGAL, encircled by a smudged blue capital E, printed underneath. In every way the teacup seemed specially right for Bill. How Edith longed for him to be settled in, having his tea, with her pouring from the new teapot warmed under its new cosy, into his special teacup!

He took two heaped spoons of sugar, she shivered with excitement at remembering.

On Bill's first night she could not disguise her happiness. They left work together that night, they came home sitting side by side on the top deck of the bus, they walked together from the bus stop down and along the road to the house. His luggage had already been delivered; it stood in the corridor, strapped and bulging, mysterious, exciting, with foreign labels.

And now there was the bliss of showing him his room, the ins and outs of his new lodgings — the bathroom, telling him on which day he could bathe, showing him how to turn on the hot water.

'Up is on, Down is off . . .'

Explaining, pointing out, revealing, with her cheeks flushed and her breast rising and falling quickly to get enough breath for speech because the details, all the pointing out and revealing were fraught with so much excitement.

At last she led him to the cupboard in the kitchen.

'This is your shelf. Here is your knife, fork, spoon. Of course you can always take anything, anything you want from my shelf, here, this one here, but not from Jean's.'

'Anything you want,' she said again, urgently, 'take from my shelf, won't you?'

Then she paused.

'And this is your special cup and saucer.'

She detached the cup from its golden hook and held it to the light. He looked approvingly at it.

'Nice and big,' he said.

She glowed.

'That's why I chose it from the others. There used to be two of them, but that woman from Australia who stayed here broke the handle of one.'

She still held the teacup as if she were reluctant to return it to its place on the hook.

'Isn't it roomy?' she said, seeking, in a way, for further acknowledgement from him.

But he had turned his attention elsewhere. He was hungry. He sniffed at the food already cooking.

They had dinner then. She had prepared everything — the stewed beef, potatoes, carrots, onions, cabbage. His place was laid at the small table which was really a cabinet and was therefore awkward to sit at, as one's knees bumped into its cupboard door. She apologised for the table, and thought, I'll have to look around for a cheap table, perhaps one with a formica top, easily cleaned, Oh dear there is so much furniture we need, and those lace curtains need renewing, just from where I am sitting I can see they are almost in shreds.

And she sighed with the happy responsibility of everything.

After dinner she washed the dishes, showed him where to hang his bath towel, and where to put his shaving gear, before he went upstairs to lie on his bed and read the evening paper. Then, sharp at half-past eight, she put the kettle on (she hadn't noticed before how furred it was, and dented at the sides, she would have to see about a new kettle) and when the water was boiling she made two cups of tea, taking one up to his room and knocking gently on the door.

'Can I come in, Bill?'

'Yes, come in.'

He was rather irritated at being interrupted, and showed his irritation by frowning at her, for he had of course been in the Army and he believed in directness, in speaking out.

She stood a moment, timidly, in the doorway.

'I've brought you a cup of tea.'

She handed him his special teacup on its matching saucer.

'That's good of you.'

He took it, and blew the parcels from the top. She stayed a while, talking, while he drank his tea. She asked him how he liked his new lodging. She told him there were a few shops around the corner, two cinemas further down the road 'showing nice programmes of an evening', and that in summer the park near by was lovely to sit and walk in.

Then he told her that he was tired, all this changing around, that he was going to bed to get some sleep.

'See you in the morning,' she said.

She took the cups and went downstairs to the kitchen to tidy up for the night. Jean was in the kitchen filling her hot-water bottle. Edith glanced at her, not being able to conceal her joy. Jean had no friend to stay, she had no one to cook for, to wash for. Edith began to talk of Bill.

'I'll be up earlier than usual tomorrow,' she said. 'There's Bill's breakfast to get. He has two boiled eggs every morning,' she said, pausing for Jean to express the wonder which should be aroused at the thought of two boiled eggs for breakfast.

'Does he?' Jean exclaimed, faintly admiring, envious.

'I'm calling him in the morning as he finds it difficult to wake up. Some men do, you know.'

'Yes,' Jean said. 'I know.'

Early next morning Edith was bustling about the kitchen attending to Bill and his toilet and breakfast needs — putting on hot water for the shave, boiling the two eggs, and then sharp at twenty to eight they set out together to catch the bus for work, walking up the road arm in arm. Bill wore a navy-blue duffle coat and carried a canvas bag. The morning light caught the sandy colour of his thinning hair, and showed the pink baldness near his temples and the pink confectionery tint of his cheeks. She was wearing her heavy brown tweed coat and the fawn flowerpot hat which she had bought when her sister took her shopping at Blackheath. Clothes were cheaper yet more attractive in Blackheath; the market was full of bargains — why was it not so, Edith wondered, in her home territory, why did other people always live where really good things were marked down, going for a song, though the flowerpot hat was not cheap. Edith had long ago given up worrying over the hat. She had felt uneasy about it — perhaps it would go suddenly out of fashion, and although she never kept consciously in fashion, whenever there was a topsy-turvy revolution with waists going up or down and busts being annihilated, Edith had the feeling that the rest of the world had turned a corner and abandoned her. She felt confused, not knowing which track to follow; people were pressing urgently forward, their destinations known and planned, young girls too, half her age . . .

Edith felt bitter towards the young girls. Why, the tips of their shoes were like hooks or swords, anyone could see they were a danger.

But everything was different now: there was Bill.

Each night they walked home, again arm in arm, separating at the shops where Edith bought supplies for their dinner while Bill went on to the house, put his bag away, had a wash, and sat cosily on a chair in the kitchen, reading the evening paper and waiting for his dinner to be prepared. They had dinner, sitting awkwardly at the table-cabinet, with Edith each night apologising, remarking that one weekend she would scout around at Blackheath for a cheap table.

'The wallpaper wants doing, too,' she said one evening, looking thoughtfully at the torn paper over the fireplace. To her joy Bill took the hint.

'I'm not bad at decorating,' he said. 'Being in the Army, you know.'

She laughed impatiently and blushed.

'But you're not in the Army now, you're settling down!'

He agreed. 'Yes, it's time I settled down.'

He spent the following weekend papering the kitchen, and although it was Edith's usual time for visiting her sister, she did not go to Blackheath but stayed in the kitchen, making cups of tea for Bill, fetching, carrying, admiring, talking to him, holding equipment for him, and by Sunday evening when the job was finished and the kitchen cupboard had been painted too, and the window sills, and even new curtains hung on plastic hooks which were rustproof and could be washed free of dust and soot, the two sat together, in deep contentment, drinking their cups of tea and eating their slices of white bread and apricot jam, homemade.

But Edith's satisfaction was chilled by the persistent thought, It isn't even my own home, it isn't even my own home. Still, she consoled herself, in time, who knows?

Their routine was established. Every evening it was the same — dinner, apologies over the awkward shape of the table (but why, she thought, should I spend money on a table when it isn't even my own home?), meagre conversation, a few exclamations, statements, revival of rumours; the newspapers to read . . . They each bought their own evening paper, and after they both had finished reading they exchanged papers, with a dreamlike movement, for they were at the same time concentrating on their stewed beef or fried chops or fish.

'There's the same news in both, really.'

'Yes, there's not much difference.'

Nevertheless they exchanged papers and settled once more to eat and read. When they had finished she would say, 'I'll do the dishes.'

At first Bill used to walk around with a tea towel hanging over his arm. Later, when he realised that his help was not needed, he didn't bother to remove the towel from the railing behind the kitchen door. There were three railings, one each for Edith, Jean, and Bill. Edith had bought Bill a special tea towel, red and blue (colourfast) with a matador and two bulls printed on it.

One evening when Edith was not feeling tired she said she would like to go to the pictures, that there was a good one showing down the road, and if they hurried they would get in at the beginning of the main picture, or halfway through *Look at Life*.

Bill was not interested.

'Not for me, not tonight.'

He went upstairs to make the final preparations and judgements for the filling-in of the football coupon, while Edith retired to her room, switched on the electric fire, and sat in her armchair, knitting. The glow from the fire sent bars of light, like burns, across her face. Her eyes watered a little as she leaned forward to follow the pattern. The wool felt thick and rough against her fingers.

I must be tired after all, she thought, and put down her knitting. At half-past eight she went to the kitchen to make the usual cup of tea, and as she said good night to Bill she thought, He's tired after that heavy packing at work all day. Maybe in the weekends we'll go out together somewhere, to the pictures or the park.

The next morning when it was time to set out for work it seemed that Bill was not quite ready, there were a few things to see to, he said. So Edith went alone up the road to the bus stop, and later Bill set out for work alone. And that night they came home separately. And after that, every morning and evening they went to and from work alone.

In the weekend Bill mentioned that he knew friends who kept a pub in Covent Garden, that he would be spending the weekend there. Soon he spent every weekend there. At night he still came home for meals, but sometimes he neglected to say that he wasn't coming home, and Edith would make elaborate preparations for dinner, only to find that she had to eat it alone.

'If only he would tell me,' she complained to Jean. 'I see him at work during the day, and for some reason he's even ashamed to let on that he stays here. Afraid the others will tease him.'

She smiled wistfully, a little secretively, as if perhaps there might be cause for teasing.

Well, she thought, at least he sleeps here.

And was there not all the satisfying flurry in the morning of heating his shaving-water, putting the two eggs to boil, leaving the kettle on low gas in case he needed it, setting his place at the table with his plate, his knife, and, carefully at the side, his special teacup and saucer? And then taking possession of details concerning him, as if they were property being signed to her alone? He eats far too much salt. One drum of salt lasts no time with him. How can he eat so much black pudding? He's fond of sugar, too.

He likes, he prefers, he would rather have . . .

He'd be lost without his cup of tea.

Yes, that was one thing he was always ready for, she could always make him a cup of tea.

And then there were his personal habits which she treasured as legacies, as if his gradual withdrawal from her had been concerned, in a way, with death, wills and next-of-kin, with her being the sole beneficiary.

'Why, oh why, does he leave all his pairs of socks to be washed at once?' — said in a voice at the same time complaining and proud — 'I've told him to bring his dirty clothing down for me to wash, but he persists in leaving it in his room, and there I have to go and search about in his most private clothing, and I never know where he keeps anything!' — said in a voice warm with satisfaction.

It was true that her washing seemed endless, and lasted all Saturday morning, and the ironing took all Sunday morning or Monday evening. She liked ironing his shirts, underclothes and handkerchiefs. She tried to accept the fact that he was not inclined to take her out anywhere, not even to the pictures or the park, that he did not care to accompany her to or from work. Once or twice she reminded him that he was getting old, that he was forty-seven, that she was about the same age . . . perhaps they could spend the rest of their lives together, life was not all dizzy romance, perhaps they could marry . . . she would look after him, see to him . . .

'But I like my freedom,' he said.

Then she tried to frighten him into thoughts of himself as a lonely old man with no one to care for him and no one to talk to.

'If it happens,' he said, 'it happens. I've been in the Army, you know, around in Japan, India, Germany, I've seen a thing or two.'

As if being in the Army had provided him with special defences and privileges. And it had, hadn't it? He could speak his mind, he knew what he was up to . . .

So the wonderful hopes which had filled Edith's mind when Bill had first come to stay, began to fade. Why won't he see? she thought. I'm trying to do my best for him. It would be nice, in summer, to walk arm in arm in the park.

Meanwhile her stated attitude became, I don't care, it doesn't worry me.

The Council were starting a course of dancing lessons for beginners over thirty. She began to go dancing in the evenings, and when she came home she would tell Jean about the lovely time she had enjoyed.

'I go with the girl from work. Her father has that grey Jaguar with the toy leopard in the back.'

'You want to go dancing,' she suggested one night to Jean.

'Oh,' Jean replied. 'I had a friend to visit me.'

'A friend? A man?'

'Yes. A man.'

'I didn't see him.'

'Oh, he came to visit me.'

Sometimes Edith went dancing twice a week now, and Bill came home or didn't come home to dinner. Still, rather wistfully, Edith prepared food for him, peeled the potatoes (he was fond of potatoes), cleaned the Brussels sprouts, or left little notes with directions in them: 'The sausages from yesterday are in the oven if you care for them. There's soup in the enamel jug. There are half a dozen best eggs on my shelf . . . or if you fancy baked beans . . .'

Edith noticed that Jean's new friend seemed to bring her a plentiful supply of food. Why, sometimes her shelf was filled to overflowing. She hoped that Bill had remembered not to touch anything upon Jean's shelf.

'My friend's good that way,' Jean said. 'And he always lets me know when he is coming to visit me.'

Edith flushed.

'Bill would let me know about dinner and suchlike, but I don't see him much during the day, not now he's working upstairs. He's very thoughtful underneath, Bill is.'

'My friend bought me underwear for Christmas. Do you think I should have accepted it?'

'It's rather personal isn't it?'

Bill had not given Edith a present.

'Oh there's nothing between us,' Jean assured her.

'Bill wanted to give me something but I wouldn't have it. I said I enjoy what I'm doing for him and that's that. You say your friend came on Saturday? I've never seen him yet.'

'You always miss him, don't you?'

That was Monday.

That night when Bill had come home, eaten his dinner, and gone to his room, and Edith had put the kettle on the gas and was setting out the cups for tea, she noticed that Bill's cup was missing, the big teacup with the gold, dark-blue and light-green decorations and the words printed at the bottom, the big teacup, Bill's cup, that hung always on the golden hook.

With a feeling of panic she searched Bill's shelf, Jean's, her own, and the cupboards underneath, removing the grater and flour sifter, the cake tins, and the two battered saucepans which had belonged to the woman from Australia.

She could not find the teacup.

She hurried from the kitchen and up to Bill's room.

'Bill,' she called, 'your cup's missing!'

A sleepy voice sounded, 'My what?'

She opened the door. He was lying fully dressed on the bed.

He sat up.

Edith's voice was trembling, as if she were bringing him bad news which did not affect him as much as it affected herself, yet which she needed to share.

'Your big teacup that hangs on the hook on your shelf. Have you seen it?'

He spoke abruptly. 'No, I haven't seen it.'

She looked at him with all the feelings of the past weeks and months working in her face, and her eyes bright. Her voice implored him, 'Now Bill, just stay there quietly and try to remember when you last saw your cup!'

He got up from the bed. 'What the hell?' he shouted. 'What the hell is the fuss about?'

He lowered his voice. 'Well I last saw it on the ledge by

the cupboard. I had a cup of tea in it,' he said guiltily.

Then he saw the marks where his shoes had touched the end of the bed. He brushed at the counterpane. 'I should have taken my shoes off, eh?'

Edith was calm now. 'So you haven't seen your teacup?' she said, but she could not bear to dismiss the subject, to make an end of it all, without saying, 'Your teacup, Bill, the one with the gold, dark-blue and green that hangs on the hook on your shelf?'

Then she suddenly left him, and hurried down the stairs, and knocked sharply on Jean's door, and almost before she was invited, she opened the door and looked searchingly around the room. Her face was flushed. Her eyes were glistening as if she had been leaning too close to the fire. At first she did not speak but glanced meaningly at one of the kitchen cups which Jean had borrowed for a drink of water.

'Have you seen Bill's cup?' Edith asked, staring hard at the cup of water as if to say, 'If you borrow this you might surely have borrowed Bill's cup!'

Jean felt a pang of guilt. She had not seen or borrowed the cup but she felt sure that suspicion rested on her.

'No,' she said. 'I haven't seen it. Isn't it in the kitchen?'

'No, it's not there.'

Edith's voice had a note of desperation, as if the incident had brought her suddenly to the limit of her endurance.

'No, it's not there,' she said. She felt like weeping, but she was not going to break down, she had her suspicions of Jean. She looked once more around Jean's room, as if trying to uncover the hiding-place.

'I last saw it,' she said, 'on Saturday at lunchtime when I washed it. Then I went away to my sister's at Blackheath, as you know, and Bill went away for the weekend, and the family was away. That means you were the only one in the house.'

'My friend came,' Jean reminded her.

Edith pounced. 'Perhaps he used Bill's cup?' No, Jean told her, he hadn't.

'Well you were the only one in the house from Saturday at lunchtime.'

'Perhaps Bill knows where it is?' Jean asked.

Edith's voice quavered. 'He doesn't. I've asked him. I said to him, "Now just sit quietly and remember when you last saw it."'

'What did he say?'

'He said when he last saw it, there were dregs of tea in it, and it was on the ledge by the cupboard in the kitchen. And that's correct,' Edith said triumphantly, 'for I washed it — you were the only one in the house with it until Monday, today, and between Saturday and today it vanished. There was your friend of course,' she said accusingly.

'Oh, he didn't touch it. I don't know what to do with him, he brings me so much food. And he always writes to tell me when he is visiting me.'

'Bill is a typical man,' Edith said coldly. 'He has no idea what food we (he and I) need. If he did he would buy it, and see to things. And now that he's upstairs at work during the day he can't see me to say whether or not he's coming home to dinner.'

Then she made a stifled sound, like a sob. 'I don't know where his cup has got to, his teacup.'

It seemed that the teacup hanging on its golden hook had contained the last of Edith's hope, and now it was gone, someone had taken it. She suspected Jean. Who was this mysterious friend who came to visit Jean? Jean hadn't discovered this friend until Bill had come to stay in the house. It was all Jean's fault, everything was Jean's fault, Jean was jealous of her and Bill, she has stolen Bill's teacup, his special teacup with the gold, dark-blue and green decorations, and the writing underneath . . .

For the next few days there was tension between the two women. Edith left a note before she went to work, 'Dear Jean, If you are ironing please will you run over Bill's two towels?'

Jean forgot to iron the towels.

Each evening the same questions and answers passed between them.

'Bill's cup must be somewhere. It just can't vanish. You didn't break it by chance, and put it in the rubbish tin?'

'If I had broken it I would have said.'

'That woman from Australia broke the handle of the other one, if that woman from Australia hadn't broken the other one Bill could be using it now.'

'*I* broke the other one.'

'Then you could have broken this one as well. But I thought . . . that handle . . . I thought it was the woman from Australia. I tried to emigrate to Australia once. I went as far as getting papers and filling them in . . .'

She spoke longingly as if emigrating to Australia were another of the good things in life which had been denied her at the last moment, as if it were somehow concerned with the affair of Bill and the lost teacup and never ever walking arm in arm in the park, in summer.

By the fourth day the kitchen had been thoroughly searched and the cup was nowhere to be found. Bill was now spending many of his week-nights away from the house, and the two women found themselves often alone together. They spoke little. They glanced grimly at each other, accusingly.

Sometimes at night in her room in the middle of reading her romantic novel from the library (*Set Fair for France, All My Own, Love and Ailsa Dare*), Edith would break down and weep, she could not explain it, but the disappearance of the teacup was the last straw. She said the phrase to herself, drying her eyes, 'The last straw.'

Then she chided herself, 'Don't be silly. What's the use?' But the people in the novels had everything so neatly provided for them. There was this secretary with the purple eyes and trim figure, and she dined by candlelight with the young director, the youngest and wealthiest director of the firm; everybody was jealous of this secretary; all the men made excuses to visit her at her desk, to invite her out . . .

Edith was heavily built; she bought a salmon-pink corset once a year; she needed to wear it. Her eyes were grey and chipped, like a pavement. Her back humped.

'I'm ugly of course,' she said, as she closed *Love and Ailsa Dare*. 'I don't mind that so much now I'm used to it, but the teacup, Bill's cup, who has taken it?'

After the week had passed and the cup had still not been found, and there was no clue to its hiding-place, Edith gave up preparing meals for Bill. She even neglected to go to his room to collect what he referred to as his 'mid-week smalls'. And the following week, in an effort to cheer herself, she went dancing three times to the Council class, but she found little pleasure in it. She had tried to buy a pair of white satin shoes such as everyone else wore, and when she did find a pair they nipped and cramped her two toes, causing a pain which was so prolonged that she visited the doctor (the one around the corner with his house newly decorated, and his smart car standing outside the gate; everyone went to him) who said to her, 'I can do nothing about it, it's your age, Miss Rogers, the best thing is for you to have a small operation which will remove those two toes; it's arthritis, it attacks the toes first, with some patients; the operation is quite quick and harmless.'

When Edith came home from the doctor's she burst into tears. Two toes removed, just like that! It was the beginning of the end. They would soon want permission to remove every part of her, they did that sort of thing, gradually, once they began they never knew where to finish.

She stopped going to dancing class. She stayed inside by the electric fire, knitting, and sewing at the sewing machine, pedalling fiercely until her legs ached and she was forced to rest them.

One weekend when she returned from her sister's at Blackheath she found that Bill had changed his lodging, had gone to stay with his friends who kept the pub in Covent Garden. He had gone without telling her, without a word. But he never told people things, he was secretive, he didn't understand, he had been in the Army . . .

That Monday evening on her way past the shops Edith saw Jean in the grocer's; she was buying food, mountains of it. So much for her mysterious friend, Edith thought, as she hurried home.

The two met later in the kitchen, filling their hot-water bottles.

'Have you been dancing lately?' Jean asked.

'Yes,' Edith said. 'I go often. In fact I went during the weekend. I had a wonderful time. Smashing. Did your friend come?'

'Yes, my friend came, with stacks of food, look!'

Jean pointed to the bread, fruit salad, ham, which she had just bought at the grocer's.

Then, without speaking much — for what was there to say? — they filled their hot-water bottles and said good night.

And no one ever found the dark-blue, gold, green teacup with the writing ARKLOW POTTERY EIRE DONEGAL underneath, that used to hang — an age ago, it seemed — in the kitchen on the special shelf on the shining golden hook!

The Advocate

If you stop Ted in the street and ask him the way he is always eager to direct you. He helps the aged, the blind, the crippled. He will rescue children in distress separated from their mothers in a crowd. At the scene of an accident he is among the first to restore calm, to comfort people, ring for ambulances, distribute hot sweet tea.

He will reprimand or report to the police anyone making himself a public nuisance or breaking the law. Ted has deep respect for the law.

If you say good morning to him he returns your greeting with a cheerful smile.

That is Ted.

At work he is willing, eager; he goes out of his way to please, he stays behind in the evenings to give extra attention to his tasks and prepare for the following day. How courteous he is, how efficient.

In his conversation he refers to his many friends, to his popularity among them.

'They will do anything for me,' he says.

He tells you of the liftman at work who is always ready to take him to any floor, to give him service before all others; of the manager who calls him by his Christian name and gives him a friendly wink from time to time, there being definite understanding between them; of the Director who chats intimately with him in a manner which he does not adopt with the other members of the staff; of the shy young office girls who are delighted to be taken 'under his wing'; of the Chief Security Officer who, relaxing the principle of keeping aloof from the staff, invites him to his room for coffee, talking to him as an equal.

He likes to make it known that he is given certain privileges: he is allowed free time whenever he chooses; he is trusted, taken into the confidence of others, consulted on personal problems. He has so many friends. If you spend enough time with him you soon learn that he seems to have more friends than most people; you learn too of his illustrious relatives, of famous people who have spoken to him or corresponded with him, of high-ranking officials in other countries whom he has known intimately. In case you do not believe him (but who would doubt his word?) he has a supply of anecdotes, dates, Christian names. And in all his stories he features as the man with many friends, the man to whom people turn for advice and comfort.

Then why is he so alone? Why does he go to bed each night hoping for immediate sleep to ward off his loneliness? Why does he go every Sunday afternoon to the pictures and sit alone in the dark through two showings of the programme, and then return to his deserted flat and once more go to bed, trying to evade the loneliness?

He hasn't a friend in the world, and he knows it.

When his back is turned they label him bumptious, overbearing, conceited, nosey-parker, poke-nose, opinionated, bigoted . . .

Over his dead body, before he is taken to be buried in the grave of a suicide, they praise him as helpful, kind, courteous, willing, conscientious, a noble and good man . . .

Which judgement is correct? Is there a correct one? How can one be judged truly unless, like Ted, one hires the services of the Advocate Death?

The Chosen Image

In late winter when the seed catalogues were thrust through the letter box, the poet, having a spare hour or two, gathered them upon his table, studied them carefully, and from the many magnificent illustrations he chose the bloom which he had decided to plant in a wooden box upon his window sill, for he did not possess a garden. That same afternoon he went to the local post office and after waiting in the queue which extended from the stationery beyond the frozen foods to the cheeses which were next to the door, the poet bought a postal order for two and threepence, put it in an envelope with the number of the packet of seed, and sent it to the seed company. Then he returned home and for three days waited impatiently for the seed to arrive. At night after he had gone to bed he would take the catalogue and read it, and on the third night when he was gazing at the picture of his chosen seed which he already loved very dearly, he happened to read the small print beneath the advertisement.

'Hothouse bloom only,' he read.

For a moment he was alarmed. He knew that his room would not provide much warmth for the plant, because he did not earn much money as a poet, in spite of the occasional television interviews where he was asked, What do you think of the world situation? Do you think Success comes too early in this modern age? If you had to live your life over again which one thing would you change? And in spite of the occasional poem printed in a literary journal, and the advertisement jingle which he wrote for a friend in an agency, his slight income did not allow for central heating. How would a hothouse bloom ever survive? he wondered.

'Well,' he said at last to himself, 'I will breathe on it. My body is warm, well stoked, blood flows from rafter to basement and even the rats have been driven inside this winter to seek shelter in me. By the way, one day when I am free of dreams and light, hawkers, carrion crows and enchantments I shall take time to sprinkle an appetising sweet poison for the rats in my sealed cabinet. In the meantime I shall await my packet of wonderful blossom.'

So he waited, sitting down to work the next morning with his mind continually straying to the thought of growing a hothouse bloom upon his window sill.

In due course the packet of seed arrived. The poet planted it, following the instructions as carefully as his individual temperament would allow. He resolved to breathe upon the soil, the seed and the resulting plant as often as he remembered or was free to do so when he took time from writing his poems to walk about the room counting the faded leaves upon the carpet or looking from the window at the man in the battered grey cap who walked from door to door asking, 'Have you any old watches, old gold, bracelets, wedding rings?'

The poet was not married, although like all poets he possessed an invisible muse, a mistress and wife to him, and a wedding ring with which he pledged his devotion to the Chosen Image. Unfortunately, when he turned the wedding ring three times upon his finger it did not provide him with a poem. There had been much controversy. Some poets had said that the wedding ring should provide poems in this way.

Nor could the poet give to the man in the grey battered cap any old watches, old gold or bracelets. How could he possess such valuables? He lived in a small flat where his only treasures which were yet not his alone but were accessible to all, lay arranged in dictionaries and grammars upon his bookshelves. Strange, wasn't it, that no burglar had been known to raid the premises in order to steal suitcases of words?

As for old watches, well, the poet owned a wrist watch which he preferred to keep in his pocket or upon his table. Strapped on his wrist it reminded him of a too genial handcuff to which he had no key, for which no key had yet been made.

Did I tell you he was a poet who could not write good poetry (there are many such) but unearthed clichés as if they were archaeological treasures arranged on a silver spade? After he had written each poem he was pleased with it, he confused the warmth and excitement which the act of writing gave him with the feelings naturally provided by a thing of beauty; therefore he thought his poem beautiful, and was most distressed and could not understand when later, from somewhere in the cave roof, the dampening idea leaked through that his poem was bad. Yet he could not stop writing just as he could not stop counting the leaves on the carpet or looking from his window at the man calling for Old Watches, Old Gold, Bracelets; or breathing warmth upon the tender leaves that had sprung from his chosen seed.

One evening when he looked at the plant he noticed a tiny bud with its petals beginning to open, and he knew that when morning came the plant would be in full blossom. So he went quickly to bed, pulling the blankets well over him in the belief that concealment means escape and acceleration of time, and soon he was fast asleep and dreaming, but the anonymous voices which inhabit all dreams said to him, 'What can you call entirely your own? You cannot write a poem without using the words, often the thoughts, of others. The words of the world lie like stagnant water in the ponds for the poets masquerading as the sun to quench their thirst, spitting out the dead tadpoles and the dry sticks and stones and bones. If ever you have precious thoughts of your own which do not lie accessible to all beneath the sky, how can you safeguard them? Where are your security measures for putting thoughts under lock and key?

'But then no thoughts belong entirely to you. You have no talent for your work. Your only talent and personal possession is breath, and yet since late winter when the seed catalogues were thrust through your letter box you have bestowed your breath upon a mere plant in order that it should give you pleasure by blossoming on your window sill. Do you think that is wise? Should you not conserve your breath, issue it according to a planned system of economy, and not waste it upon objects like flowers which perish almost as soon as they have bloomed?'

The poet heeded the voices in his dream and the next morning when he looked at the plant, although he knew that the flower was almost in blossom, he refused to breathe upon it, and all day it shivered upon the window sill, feeling for the first time the bitterness of the March winds that moaned up and down the street, and the chill touch of the tendrils of frost and fog that crept down the chimney, under the door, and through the top of the window into the poet's room. And the petals of the flower never opened, their promise was never fulfilled. By nightfall the leaves had blackened at the edges and the bud was a shrivelled silken cocoon of nothing.

The saddened poet gazed at the corpse of his Chosen Image, then uprooting it from the window box and taking it outside onto the landing, he thrust the plant and flower down the chute which extended from the top floor to the basement and which carried away all the refuse of the block of flats where he lived — cataracts of detergent packets, drums, soup tins, sardine keys, torn letters, parcel wrappings, newspapers, ends of bread, eggshells, orange peel, used cotton wool. Sorrowfully the poet watched the plant join its travelling companions, finding its place almost as if it belonged there, taking up the new rhythm of its journey, jostling, struggling in the narrow chute, being trampled and crushed by overbearing jam jars, bottles, and a rusted paraffin container.

For a moment the poet regretted his action. He longed to be in his room again with the plant there on the window sill, almost in blossom, and with him breathing tenderly upon it to provide it with the warmth it needed in order to survive.

Then he shrugged, and smiled cheerfully. What was the use of feeling dejected when one had only done what was right, and refused to waste one's breath upon a negligible hothouse bloom which had been deceitful anyway as its real nature had not been known until the small print of the contract was studied?

'I will forget the whole episode,' the poet said.

And he tried to forget.

He returned to his room and began to write his new poem. Now and again he glanced at the empty window box and sighed. The poem refused to be composed. The poet turned his wedding ring three times. Still the poem refused to be composed.

Well, that was nothing unusual.

He glanced once again at the empty window box and stilled his conscience by remarking to himself, 'Anyway it was a hothouse bloom and would never have survived the rigours of this climate; not even if it had been allowed to blossom. It was not selfish of me to deny it my breath, to dispose of it. Rather was it an act of thoughtfulness which is rare these days.'

He smoothed the paper before him, ready to imprint his poem.

Then a fit of coughing seized him, and he died.

In her silk and ivory tower the Muse turned from her window. 'He was a hothouse plant, anyway. I chose him at random without reading the small print at the bottom of the contract. He would never have blossomed. In future I shall keep my breath to myself — well at least I shall not be tempted when aspiring poets thrust their souls catalogued, numbered, illustrated, through my letter box.'

The Linesman

Three men arrived yesterday with their van and equipment to repair the telephone lines leading to the house opposite. Two of the men stayed at work in the house. The third carried his ladder and set it up against the telegraph pole twenty-five yards from the house. He climbed the ladder and beyond it to the top of the pole where, with his feet resting on the iron rungs which are embedded at intervals in the sides of the pole, he began his work, his hands being made free after he had adjusted his safety harness. He was not likely to fall. I did not see him climb the pole. I looked from my window and saw him already working, twisting, arranging wires, screwing, unscrewing, leaning back from the pole, dependent upon his safety belt, trusting in it, seeming in a position of comfort and security.

I stared at him. I was reluctant to leave the window because I was so intent upon watching the linesman at work, and because I wanted to see him descend from the pole when his work was finished.

People in the houses near the telegraph pole had drawn their curtains; they did not wish to be spied upon. He was in an excellent position for spying, with a clear view into the front rooms of half a dozen houses.

The clouds, curds and whey, were churned from south to north across the sky. It was one of the first Sundays of spring. Washing was blowing on the clotheslines in back gardens; youths were lying in attitudes of surrender beneath the dismantled bellies of scooters; women were sweeping the Saturday night refuse from their share of the pavement. Perhaps it was time for me to have something to eat — a cup of coffee, a biscuit, anything to occupy the ever marauding despair.

But still I could not leave my position at the window. I stared at the linesman until I had to screw up my eyes to avoid the bright stabs of spring light. I watched the work, the snipping, twisting, joining, screwing, unscrewing of bolts. And all the time I was afraid to leave the window. I kept my eyes fixed upon the linesman slung in his safety harness at the top of the telegraph pole.

You see, I was hoping that he might fall.

How Can I Get
in Touch with Persia?

Early in his life he grew mistrustful of messages borne to him by word of mouth or letter. He became concerned with invisible communications and the sly cryptic evidence of them in telephone wires, radio aerials, valves and switches, and, lately, the four hundred and five invisible lines of a television picture. Electricity fascinated him. When his parents talked of the 'old days' of gas lamps in the street and candles burning with their leaf-shaped flame at the foot of the stairs, he felt a special pride in the fact that he had always known electricity, the power of turning the switch and invading the room with probes of light or condemning it to darkness. When his mother plugged in the electric iron he used to rub his finger along the bottom of the iron, collecting the evidence, the mystical vibrations, tracing them along the cord to the unobtrusive three-pin plug above the baseboard, just inside the door. The repeated warnings BE CAREFUL OF ELECTRICITY, THE INVISIBLE KILLER, only increased its fascination. He became preoccupied even in sleep and dreaming with its mystery. He longed to seek out the reality of it, to put his hand into the dark and touch it.

He constructed his first transmitting and receiving set. He was filled with wonder and love at the variety of messages in the air. Sometimes messages came to him even while he was walking in the street or at work. While other boys of his age sought the company of girl friends and found their escape and pleasure in clubs, gangs, the telly, the dance hall, the cinema, he derived his entertainment and solace from the workbench in his tiny room on the top floor of the house where he had an increasing supply of electrical gadgets, wires, plugs, and his transmitting and receiving set. Often he would stay into the early hours of the morning, tapping in code and talking to people in the distant countries which could only be located on the map by searching the index and then carefully trapping the area between its bonds of latitude and longitude. Every country was trapped in this way. Not one could hide or fake death in order to escape notice, such was the ruthlessness of the map of the world.

But all things were ruthless, all men and their instruments.

And what of Death?

He used to sit in the dark, sometimes not attending the signals on his wireless, considering the problem of death and the means of solving it with his one ally — Electricity. Then he would switch on the BBC and laugh when the late-night clergyman entreated him to Lift Up Your Hearts For God Dwells on High, Come Unto Him All Ye that Labour and Are Heavy-laden and He Will Give You Rest.

Well, he was not heavy-laden, anyway. He was selected to receive special messages. The sound waves eddied about him, touching his skin, the palms of his hands, caressing him, even underneath his clothing; he throbbed with messages.

He worked as a packer in a Mail-Order Firm at Brixton. He applied for that job after the episode of the sea holiday when the family doctor had said that he needed rest, he had been growing too fast, and now that he was in his early twenties he should be leading a 'more normal' life.

Sometimes he stayed in bed all day.

'You great lout,' his father said. 'When I was your age . . .'

That was when he was working at the self-service store, on the adding machine, for he was interested in numbers and sympathetic to machines. Then for a while he stayed at home while the doctor persisted in telling him to get to the seaside.

But who would supply the money? He grew tired of hearing of the seaside.

For three days and nights without ceasing he communicated with foreign places. He called it his seaside holiday. It refreshed him. Besides, he had a plan in mind. It would astonish the world, it would show everybody. He slept with wires round his wrists to collect and store messages which came while he slept, for it would take much time and study to complete his plan, there was not a moment to be lost because the life expectation of every human being had lengthened and branched out at the edge with poisonous blossoms, wire flowers lit by concealed bulbs which flashed their urgency, red, gold, and dark green.

It troubled him that when he applied for the job at Brixton he was asked to sign a form stating that he was willing to be searched every evening before he left the factory. Why should he say that he was willing to be searched when he was not willing to be searched? What were they trying to seize from him? He was grateful that his messages, the receiving waves, were invisible, and his heart was learning to beat in Morse code, so as to transmit secret answers, and not a soul at the Mail-Order Firm knew of his secret preoccupations or of his growing power and alliance with electricity.

'Get out and about,' his father said, 'instead of tinkering and talking to Persia.'

So he went one night to the wrestling, and although he listened carefully to the names of the holds — Full Nelson,

Drop Kick, Toe Hold, Body Scissors — and tried to grasp the special significance of them when applied to his secret plans, the spectacle of wrestling did not interest him. He had gone there only to please his mother when she said, 'Yes, do as your father says, have an evening out, to the stock-car racing or somewhere.'

His heart had beaten fast with dread when she said, 'or somewhere', for the expression was so vague that he knew she was trying to convey a special meaning, perhaps a warning. Had she intercepted a message intended for him?

Sometimes when he came home at night he found that his father had gone down to the pub and he was alone with his mother. He enjoyed these evenings. He sat in his father's chair by the stove and watched his mother bending and twisting the wire to make the frames of the lamp shades which she afterwards fleshed with stiff material, like parchment, painting flowers and scenes and faces upon it. Making lamp shades was her hobby. She had orders from so many people that she could hardly keep up with the demand. Some she gave away, others she sold; it depended. As he sat there watching and talking to her, telling her about the latest messages from Persia, and about his job in the Mail-Order Firm, he would at times be overcome by a haunting fear at the sight of his mother's face and the used look of her skin, as if someone in the Mail-Order Firm had charge of her, stamping wrinkled destinations upon her face in a crude impersonal way, as if she had changed into one of those dull-coloured envelopes which are issued by the Post Office with the instructions, RE-USE, ATTACH FLAP AND RE-USE TO ASSIST ECONOMY DRIVE. What did it mean? He would try to forget his fear. He would renew the conversation, giving detailed accounts of his day at work, but when the silences came his mind would be occupied with the problem of destinations, areas of land

and their ownership, human mortgages, electricity; chiefly electricity.

When his father returned from the pub, he would stop talking to his mother and get up from his father's chair, and go quickly to his room, close the door carefully, lock it, draw the curtains, and sit at his workbench considering the wonderful prospects of electricity. Once, he heard rumours that his enemies were closing in upon him but he suppressed his immediate panic and smiled with scorn — was not electricity his lifelong ally?

But I need to catch up, he thought, with urgency. I should have studied it from the very beginning. In the medical world it is a miracle. I should have gone on and been a doctor.

Gone on? Where? To Persia?

Splutter, peep-peep, dot-dot-dot.

That was the language which he had learned and which he could now understand more easily than the language of people, of his mother and father. He could hear their murmurs to each other on the stairs, a rustling sound, like a straw broom sweeping debris or other messages of a hard substance, metal or stone, being shaken to extract them from the bottle in which they had drifted thousands of miles across the ocean.

He turned from listening to them and switched on his receiver.

Splutter, peep-peep, dot-dot-dot.

He felt lonely. The language infuriated him suddenly. He switched off and sat on his bed and listened to the BBC. Any Questions? Does the Team think? Will the Panel tell me?

'Go on,' he said, and lay down on his narrow bed and closed his eyes.

It happened that there was an epidemic of flu in the

district. Everybody seemed to be catching it. Some of the workers at the Mail-Order Firm were taken ill, and were sent home, and calling on their doctor on the way home they were put on the panel and given prescriptions for fancy nose sprays, bottles of medicine, boxes of pills.

First his father had flu and recovered.

He knew that he would be immune from it as he needed all his strength for the important work which was to decide his destiny. He realised that he could not be spared from his nightly conversations with far countries, and from the time-devouring problems of electricity.

The flu avoided him, and arrived at his mother. Quite surprisingly she talked in her sleep one night and his father called him, saying stupidly, 'Mum's talking in her sleep. She's delirious. We'll get the doctor.'

He did not approve of his father's suggestion. He was seized with jealousy which raged in him, making his face turn a violent red and his heart thud and throb against his chest. Why was his father not consulting him, instead of a doctor?

His jealousy subsided, his face paled; his heart was heavy with disappointment. No one knew of his secret qualifications; he would have to take action, prove himself; human lives were in the balance, the entire human race depended upon him. It was time; he would act; how?

The doctor came, after four hours. And by morning his mother was dead.

When he heard the news he went to his room and tuned in to Persia.

His mother was dead. Her unfinished lamp shades lay upon the table, beside the useless twists of copper wire. Her face was at last franked and cancelled with free death. Or so the world believed. He could not understand, he could not think clearly. He stayed all that night and the night before the funeral, leaning over his transmitting and receiving set, trying to interpret the new signals which had found their way amongst the splutter, peep-peep, dot-dot-dot.

The day of the funeral was as sunny as a Bank Holiday, and the ride to the cemetery had a festive air about it, with the hearse speeding along so that his mother might keep her last appointment.

But his mother disliked appointments; she had never kept them; and this was not her last, oh no, oh no. He burst out laughing in the back of the car.

'It takes people in different ways,' his father said.

'We all need a good cry,' said his aunt from Liverpool.

And when he saw them lowering his mother's coffin into the grave he still did not cry, and after the funeral he went straight home and got in touch with Persia.

He was talking to Persia, and trying to understand the complexities of the strange new code when he conceived his plan. When his father, as had been arranged, went north to Liverpool to stay with the aunt, he would be alone in the house. That was his opportunity.

Two days later he hired a Self-Drive car. He drove in the evening to his mother's grave, dug up her coffin, opened it, removed his mother's body which he wrapped in a blanket and laid gently in the back of the car.

He kissed his mother. He began to cry. 'Don't worry,' he said. 'I've never believed it. Even when they wanted to search me to take my life away from me, I've never believed it. All the messages have proved it is not true. There is no death, now that I have solved the mystery. You did not guess, did you, that I had solved the mystery, all this time in my room with the copper wire and switches and a few strips of aluminium? I'm going to bring you back to life. You can't die, not any more; besides, the people are waiting for their lamp shades to protect them from the light, all up and down the street they are waiting for their lamp shades, and soon you'll be making them, and I'll be sitting by the stove, watching you, talking to you.'

He drove the car home, and carried his mother to her room, and laid her on his bed. Far into the night he worked to attach the wires and switches to her body. She lay with gold and silver insect-scaffolding over her; like Gulliver wired to earth by the little people.

'She is regaining her strength,' he said confidently, distributing wires, locating switches, placing a light bulb on her breast.

At half-past three in the morning he made a cup of tea on the gas ring in the corner of his room. He offered the tea to his mother, first taking a few sips to test whether it was too strong or too sweet as she did not fancy it that way. She did not move. She did not even raise her head to drink the tea. He switched on the electric current. A slight shock trembled through his fingers and along his arm as he touched the network of wires, but still his mother did not move. He drank the tea himself. Then he kissed the cold grey face; there was a blue tinge under the skin, like deep water. He crumbled a piece of Rich Tea Biscuit over the mouth in the hope that her tongue would dart forth, like a lizard's tongue, and seize it. But there was still no movement. He rechecked the wires and the switches. His face was dazed and pale; his cheekbones felt massive, seized by a clamp; his mouth was dry.

'She is regaining her strength,' he repeated.

He sighed. He found another blanket, and lay beside his mother on the narrow bed. 'When I count twenty,' he said to himself, 'she will come alive.'

He counted twenty; she was not breathing.

'If I hear a motor bike while I am counting fifteen,

and if the edge of the curtain moves during the following fifteen and the light from the street lamp outside shines in a slit upon the wallpaper, then she will be alive.' He counted fifteen, listening anxiously for the motor bike, and opening his eyes to observe the patch of wallpaper where the street lamp would shine.

He heard a motor bike. A wind blew the edge of the curtain, letting in the light. But nothing persuaded his mother to wake.

'It takes time,' he said, his heart heavy with the humiliation of needing to include motor bikes, numbers, street lamps, in his perfect plan, to rely on ordinary visible objects when the secret world of electricity was under his command, as his agent and slave.

He drew another blanket over him and slept. He lay there for two days, never entirely losing his faith in the power of the electricity, but relying more and more upon chance happenings, shadows, noises, radios in the next house, to influence his mother, to compel her to wake. But the motor bikes, the lorries, cars, roared up and down the street; shadows formed and dissolved and the light made patterns on the wallpaper; and his mother stayed dead. From time to time he still switched the current on and off in the hope of reviving her.

It only needs time, he thought. A season, a spring or summer.

His head felt unearthed, ancient, like the skull of a mammoth. Drums beat in the sky; his skin was too tight, it would not fit.

At three o'clock the next afternoon when the man from the Self-Drive Hire Company called, knocked, and got no answer, when neighbours saw the accumulating milk bottles outside the door and the paper boy found his papers not collected, when the world, as it does in a feat of intensely interested arithmetic, put two and two together, the police were called. They forced an entry to the house. They searched. When they came to his room they found his mother lying on the bed, laced with wires and switches. He was leaning over the transmitting set in the corner of the room. Tears were streaming down his face. He was trying to get in touch with Persia.

A Relative of the Famous

If you happen to be a relative of the famous you are granted certain concessions and privileges, although you understand that your claim or the claim of others on behalf of you must first be recognised. Imposters are frowned upon. The question is, how does one decide in the first place which of the famous are imposters?

After death is best; time, sprung free of the trap, exercises itself day and night in long division, subtraction, blinding itself in the poor light of the grave where the little worms patrol the corridors carrying torches past each darkened room.

The remainders are framed in gold.

Now there was once a woman painter who became famous after her death when bearded men plunged swords in each other's hearts to possess one of her paintings or to donate one, suitably inscribed and recorded, to the local gallery which was dark brown, opening and closing with a faulty catch, like a broom cupboard where in spring and summer the dust is elbowed away and the shapes of paint are temporarily revived, with the sun warming the creaking damp joints of colour, the drip-dry bones of light blazing.

Now after the death of the painter, after her biography had been written, the memoirs of her friends printed and her work appraised as successful communication, a tunnel through dense mountain walls where the penalties of work are loneliness, suffocation, drowning in underground streams, pit-blindness, those who recognised her work and were grateful for human routes at any cost, for burdened ants who never swerve, decided to extend their interest.

'Has she any relatives?' they asked.

'None,' was the answer.

Then suddenly they heard of Wilfred, the nephew, the eccentric beachcomber with the encyclopaedic knowledge of flora, fauna, conchology.

They were amazed and excited.

'Why didn't someone tell us before?' they cried. 'To think that Wilfred has been living all this time in a remote northern seaside town, and not a word has been breathed that he was a relative of the famous!'

Few people knew.

'Wilfred?' they said. 'Dirty, evil, wandering day and night along the beach gathering shells, naming them like dynasties, tracing their kingdom.

'Wilfred feeds on the sea.

'But that is not all. Look at him standing day after day in the main street outside the Post Office, abusing people, throwing stones through the letter boxes.'

It is one of the most insulting acts possible to stand outside a Post Office, cursing and throwing stones!

Wilfred smelled like a decayed forest; he would have to be put away soon, everyone knew where, behind high walls where day and night are striped and the sun sets with the porridge in a little white china bowl.

But when Wilfred was discovered to be a relative of the famous, everything was all right; they did not put him away, there was no one to pry and ask if he knew where he was and what was his name; instead they gave him a Social Security Allowance which came in a clouded blue envelope every Monday; they let him live in his tiny beach hut by the mud flats and the grey mangroves, and those who were interested no longer spoke of him as dirty and evil, but they shook their heads, saying, 'How sad! How sad, yet fascinating! You know his aunt is the famous painter.'

Then they whispered their final remark, 'An accident of birth!'

How does one know whose infirmity one carries?

As if birth were a left-luggage department where the parcels sometimes became confused.

And there was Wilfred, with his skin lined with the same substance as that of his aunt, a famous painter — who knows what luggage had been checked in for her to be collected by others, to burden their lives?

But Wilfred did not heed these searching discussions. Wilfred was enclosed in his own world. He was not a dung beetle or mole making person to person calls through dangerous territory; his life contained enough peril. Wandering the beach gathering shells, cursing and throwing stones in the main street remained his right and privilege.

Now a rich woman of esteem lived in the town. She was shaped like a sonnet, with piled white hair. She planned her life and the lives of others; she could afford to, for much wealth is required for planning. She contributed generously to the Church, the Red Cross, the Mothers' Union, the Women's Division of the Farmers' Union, but her particular interest was directed to the famous, many of whom she knew personally, and although her husband who was also a person of esteem liked to be private, sitting in his armchair, wearing an old grey cardigan of humility, she preferred her intimate knowledge of the famous to be made known. You can imagine her surprise and the quickening of her interest when she learned that Wilfred, a relative of the famous, was living almost on her own doorstep.

'In the same town, I can hardly believe it!' she exclaimed with delight.

'To think that we have been living here all this time, and never known about Wilfred!'

She invited Wilfred to tea.

He accepted the invitation. He came to her house at five o'clock one evening (though it was impossible to tell how he knew the exact time) and stood all evening in the centre of her living room, his blue eyes wide, the curses flowing from his lips, brisk, playful, terrible, like sporting sharks in summer waters. The curses tore the esteemed woman's flesh to pieces; she looked embarrassed and went to find the Elastoplast with the built-in dressing. And still the curses flowed! And Wilfred was not even standing in the main street outside the Post Office! But they served him tea and smiled at him and listened to him, yet they were relieved when he began to glance anxiously around the room, as if it were time for him to go home. He grew suddenly quiet. Not once had he smiled in answer to their smiles. Then he spoke the esteemed woman's name.

'Mrs Allcloud,' he said. 'Between the cat's-eyes, the cockle, the fan shell, the lamp shell, stars that may brag may brag.'

'How delightful,' she said, trying to concentrate. 'Well, you'll be on your way I suppose, Wilfred.'

She spoke as one might to a traveller who was leaving for a long night's hazardous journey through frost and fog.

Wilfred put down his teacup which he had held all evening, and without saying Thank you or smiling goodbye he went from the room, along the passage, and out the front door.

Mrs Allcloud followed him to the door. 'Good night, Wilfred.'

He did not look back. He walked along the road with his head high, his steps mincing, if by mincing one means that footsteps grind the flesh of the earth, churning it into little heaps like worm casts.

'Well,' Mrs Allcloud sighed, returning to her living room and mending with one wholesome knitting glance the cracks in the windows, walls, roof, made by an evening of well-directed curses. 'He didn't say Thank you, or seem pleased. His manners are frightful. But we must learn to understand him, mustn't we, Anthony?' — she glanced apprehensively at her husband and fear looked through the lines of her rhyming body — 'We must understand him, cultivate him, for poor Noeline's sake. It is sad that I missed making her acquaintance, but I recognised from the first the value of her art, I was on the committee, remember, who chose her painting for the gallery, and though there was a storm, with the public labelling the painting as obscene, I stood firm. Poor Wilfred! It is not as if he were *nobody*!'

And the next day, having spread her evening's memory with golden syrup, Mrs Allcloud talked gaily and brightly at the Ladies' Club, mentioning, only by the way, that Wilfred (nephew of the famous artist) had visited her for tea, that she knew him well, that he was a close friend of the family.

And in future, every month, sometimes twice a month, she made a point of inviting Wilfred to tea. She would stop him outside the Post Office where he was engaged in his curses. He would pause when he caught sight of her.

'Building negotiations!' he would shout. 'The lowest or any tender not necessarily accepted!'

She would smile kindly.

'Will you come to tea, Wilfred, on Saturday evening at five?'

'As a dome of shells is ground to sand, soft bodies within, the resentment of water against temples, give a dog a bone a bone to carry home, to bury — purport, purport, fangs, change, prayer to pulp . . .'

'Will you come to tea? Fifty-five East Street.'

It was as well for him to be reminded of the address.

Then she would smile at him once more, and he would stare with his blue eyes unsmiling, then resume his fury against the Post Office.

But he always accepted the invitation to tea, behaving on each occasion as he had done the first evening. Once, though, he brought Mrs Allcloud a mountain orchid which he had gathered from the bush-clad hill overlooking the sea.

Mrs Allcloud flourished with goodness and interest.

'His aunt,' she would say, 'the famous painter, you know . . .'

'Have you read her biography, the definitive edition?'

'Have you read her collected letters?'

Once when someone remarked that no mention was made of Wilfred in the biography, she said warmly, 'I am so fond of Wilfred. You know how he is, but somehow one can sense the family trend, underneath everything he is gifted, so gifted.'

'You remember the famous painter? I know her nephew, he often comes to tea.'

The one flaw in Mrs Allcloud's happiness at this time was her inability to mould Wilfred's life, to plan for it as she had done for so many others. She had helped artists by giving them money, buying their pictures. She had encouraged writers, subscribed to the publication of their books. She longed to help Wilfred in some way, to possess him, to stake her claim in his life. She had never been faced with anyone like Wilfred. He was a mountain wall, she could make no impression on him, her fingerprints, her footprints did not show; his secret inward weather covered all her tracks.

It was a serious and disturbing occasion when Mrs

Allcloud discovered that Wilfred was not after all a relative of the famous. She had been studying more closely the family history of the painter. She realised that somehow a mistake had been made, that Wilfred was no relation at all, that he belonged to the South Island Vincents, the Racing People in Southland, a notable family certainly, but no connection, no connection at all with the famous painter. She still felt bound by her conscience to invite Wilfred to tea — he was so helpless, so strange, what could one do? — but the filth of his unwashed body and clothes appalled her, and his curses, there in her living room, were an abuse and insult which no sensitive person, like herself, could be expected to endure. And he showed no gratitude for the interest in him, he made no response to sympathy and kindness. There had been the gift of the mountain orchid; certainly that had been touching, but now, seen in its proper perspective the encouragement and cultivation of Wilfred had not been altogether wise.

But Mrs Allcloud kept her discovery to herself, although she did not make it known now that Wilfred was a relative of the famous. And who was to know? Who was interested enough to delve into the Vincent family history?

Many people were interested. She realised this almost as soon as she denied it. Her discovery would not for long remain secret. Oh how confusing one's life became, she thought. How could one act for the best, taking all things into consideration?

All things?

Public safety, concern, hygiene, for instance.

And Wilfred?

How could she deal with Wilfred? How can you deal with someone who is less concerned with your presence, your power, your riches, than he is with naming shells, following the tides, cursing and throwing stones in the main street outside the Post Office while the letters flow backward and forward, here and there, with the correct number of stamps on them and the correct address and the enclosed lucid notes between person and person, How pleased I was to visit you on Saturday for tea, how a warmth flows through me when I realise your interest and kindness, your desire to befriend me, whether on behalf of a mythical aunt who laid submarine cables or of myself who am enclosed for ever, hermetically sealed, or on behalf of humanity biting its tongue in two, what do I care about your snobbish excuses, when you invite me, befriend me, but I regret I cannot accept your invitation, your life is adrift on the beach, you have gone out with the tide, I am alone in the world, even with daisy chains of aunts who are famous or unknown, I am alone in the world, yet I am the Saviour in the main street, I will defend the whole of humanity against the evils of the Post Office, but help, rescue, what am I to do?

The Triumph of Poetry

When he was born they named him Alan, meaning that in future the area of himself would be known as Alan. The area of oneself is like a drop of ink absorbed by blotting paper, gradually spreading, blurring at the edges, receiving upon it other blots in different shapes and colours until finally the original is dim, indistinguishable, while the saturated sheet of humanity upon which it lies is cast as worthless into the wastebasket, and another sheet, a clean sheet provided by the advertisers, is placed upon the desk.

Alan was a bright boy at school. He was Junior, Intermediate, and Senior Chess Champion. He could play tennis and swim well. He was liked by his classmates. He enjoyed school.

'What do you want to be?' they asked him.

He was not sure. In the holidays when he was fourteen he began to write verse, prospecting a trampled earth with a seam of gold shining through it. The gold was his cousin Lorna's hair, fluffed like wattle, rubbing gold dust on his fingers when he touched it, but only in his dreams. During the day he swam in an ice-cold mountain pool, with a knife between his teeth.

In his final year at school they repeated their question because they preferred to watch their pupils heading, like runners emerging into the sun, each to his separate lane with his number in bold letters printed on his body. They preferred the course to remain clear in order that, should they have occasion to cheer their pupils in times of darkness or dim light, they should not discover to their humiliation, when the course was again visible, that they had been giving encouragement to pupils running in strange lanes, wearing strange colours, or even to those who were refusing to run at all, those who lagged, content with musing on the scenery, even breaking away from their course, running cross-country where no tracks had ever been marked, and no flags were flying, and there was no one, no official, to greet them at the end!

'What do you want to be?' they asked him again.

He told them that he had decided to be a poet.

'That's not exactly a career,' they said.

'We mean what do you want to spend your life doing? Teaching, medicine . . . ?'

'I will get my degree,' he said (he had won a scholarship to a university), 'and then write poetry as my life's work.'

'But how will you earn your living?' they asked him. 'You can always be a poet as a side line, in your spare time — but how will you keep yourself?'

One needs to be kept, swept, turned inside out, shaken free of insects, polished, pleated, trimmed, preserved in brine which is collected in opaque green bottles from the sea or from tears which fall in the intervals between each death.

They said goodbye to him at school. They smiled kindly as he went out into the sun.

'You go ahead, get your degree, perhaps take up teaching; then you might decide what you really want to do.'

He did not cower in the sun's blaze. He turned and spoke angrily. There was also a note of puzzlement in his voice. Why did they not understand?

'But I already *know* what I want to do. I am going to be a poet!'

The First Assistant, standing at the door, walked a little way towards him; there was a smell about him as if he had emerged from a stable where he had been fed on chalk; his gown lay like a bridle over his shoulders, and his eyes were trained not to stare distracted at the revelations in their corner mirrors.

'I used to write poems myself once, Wakefield. Who doesn't? I had a few published, in little magazines here and there. Of course I'm ashamed of them now. I had enough sense to leave that stage behind, get a safe job, regular income, marry, have a family, occupy my time in normal ways. I've seen boys like yourself go off to the University with bright ambitions. The important thing is to have something to fall back on.'

The First Assistant glanced a moment at the door behind them, then he frowned; a gust of wind had banged the door shut. He stepped a few paces back towards the door, hitched his gown where it had fallen from his left shoulder.

'It's a phase, a phase, Alan,' he said. He looked apprehensively behind him at the closed door. He seemed to be listening, as if his statement, 'It's a phase, a phase,' had assumed animal shape and was waiting inside to challenge him.

Then he opened the door and boldly walked in, out of the light.

Alan began his studies at the University. He wrote poems which were published and praised in the University Reviews and in a number of little magazines which kept bursting, pop, on the literary scene, and then folding, like delicate flowers, their petals leaning solicitously over their own broken hearts. It troubled Alan that there was so little time for writing. He wanted to write, of course he wanted to write, was he not bursting with ideas for poems, for stories and novels, yet where could he find the time between attending lectures, studying, flirting, making love, holidaying at the beach? Almost before he realised it, the University year had ended, and although he gained First Class Honours in his examinations, the amount of his literary work was very small.

'Why don't you take a job on the wharves in the holidays?' asked one of his friends. 'I know someone who is writing a novel that way. He has chucked University and is working as a wharfie during the day and writing at night.'

The proposal sounded interesting. Another friend told Alan of a poet who was working as a postman and writing in his spare time. In fact, the friend said, it was the fashion for poets to work as postmen; indeed, housewives were beginning to look suspiciously at the uniformed civil servants who flung their letters through the regulation letter boxes; for poets were questionable characters whom you could not see working, as you could see other people, in whirling activity like washing in a washing machine.

Poets no longer brushed the passion from their souls like dust from a plum, by writing about kowhai trees and the felling of the bush; no, they retired to their own houses, pulled down the blinds, disconnected the telephone, cut off the electricity, and in the darkness and isolation they were sitting down like Little Jack Horner to try to crack the stone of the plum, and everybody knew that fruit stones contained arsenic which was of course a safeguard against the self-congratulatory phrases of Little Jack Horner, What a Good Boy Am I . . . But the secretive way of writing was inclined (Alan's friend told him) to rouse envy in people, to make them wish that they too could work in secret instead of being exposed like washing in a washing machine; and this (Alan's friend told him) made them inclined to sabotage washing machines — and poets!

'I'm a novelist myself,' Alan's friend said. 'But a poet

working as a postman is a risk, and housewives know it. Can poets be trusted to carry and deliver private communications? Ever, even in their own writings?'

And Alan's friend pointed out the dangers to poets and to the public (multiple dangers if the identity of the two coincided) of sorting mail in small caged rooms; of franking with strange marks invitations accepted or rejected, summonses to appear in court, eviction orders, declarations of love and hate, notifications of death, and the dead letters themselves, address not known, addressee departed leaving no trace, deceased . . .

For the holidays, then, Alan did not work as a postman. He found a job as porter in a hospital morgue, attaching tickets and tying toes together, and looking for vacant spaces on the shelves of the refrigerator in order to keep a state of efficiency. He found that the atmosphere stimulated his thinking, but only while he was among the corpses, for as soon as he went to his digs to carry out his plan of writing at night, his thoughts seemed to vanish. It's the revenge of the dead, he complained, being at that time inclined to generalisations and simplifications, chiefly because he was tired and felt in need of a milestone to rest against, or if not a milestone as they were now historical treasures and no longer legitimate resting-places, a road signal, ROAD UP, DANGEROUS CORNER.

But he knew it was not the revenge of the dead. Their toes were tied with pink tape, in bows, as for a festive occasion. Their faces were in unsealed envelopes, forwarded at half-rates with five conventional words of greeting. All was in order. The dead did not need revenge.

Before the beginning of the next University year Alan found it hard to decide between continuing his studies and finding a job as a wharfie, farm rouseabout, shearing hand, freezing-work hand, sharemilker, milk-bar attendant, or waiter in a tourist hotel. Or postman. Then he met Sylvia and instead of being afflicted with the recklessness of a lover, climbing hazardous mountains, plunging into milling torrents, he put on his oldest clothes and sat all night on the beach, threading and tightening possibilities, like a poor fisherman mending a hole in his net.

He decided to be cautious, to continue his studies, for he realised that the net and the mended hole in it would be needed to keep out the rain when rain had the impertinence to fall upon Sylvia.

Do nets keep out the rain?

Alan decided Yes, after he had spent all night on the beach.

Such decisions are not taken lightly which does not prove that they are correct because their birth has caused inconvenience, only that they are defended with more passion than reason, as statesmen know, who carry tight-lipped umbrellas and receive blows to their pride.

Alan loved Sylvia. He courted her on the beaches and the riverbanks and over the desk of the University library where she worked. They married and rented a washhouse which they converted into a tiny flat They had a folding bed, an electric cooker, two chairs, a table, a bookcase which held books instead of ornaments, and they shared a bathroom and lavatory with the young couple, Tony and Leila, living in the adjacent washhouse. Tony had been a stock hand in Australia and was now working on the wharves and writing short stories in his spare time.

'As soon as I see my way clear,' he told Alan, 'I'll be writing a novel. How's your poetry coming along?'

'If conditions are favourable . . .' Alan began. 'We might be talking about prize flowers or a proposed truce in a long-drawn-out civil war . . .'

'Perhaps a harvest of opportunities; reaped and bound,

stacked by machine, but with no mechanical device for grinding; only two stones, gravestones . . .'

Alan and Sylvia, Tony and Leila, were enjoying their married life although making love gave little time for study and less time for writing the poems and novels which it inspired. Then the long summer evenings were so pleasant! How lucky they were to be living so close to the beach where they could have picnic meals, dig down to Spain if they were so inclined, romp in the water, surfing, swimming, fishing from the rocks, or wandering hand in hand by starlight and moonlight, plodging their toes in the wet sand, their ankles entangled with seaweed, the stink of salt in their throats. Summer was wonderful and warm, no one could stay inside chewing at books, the sky in the daytime was pure blue, now solid, like rock so that you might have hammered it and been showered with lethal stones and pieces of blue cliff, now like bright blue glass that endured the sun until it shattered in a storm with lightning and thunder, and silver-wet outer space seeped through crackling like cellophane, sheeting the hills with rain and mist.

Who could study and pore over novels in the summer?

Yet when the two young couples wandered along the beach in the evenings they liked to recite poems, but they were not poems which Alan had written.

'You have to get your voice right for mine,' he said, laughing. 'The salt air pickles my language, shrivels the skin of it; the roots lose their grip; my words are not endowed with prehensile characteristics.'

They skimmed stones on the sea, stones cold as a turned-aside human cheek, if death can be defined as the lure of a new direction where eyes and face target the unseen.

They set crabs on one another, laughing when the

pincers closed on the loved skin. They stamped and shouted; dived in the water and made floating love, merman to mermaid above the crusted wrecks of nothing and the discarded bicycle wheels and car bodies.

Life was idyllic. At one time Sylvia discovered that she was pregnant. Her heart flurried with alarm. How could she rear a child in a washhouse? Besides, Alan was still studying, she would have to give up her job . . .

Alan wanted her to have the child. He began (when he found time) to write poems about it, 'Lines to my son, Aged Three'; 'To My Daughter Lying in Her Pram' —

> My wild-west daughter in your covered wagon
>   sombre
> waterproofed against the sky and the tears of your
>   mother . . .

One afternoon, however, Alan and Sylvia kept an appointment in a house in Freeman's Bay where both were blindfolded, and Sylvia underwent an operation. That evening Sylvia lay seriously ill in the local hospital, but after a few days she recovered, no questions were asked, and she and Alan resumed their idyllic life, less forty pounds of their savings, and with an unidentified fear which greeted them each evening in their tiny washhouse flat as if it were lord of their mansion. They chose not to identify their fear. Names, they realised, bestow space, keys, power on the nameless which encircle human lives, waiting their chance.

'How fortunate we are to be so intelligent,' they said to each other when one night they came home to find their fear standing waiting for the double bed to be unfolded for love and sleep.

Soon it was Alan's fourth year at the University. He had gained a brilliant degree and was sitting his Honours Examination. He found little time for writing poetry.

Leila and Tony had sailed overseas where Tony was to seek his fortune and where he would find time for writing his novel.

There was a prevalent idea that Time overseas was different from Time in one's own country; it could be juggled, coaxed, extended in a most extraordinary and satisfying manner. Leila and Tony were already installed in a tiny flat in London and their first letter (they had written no more since their arrival) had been enthusiastic and full of plans for the future. It did seem, Alan thought wistfully, that Time overseas was more abundant, looped and lazy like spaghetti, dangling everywhere, one only needed to twirl a fork of thought and hook an endless length of Time.

Occasionally, however, Alan would set to work and produce a poem which he sent to one of the literary magazines. He was beginning to gain a reputation. One or two people spoke of him as 'that promising young poet Alan Wakefield'. Another had remarked, in rather sinister fashion, Alan thought, 'Alan Wakefield is a poet who should be watched'; while yet another critic noted that it was 'impossible to judge Alan Wakefield until he has given us a small but representative volume of his work'.

I wonder, Alan thought, reading the critics' words, if I have enough poems to make a book, to submit to a publisher? Oh, if only I had more time! What would I not do with more time!

How excited he became when he thought of the prospect of more time! It's like the old days, he would think, feeling a quickening in his blood and an acceleration of thoughts in his mind.

The old days, and he was only twenty-four!

Still, life was good, life was satisfying. He was studying hard for his examination. He was very much in love with his wife. He had many friends. There were parties, picnics, expeditions to the bush, to the mountains. People called at all hours to their tiny flat, 'Hey Alan, anyone home? Hey Sylvie!'

Sometimes at night when all the visitors had gone and Sylvia, exhausted, had already fallen asleep, Alan would go to the tiny window of the washhouse flat, draw aside the skimpy lace curtain, and look down at the sea crouched moaning and restless at their back door. He would time his breathing to the sighing rise and fall of the water, and find himself sighing also, or moaning.

The patience of the sea depressed him. Why should it go on waiting and waiting, moaning and beating its forehead, shedding a fury of tears or, placid, swallowing them and shining with pretended peace, yet always waiting and waiting as if it were so sure of the outcome and the end?

Often Alan would watch the sea until far into the night. Then he would start from his dream and think guiltily, I could have been writing a poem. Then he would try to console himself. 'Still,' he would say, 'it's worth it to be able to observe all that beach in all tides and seasons.'

'Worth what?' his muse and his conscience asked together.

Yes, he would think, I could have been writing a poem. He was beginning to think more often of writing poems than of the poems themselves. People talked to him of poetry. He began to feel hemmed in, as if people were trying to decide his life for him. 'I don't have to write poems just because they ask me to,' he would say. It seemed as if people were invading him, his private territory and putting up their own signposts. He resented this. There were times now when he stayed silent for days, and one or two of his acquaintances began to whisper amongst themselves and tap their foreheads, which was a means of charming themselves against their fate, or of waking up their thoughts which had overslept, or of trying to enter the perpetually closed mountain skull. Who knows?

Alan gained his Honours degree and was appointed to the post of lecturer at the University. Life was gay once more, social, controversial. Lectures took a long time to prepare. The weather that summer was again very warm. There were swimming parties to the beach, morning, noon, and night, moonlight bonfires and barbecues. In a quarterly review of literature one of the critics asked, 'What has happened to our promising younger poets?'

That means Alan, of course, Sylvia thought as she read it, but she did not say so directly to Alan. Besides, he could no longer be called 'one of our promising younger poets'. His hair was thinning at the temples and a bald patch had appeared at the back of his head. It was early for Alan to be losing his hair, many kept theirs well into middle age or did not lose it at all, but Alan seemed to be subject to the pressures of a personal age which took its toll not by years but by a secret ringing, as of trees, of the life of his heart. The thinning of his hair was merely a concession to recognised Time, to allay the suspicions of those who, tiring of the marks of chronological age, might seek to explore the more secret areas of a man's life where Time is personal with its own rules and measurements.

The fact remains, Sylvia thought, that Alan can no longer be regarded as 'one of our promising younger poets'. Sylvia had an increasing desire to care for his poetry, to dress it to appear in public, to attend to the toileting of its language.

Also, a number of new poets were emerging from the

schools and universities, and these were now appearing regularly in the literary magazines. Sometimes entire issues were devoted to 'the new young poets'. Once, when Alan was flipping through the pages of one of these magazines, he was touched to read a tribute to himself as 'one of the country's established poets, Alan Wakefield, who pursues his own quiet line of thought'.

Yes, Alan thought bitterly, a quiet line all right, a branch line about to be closed because nobody travels there any more and weeds are growing over the track; and everybody dizzies back and forth on the Main Trunk Line with stops for organised refreshment at fixed prices — yes, a branch line with no train and no timetable, no flags, no signals.

Yet the reference to his work inspired Alan to write a poem for the next issue of the magazine which was called *Trend III*, following upon *Trend I* and *Trend II* which had ceased through lack of financial support because poetry was not yet as popular as the TAB and there was no legitimate reason why it should be unless it flashes winners and numbers in orderly and accurate gold lights that peck and stab like a surgeon's knife where one keeps one's heart wrapped snug against the fivers . . .

Alan's poem, which was not printed by the magazine, began:

> For drowning in rock-pools the face-downward men
> find cupful of tide enough to evict from their
>   human home
> the put-you-up and put-upon generations of
>   breath . . .

His poem was confused and chaotic. It dealt with the stifling effects of teacups, teaspoons, phials, eggcups, eye-baths . . .

Then came verses which Alan would have been ashamed of writing five or six years before.

With the hairs of my head I trap
the night-flying thoughts.
My hair, like grass, covers the mountain
where insects, knocking in the dark, are bruised
   upon the stone.

Nude statues overgrown with glances,
silent temples biding their time in the forenoon of
   civilisation,
weapon-crammed outposts of the guiding touch,
aphasic cities unable to extricate the knives and
   bullets of past utterance . . .

Justice like an oilstove must burn
with the correct blue flame
or the inhabitant of the room will die,
and the maker shed all responsibility . . .

Green moss in the hollows between person to
   person calls,
drifts of snow, the telephone wires blown down;
beasts of prey encircling the stranded town . . .
Nothing has changed since I stood
in the Hangman's Wood.
Between thefts of death, night, and the arson of love
sounds the automatic alarm of light.
Still waits the noose on the hanging-tree,
still creeps the hooded assembly
of the declared honest brave and good,
still the sun carries its golden opinions and witnesses
   in the sky,

No, nothing has changed since I stood
in the Hangman's Wood.

Neptune, loyal to his nature, drives three white
   precepts home.
They are
Rest, Punctuality in meeting whirlpools and
   lagoons,
Patience in retaining more than a fair share of
   death.
These, say Neptune, are the trident of success
to sustain, to lean upon,
to thrust in three places through the hearts of
   enemies.
But I say, only jocularity and age
would burden my loneliness with three white
   precepts.
Salt grinds in the great wound everywhere,
more than two-thirds the surface of life.

Alan's poem rambled on thus. When it was returned to him he tore it to pieces and flushed it down the lavatory. He rarely wrote another poem, but now from time to time he reviewed books of poetry, and his reviews were printed in the back pages of the small literary magazines.

'Mr Walters,' he wrote in one review, 'has twenty-two wombs, seven bloods, eight, six, nine, fires, ices, bones, respectively, three thighs, one cornucopia. Mr Walters is indeed a composite wonder with immense physical, geological, decorative, but few poetic possibilities.'

The reply came from Mr Walters in 'Letters to the Editor'.

'There is nothing left but sour grapes to quench the dry mouths of a certain academic coterie.'

Mr Walters (Ted) was a promising young student who had abandoned his university career for poetry and who earned his living working as a shearing hand, a rabbiter, sharemilker, and, at Christmas, a postman, furthering the exchange of robin-stained holly-festooned blood-robed platitudes.

Two, three, four years passed. Alan was now a Ph.D. Sylvia still worked in the University library. With an increase in Alan's salary they bought an old colonial house in the fashionable suburb of Tuapere. They had enough money now to buy books, records, to attend concerts and plays, to give parties. Although Alan worked hard preparing his lectures, and although they were witty, insightful, his manner of delivery had grown increasingly hesitant. Where he had once been noted for his forthright delivery, his clarity of speech, now he was often inaudible; he had picked up irritating gestures, such as waving his hand vigorously before his face as if he were trying to remove not a massive obstacle but a congregation of small ones which clustered in more formidable solidity, threatening his line of perspective; sometimes he would draw his head briskly back as if in bending it forward he had thrust his face into invisible prongs. He would gaze towards the far wall of the old-fashioned tiered lecture room, at the students sitting in the distance, close to the roof, staring down at him like planets. A feeling of irritation and dismay would come over him as he wondered exactly what they scribbled on the notes which they passed endlessly to and fro during the lecture. Perhaps one of them had ideas of being a poet? Perhaps he was writing poetry? If this thought occurred, Alan would be seized with a sense of responsibility, as if it were his duty to perform a particular act, to give a certain piece of advice, but always the urgency faded and he was left standing there, slightly dazed, with his notes propped on his lectern and the students waiting, some politely, others restlessly, for him to conclude his lesson. In appearance he seemed now far more than thirty. He was stooped. He was almost bald. The blue veins of his head intertwined like lines on a map of the world.

Sylvia had grown more beautiful over the past years. She was plump and matronly. She had the appearance of being a mother though she had borne no children, a fact which was outwardly accepted and faced by herself and Alan, but which was the cause of friction with relatives, for their respective parents grew more impatient as year by year they failed to achieve the status of grandparents (both Alan and Sylvia had been their only children). There were from both the Wakefields and the Simpsons, visits, whispers, suggestions, remedies, hints; clothes were knitted, toys were bought; even lists of names were drawn up.

'We are happy, aren't we?' Sylvia said to Alan. 'We have almost everything. And we love each other.'

Yes, they loved each other, and every night when they went to bed, the fear which they were intelligent enough not to endow with a name and power, crept between the sheets with them and lay next to each of them, warming itself at their skin and picking at the leftovers of their day's thoughts, lifting the flaps of their dreams to read their secret desires, trying with all its tiny power to find an identity.

But Alan and Sylvia were wise. Don't you think they were wise?

How happy they were!

'Fancy,' Alan said, 'Can you imagine that I wanted to be a poet?'

Suddenly he yearned for Sylvia to say quickly and

fiercely, 'Yes, Yes.' But she laughed and looked at him fondly and said, 'No, I'm afraid not.'

They were very devoted.

She kept the home neat and employed a gardener to attend to the shrubs, for their section was nearly two acres, while she often worked in the garden with the flowers. She bought packets of seed and planted them in borders, and was so disappointed if the blooms did not match the illustrations in the catalogue.

'I should learn from experience, shouldn't I?' she said to Alan one day when one of the dahlia blooms was attacked by disease and died.

He smiled affectionately at her. He knew that she was particularly clever with dahlias. He was sitting in the corner by the bookshelf, opening the packet containing the latest edition of *Seascape*, the literary quarterly, and wishing that the dispatch department had not made such a complicated parcel with so much useless string. There were none of his poems in this edition. He rarely wrote poems now. Sometimes, in a panic, in the night when Sylvia was asleep and the house was quiet, he tried to discover his excuse for not writing any more. It was not lack of time; it had long ago ceased to be lack of time. What was the excuse now? He tried desperately to find it. Age? Glands? Contentment? But who was contented?

He would have been happier if he had written a book of poems — just one book, a slim volume between hard covers — with the title on the outside and the dedication on the appropriate page. 'To Sylvia, my wife'. Or 'To Sylvia'.

He loved Sylvia more than ever. He loved the way her body had acquired a plump stored look, like a well-filled larder. He had the feeling that in some way she would provide for him. He was alarmed one evening when he was considering his dream of a book of poems with a dedication to her, 'To Sylvia, my wife', and he found himself murmuring instead, 'For self-service stores everywhere, for the brave, for the watered-down dreamer, for dried-up ponds full of dead frogs, caked with mud . . .'

No, no. For Sylvia. Her dahlias are more wonderful this year than ever before; she has green fingers in the garden; she has been born to it.

Then from his seat in the corner by the bookshelf he had smiled fondly at her. He told himself how intelligent she was. Two intelligent people. They kept up with the trends in modern art and literature. When the National Orchestra played at the city festival each year they always bought tickets. They visited the Art Galleries. He subscribed to overseas journals, to poetry magazines from America, to one in particular called *The Triumph of Poetry* where in his student days he had been given a commendation in an annual award. 'Just imagine. Alan Wakefield, a commendation in America,' people had said. Now, each year when the award was made Alan would eagerly turn the pages of *The Triumph of Poetry* (Has my *Triumph of Poetry* arrived? he would ask Sylvia as soon as he came home on the twenty-fifth of each month) and study the winning and commended poems and compare them with his own of so long ago. How absurd, he would think. But people in literary circles still spoke of his poem. It had gained him a kind of national distinction. After all, America . . .

He sometimes felt ludicrous when he had been asked to take part in a radio book panel and the chairman's introduction referred to him as 'the poet who was commended in *The Triumph of Poetry* award for promising young poets', while the other members of the panel, waiting impatiently for their own credits, would gaze incredulously at his thinning stooped figure and his bald head. Alan was a valued member of the book panel. He was an astute critic. His wit was sharp. Only his voice lacked the sense of urgency which made it compelling to listen to in the days when he had not enough time to write. He talked ramblingly as if all urgency had lost itself within him, or as if in travelling from him it had suddenly disappeared, like something wading out of its depths in unknown seas.

Alan Wakefield. One of the trees of lost poets who contribute to the shade, magnificence, density of the forest, who give concealment, food and space to tiny hibernating metaphors, the parasitic clichés, the feathered notions, the furred images that are so often slain and their coats transformed into collars to protect the necks of human beings from strangulation, and into muffs to warm in the winter season the pickpocket pickheart fingers.

A lost poet. A man with a little talent and not enough time; the promising poet who never fulfilled his promise; thwarted by sociology, circumstance, self.

But is not his life happy? He has a loving wife, a home, a secure job, an academic reputation. He interests himself in current affairs, oppressed peoples, decimal coinage, imports and exports, swimming (they own a beach house in the subtropical north where they spend every Christmas); and he is passionately devoted to literature, painting, music, the theatre. He and his wife know how to cook continental food . . . Some day they will travel overseas, perhaps visit Tony and Leila who have a luxury flat in Kensington, since Tony saw his opportunity and joined a literary agency of which he is now a director, marketing the works of scores of well-known and flourishing authors . . . Tony and Leila go for holidays on the Continent; once they visited the United States . . .

Yes, Alan is surely happy! He and his wife are intelligent, they enjoy good conversation, they have interesting tolerant friends who prefer to send ideas rather than people to the scaffold for murder, to lash intolerance and bigotry rather than the flesh of human beings. Every day brings so much to do, so much to discuss, plans to be made, letters to write, invitations to answer, lectures to prepare. And for Sylvia there is always the garden. How enthusiastically she prepares for each season!

It was late summer, merging into autumn with the lack of drama which disappointed Sylvia when in her gardening diary she checked the outlines of the seasons and their characteristic flowers. Summer each year took up so much room, leaving so little time for autumn. But summer was wonderful, so carefree and warm, and you walked with next-to-nothing on when you went shopping, and you swam day and night in the warm Pacific or, across the other side of the island, in the Tasman surf, riding in on the crests of the waves, picnicking by moonlight, wandering here and there, restless, turbulent as the sea . . .

It was late summer.

Alan was on his way home from the University. He had not taken his car, and was travelling by tram. It was the last tram running in the city, the others having been replaced by trolley-buses. Alan enjoyed riding in the tram, sitting on the worn brown seats barred like washing-boards, rocking back and forth along the rails, strap-hanging when he got up to give his seat to a woman and her two children. It had been so long since he had travelled this way; it was so much easier to take the car. A feeling of exhilaration surged through him as he alighted at the stop and watched the tram rollicking by, noisy, exuberant.

'And it's not even spring,' Alan said to himself, trying to explain his joy as he turned the corner into the quiet street where he lived. But as he walked by the gate and into the garden of his home he was surprised to notice the beauty of the flowers; he had not realised, he thought, what patience and time Sylvia was putting into the garden. The dahlias lined the path, right up to the house. There was one dahlia which was particularly beautiful, hacked with fire, its ragged petals chopped with fire, lined with red silk, overskirt upon overskirt of burning silk; alone it would abolish night.

He picked the dahlia.

'I'll write a poem,' he thought, excitement surging through him.

'I'll write a poem. "To my wife Sylvia upon plucking the first dahlia."'

He hurried up to the house. Sylvia was out. He remembered that she had a meeting — a meeting where? He did not know, could not remember. He noticed when he changed from his dark suit that she must have been wearing her new dress, the one she bought for the Silverstones' party.

He did not stop to find anything to eat but went quickly to the room which he used as a study, and placing the dahlia upon the desk in front of him, he took a sheet of paper and wrote

'To my wife Sylvia upon plucking the first dahlia.'

What a pity, he thought, that the seasons are not dramatic in the north, that first flowers do not burst upon us with shock. How she must have cared for them, he thought, stroking the petals which drooped a little and had stains on their tips, like inward bruises.

'To My Wife Sylvia upon plucking the first dahlia.'

'True to tradition,' he said. 'A dedication at last. And we used to sleep like two mice in a matchbox, in a bed that dropped obligingly from the wall, in a washhouse fronting the sea!'

'A dedication,' he repeated.

It did not seem to matter any more that he had not published his slim volume of verse. He was writing a poem to Sylvia.

He began to write.

> The quick brown fox noses the earth,
> the dog is lazy,
> and where are all the good men of the world who
>   will come to our aid?
> For now is the time, now is the time,
> while the quick brown fox noses the earth

Impatiently he scribbled over the nonsense he had written, drawing a face, a childhood face with deep eyes deep inside spectacles.

'To my wife Sylvia,' he wrote once more.

> THE PRISONER
> In a dialogue with Time he said,
> You handcuff me to humankind,
> You sentence me who am the sentence.
> When will you learn that I am nothing,
> that giant mirrors are propped against your heart?
> You sleep alone in your cell.
> The twin delusional cell whose prisoner receives
>   your sympathy and rage
> is empty, thick with dust,
> its lock eaten by worms and rust.

Alan considered what he had written. 'It's poor,' he said, 'But if I start writing again something may come, I may yet write a complete book of poems. This is only a flexing of the muscles, so to speak. What is there now to hinder me from writing? Nothing, nothing at all!'

His hand trembled. He could feel his heart pounding; he knew a slight anxiety in noting his heartbeats. Too much sedentary work? he questioned.

'But I swim. The sea is my second home.'

Then Sylvia came in the door. She looked radiant. Yes, she was wearing the dress bought for the Silverstones' party.

'Writing?' she asked fondly. 'Don't stay at it too long, darling.' As a mother might talk to her child. 'Playing trains, mud pies? Don't get your nice clean hands all dirty will you?'

Sylvia was quick to see that her approach had been wrong.

'Take no notice,' she said, giving him a quick kiss. 'Go on writing as long as you like — it's the dinner that won't let you. It'll be ready in two shakes of a lamb's tail.'

Then she glanced at the desk and noticed the dahlia, and a change came over her. Her voice was shrill.

'My dahlia!' she cried. 'It's the prize one, the one I'm showing at the Society at the end of the week, I've been waiting and waiting for it to bloom. And you've picked it, you've picked it!'

She was almost in tears.

Alan was bewildered.

'I didn't realise,' he began. He was staring at her in a dazed way. Out of all the flowers in the garden, did she recognise each one in this way? And the society, which society?

'Which society?' he asked. 'What's the name of it, dear?'

'The name of the dahlia?' she said quickly. He could almost see her checking the list of names. How strange, she knew each one personally!

'The Dahlia Society, of course. Oh Alan!'

He stared. So she called them by names, she belonged to a society where they sat in a small room talking all evening about dahlias . . .

'It's the loveliest one I've ever had, Alan! And you picked it. And look, you've bruised one of the petals! And is that ink on it, ink!'

Then she leaned forward suddenly and snatching the paper where he had been writing his verses she tore it to pieces. Then she seized the drooping dahlia and held it close to her breast. Then she began to cry.

'I'm sorry,' she said. 'Do forgive me, Alan!'

She picked up the pieces of paper and without looking at them she replaced them on his desk. He took a vase from the window sill and filling it with water from the tap in the adjacent bathroom, he tenderly took the dahlia from her and put it in the vase. He noticed a brown stain spreading in the water. Then he and Sylvia embraced. Everything was all right. They were intelligent, they understood each other.

They went then to their dining room overlooking the garden. They had dinner, talking brightly to each other, making jokes. Alan told her about his journey home in the tram. How they laughed over it! How they yearned for the old days!

'Do you know,' Sylvia said, 'I passed our flat the other day, you know, the washhouse, and I couldn't resist knocking on the door. Do you know who lives there? You'll never guess!'

Of course he guessed, but he said 'Who?'

'A young student and his wife, one of your students, too. He's going to be a novelist when he has time . . . I'm sorry . . .'

'Don't pity *me*. You know that I was never much of a poet.'

He hoped that she would say, 'Yes you were, you were!'
but she looked vague and sad and murmured, 'Oh well!'

She brightened.

'Well anyway this young couple spend nearly all
their time on the beach, the sea is so tempting, oh isn't it
marvellous, quick as a wink the summer will be around
and we'll be off up north; there's the garden though . . .'

'You don't like leaving it do you?'

She was defensive.

'There's no harm in that is there? No harm in being
fond of something. It was my best dahlia, Alan.'

'I'm sorry, I've told you I'm sorry. I didn't know . . .'

Her voice became sharp.

'You should have known. Oh Alan! We were so close!
What has come over us?'

They went early to bed. He told her he had meant to
write a poem to her, and she wept, and all was forgiven.
They were very tender towards each other. They slept.
Alan dreamed that writing a poem became so easy, all that
was necessary was to take a packet of dahlia seed and spill
it upon the paper. He took a packet of seed; it fell like fly-
dirt, full-stops, pinpricks but Sylvia began to cry, it was
her best seed, she said, the packet she had saved specially.
Then she looked closer at the packet. She grinned. Her
mouth was wide like a lake, and dark. No, she said, the
best seed is at the Silverstones'; this is the cheap variety
which never blooms, I can't think how I came by it. She
took the seed and tossed it out of the window and a huge
bird flew down and swallowed it, stabbing his beak upon
each grain.

'An indemnity,' Alan said, and woke up. Sylvia was
smiling in her sleep.

Soon the house was quiet. No one was awake, that is
no one who had not his own right, like mice, travelling

beetles, moths, beams of light; and the named fear who had at last been given power, space, keys, and lay supreme between Sylvia and Alan, waiting to devour their lives.

From

*You Are Now Entering
the Human Heart*

The Bath

On Friday afternoon she bought cut flowers — daffodils, anemones, a few twigs of a red-leaved shrub, wrapped in mauve waxed paper, for Saturday was the seventeenth anniversary of her husband's death and she planned to visit his grave, as she did each year, to weed it and put fresh flowers in the two jam jars standing one on each side of the tombstone. Her visit this year occupied her thoughts more than usual. She had bought the flowers to force herself to make the journey that each year became more hazardous, from the walk to the bus stop, the change of buses at the Octagon, to the bitterness of the winds blowing from the open sea across almost unsheltered rows of tombstones; and the tiredness that overcame her when it was time to return home when she longed to find a place beside the graves, in the soft grass, and fall asleep.

That evening she filled the coal bucket, stoked the fire. Her movements were slow and arduous, her back and shoulder gave her so much pain. She cooked her tea — liver and bacon — set up knife and fork on the teatowel she used as a tablecloth, turned up the volume of the polished red radio to listen to the Weather Report and the News, ate her tea, washed her dishes, then sat drowsing in the rocking chair by the fire, waiting for the water to get hot enough for a bath. Visits to the cemetery, the doctor, and to relatives, to stay, always demanded a bath. When she was sure that the water was hot enough (and her tea had been digested) she ventured from the kitchen through the cold passageway to the colder bathroom. She paused in the doorway to get used to the chill of the air then she walked slowly, feeling with each step the pain in her back, across to the bath, and though she knew that she was gradually losing the power in her hands she managed to wrench on the stiff cold and hot taps and half-fill the bath with warm water. How wasteful, she thought, that with the kitchen fire always burning during the past month of frost, and the water almost always hot, getting in and out of a bath had become such an effort that it was not possible to bath every night or even every week!

She found a big towel, laid it ready over a chair, arranged the chair so that should difficulty arise as it had last time she bathed she would have some way of rescuing herself; then with her nightclothes warming on a page of newspaper inside the coal oven and her dressing-gown across the chair to be put on the instant she stepped from the bath, she undressed and pausing first to get her breath and clinging tightly to the slippery yellow-stained rim that now seemed more like the edge of a cliff with a deep drop below into the sea, slowly and painfully she climbed into the bath.

I'll put on my nightie the instant I get out, she thought. The instant she got out indeed! She knew it would be more than a matter of instants yet she tried to think of it calmly, without dread, telling herself that when the time came she would be very careful, taking the process step by step, surprising her bad back and shoulder and her powerless wrists into performing feats they might usually rebel against, but the key to controlling them would be the surprise, the slow stealing up on them. With care, with thought . . .

Sitting upright, not daring to lean back or lie down, she soaped herself, washing away the dirt of the past fortnight, seeing with satisfaction how it drifted about on the water as a sign that she was clean again. Then when her washing was completed she found herself looking for excuses not to try yet to climb out. Those old woman's finger nails, cracked and dry, where germs could lodge, would need to be scrubbed again; the skin of her heels, too, growing so hard that her feet might have been turning to stone; behind her ears where a thread of dirt lay in the rim; after all, she did not often have the luxury of a bath, did she? How warm it was! She drowsed a moment. If only she could fall asleep then wake to find herself in her nightdress in bed for the night! Slowly she rewashed her body, and when she knew she could no longer deceive herself into thinking she was not clean she reluctantly replaced the soap, brush and flannel in the groove at the side of the bath, feeling as she loosened her grip on them that all strength and support were ebbing from her. Quickly she seized the nail-brush again, but its magic had been used and was gone; it would not adopt the role she tried to urge upon it. The flannel too, and the soap, were frail flotsam to cling to in the hope of being borne to safety.

She was alone now. For a few minutes she sat swilling the water against her skin, perhaps as a means of buoying up her courage. Then resolutely she pulled out the plug, sat feeling the tide swirl and scrape at her skin and flesh, trying to draw her down, down into the earth; then the bathwater was gone in a soapy gurgle and she was naked and shivering and had not yet made the attempt to get out of the bath.

How slippery the surface had become! In future she would not clean it with kerosene, she would use the paste cleaner that, left on overnight, gave the enamel rough patches that could be gripped with the skin.

She leaned forward, feeling the pain in her back and shoulder. She grasped the rim of the bath but her fingers slithered from it almost at once. She would not panic, she told herself; she would try gradually, carefully, to get out. Again she leaned forward; again her grip loosened as if iron hands had deliberately uncurled her stiffened blue fingers from their trembling hold. Her heart began to beat faster, her breath came more quickly, her mouth was dry. She moistened her lips. If I shout for help, she thought, no one will hear me. No one in the world will hear me. No one will know I'm in the bath and can't get out.

She listened. She could hear only the drip-drip of the cold water tap of the wash-basin, and a corresponding whisper and gurgle of her heart, as if it were beating under water. All else was silent. Where were the people, the traffic? Then she had a strange feeling of being under the earth, of a throbbing in her head like wheels going over the earth above her.

Then she told herself sternly that she must have no nonsense, that she had really not tried to get out of the bath. She had forgotten the strong solid chair and the grip she could get on it. If she made the effort quickly she could first take hold on both sides of the bath, pull herself up, then transfer her hold to the chair and thus pull herself out.

She tried to do this; she just failed to make the final effort. Pale now, gasping for breath, she sank back into the bath. She began to call out but as she had predicted there was no answer. No one had heard her, no one in the houses or the street or Dunedin or the world knew that she was imprisoned. Loneliness welled in her. If John were here, she thought, if we were sharing our old age, helping each other, this would never have happened. She made another effort to get out. Again she failed. Faintness overcoming her she closed her eyes, trying to rest, then recovering and trying again and failing, she panicked and began to cry and strike the sides of the bath; it made a hollow sound like a wild drum-beat.

Then she stopped striking with her fists; she struggled again to get out; and for over half an hour she stayed alternately struggling and resting until at last she did succeed in climbing out and making her escape into the kitchen. She thought, I'll never take another bath in this house or anywhere. I never want to see that bath again. This is the end or the beginning of it. In future a district nurse will have to come to attend me. Submitting to that will be the first humiliation. There will be others, and others.

In bed at last she lay exhausted and lonely thinking that perhaps it might be better for her to die at once. The slow progression of difficulties was a kind of torture. There were her shoes that had to be made specially in a special shape or she could not walk. There were the times she had to call in a neighbour to fetch a pot of jam from the top shelf of her cupboard when it had been only a year ago that she herself had made the jam and put it on the shelf. Sometimes a niece came to fill the coal-bucket or mow the lawn. Every week there was the washing to be hung on the line — this required a special technique for she could not raise her arms without at the same time finding some support in the dizziness that overcame her. She remembered with a sense of the world narrowing and growing darker, like a tunnel, the incredulous almost despising look on the face of her niece when in answer to the comment 'How beautiful the clouds are in Dunedin! These big billowing white and grey clouds — don't you think, Auntie?' she had said, her disappointment at the misery of things putting a sharpness in her voice, 'I never look at the clouds!'

She wondered how long ago it was since she had been able to look up at the sky without reeling with dizziness. Now she did not dare look up. There was enough to attend to down and around — the cracks and hollows in the footpath, the patches of frost and ice and the potholes in the roads; the approaching cars and motorcycles; and now, after all the outside menaces, the inner menace of her own body. She had to be guardian now over her arms and legs, force them to do as she wanted when how easily and dutifully they had walked, moved and grasped, in the old days! They were the enemy now. It had been her body that showed treachery when she tried to get out of the bath. If she ever wanted to bath again — how strange it seemed! — she would have to ask another human being to help her to guard and control her own body. Was this so fearful? she wondered. Even if it were not, it seemed so.

She thought of the frost slowly hardening outside on the fences, roofs, windows and streets. She thought again of the terror of not being able to escape from the bath. She remembered her dead husband and the flowers she had bought to put on his grave. Then thinking again of the frost, its whiteness, white like a new bath, of the anemones and daffodils and the twigs of the red-leaved shrub, of John dead seventeen years, she fell asleep while outside, within two hours, the frost began to melt with the warmth of a sudden wind blowing from the north, and the night grew warm, like a spring night, and in the morning the light came early, the sky was pale blue, the same warm wind as gentle as a mere breath, was blowing, and a narcissus had burst its bud in the front garden.

In all her years of visiting the cemetery she had never known the wind so mild. On an arm of the peninsula exposed to the winds from two stretches of sea, the cemetery had always been a place to crouch shivering in overcoat and scarf while the flowers were set on the grave and the narrow garden cleared of weeds. Today, everything was different. After all the frosts of the past month there was no trace of chill in the air. The mildness and warmth were scarcely to be believed. The sea lay, violet-coloured, hush-hushing, turning and heaving, not breaking into foamy waves; it was one sinuous ripple from shore to horizon and its sound was the muted sound of distant forests of peace.

Picking up the rusted garden fork that she knew lay always in the grass of the next grave, long neglected, she set to work to clear away the twitch and other weeds, exposing the first bunch of dark blue primroses with yellow centres, a clump of autumn lilies, and the shoots, six inches high, of daffodils. Then removing the green-slimed jam jars from their grooves on each side of the tombstone she walked slowly, stiff from her crouching, to the ever-dripping tap at the end of the lawn path where, filling the jars with pebbles and water she rattled them up and down to try to clean them of slime. Then she ran the sparkling ice-cold water into the jars and balancing them carefully one in each hand she walked back to the grave where she shook the daffodils, anemones, red leaves from their waxed paper and dividing them put half in one jar, half in the other. The dark blue of the anemones swelled with a sea-colour as their heads rested against the red leaves. The daffodils were short-stemmed with big ragged rather than delicate trumpets — the type for blowing; and their scent was strong.

Finally, remembering the winds that raged from the sea she stuffed small pieces of the screwed-up waxed paper into the top of each jar so the flowers would not be carried away by the wind. Then with a feeling of satisfaction — I look after my husband's grave after seventeen years. The tombstone is not cracked or blown over, the garden has not

sunk into a pool of clay. I look after my husband's grave —
she began to walk away, between the rows of graves, noting
which were and were not cared for. Her father and mother
had been buried here. She stood now before their grave.
It was a roomy grave made in the days when there was
space for the dead and for the dead with money, like her
parents, extra space should they need it. Their tombstone
was elaborate though the writing was now faded; in death
they kept the elaborate station of their life. There were no
flowers on the grave, only the feathery sea-grass soft to the
touch, lit with gold in the sun. There was no sound but
the sound of the sea and the one row of fir trees on the brow
of the hill. She felt the peace inside her; the nightmare of
the evening before seemed far away, seemed not to have
happened; the senseless terrifying struggle to get out of a
bath!

She sat on the concrete edge of her parents' grave.
She did not want to go home. She felt content to sit here
quietly with the warm soft wind flowing around her and
the sigh of the sea rising to mingle with the sighing of the
firs and the whisper of the thin gold grass. She was grateful
for the money, the time and the forethought that had made
her parents' grave so much bigger than the others near by.
Her husband, cremated, had been allowed only a narrow
eighteen inches by two feet, room only for the flecked
grey tombstone In Memory of My Husband John Edward
Harraway died August 6th 1948, and the narrow garden
of spring flowers, whereas her parents' grave was so wide,
and its concrete wall was a foot high; it was, in death, the
equivalent of a quarter-acre section before there were too
many people in the world. Why when the world was wider
and wider was there no space left?

Or was the world narrower?

She did not know; she could not think; she knew

only that she did not want to go home, she wanted to sit here on the edge of the grave, never catching any more buses, crossing streets, walking on icy footpaths, turning mattresses, trying to reach jam from the top shelf of the cupboard, filling coal buckets, getting in and out of the bath. Only to get in somewhere and stay in; to get out and stay out; to stay now, always, in one place.

Ten minutes later she was waiting at the bus stop; anxiously studying the destination of each bus as it passed, clutching her money since concession tickets were not allowed in the weekend, thinking of the cup of tea she would make when she got home, of her evening meal — the remainder of the liver and bacon, of her nephew in Christchurch who was coming with his wife and children for the school holidays, of her niece in the home expecting her third baby. Cars and buses surged by, horns tooted, a plane droned, near and far, near and far, children cried out, dogs barked; the sea, in competition, made a harsher sound as if its waves were now breaking in foam.

For a moment, confused after the peace of the cemetery, she shut her eyes, trying to recapture the image of her husband's grave, now bright with spring flowers, and her parents' grave, wide, spacious, with room should the dead desire it to turn and sigh and move in dreams as if the two slept together in a big soft grass double-bed.

She waited, trying to capture the image of peace. She saw only her husband's grave, made narrower, the spring garden whittled to a thin strip; then it vanished and she was left with the image of the bathroom, of the narrow confining bath grass-yellow as old baths are, not frost-white, waiting, waiting for one moment of inattention, weakness, pain, to claim her for ever.

Winter Garden

Mr Paget's wife had been in a coma for two months. Every day he visited her in the hospital, sitting by her bed, not speaking except to say, 'Miriam, it's me, Alec, I'm here with you,' while she lay unresponsive, not moving, her eyes closed, her face pale. Usually Mr Paget stayed half an hour to an hour; then he would kiss his wife, return her hand that he'd withdrawn and held, to her side under the bedclothes, pat the clothes into their position, and then, conscious of his own privileged freedom and movement in the afternoon or evening light, he would go home to the corner brick house in the hill suburb, where he would prepare and eat a meal before going outside to work in the garden. Every day in all seasons he found work to do in the garden. His time was divided between visiting the hospital and tending his flowers, lawn and olearia hedge. When the neighbours saw him digging, clipping, or mowing they said, 'Poor Mr Paget. His garden must be a comfort to him.' Later in the evening, when the violet-coloured glare showed through the drawn curtains of the sitting-room as Mr Paget watched television, the neighbours said, 'Poor Mr Paget. The television must be a comfort to him.' Often in the evening he would phone for news of his wife and the answer would be, always, Her condition shows no change. No change, no change. He had learned to accept the words without question. He knew what they meant — that she was no nearer living or dying, that the scarcely perceptible fluctuations he noted in his daily visits were ripples only, this way and that, as the opposing winds blew, but were no indication of the surge of the tide. No change. How intently he watched her face! Sometimes he stroked it; even her eyelids did not blink; they were shut and white like lamp shells.

Mr Paget's garden was admired in the street. His roses were perfect, untouched by blight or greenfly. His lawn shone like fur in the sun. Laid between his lawn and the street his hedge looked like a long smooth plump slice of yellow cake — except that it moved; in the wind it crackled its curly dented leaves with a kindling sound as if small fires were being started; in the morning light it was varnished a glossy green; in the evening it became pale lemon, appearing under the mass of house shadow as lawns do sometimes, seen beneath dark trees at sundown.

In the corner of the garden overhanging the street a rowan tree grew that was Mr Paget's pride. It was now, in autumn, thick with berries suspended from beneath the protecting leaves of each twig like clusters of glistening beads. Everyone admired the rowan tree, and its berries cheered Mr Paget as he trimmed, mowed, staked, planted. In the early days of his wife's illness, depressed by the funereal association of flowers, he made up his mind not to take them to the hospital; but one day, impulsively, he picked a cluster of rowan berries.

He arrived early, before visiting time. He found on his wife's bedside so many instruments, tubes, needles — all the tools necessary to care for an apparently lifeless body — that at first there did not seem to be room for the berries. Hesitating, he put them on the locker next to a brick-coloured gaping-throated tube. Perhaps his wife, lying in the strange secret garden where those instruments tended her, would notice the berries.

A nurse came into the room, 'Oh, Mr Paget, you're early. I'll remove this tray and put these berries in water. Aren't they from your garden?'

Mr Paget nodded.

The nurse leaned over his wife, tucking in the bedclothes as if to arrange a blanket defence against the living, speaking creature who had invaded her vegetable peace. Then taking her silver tray of tools and the twig of berries she went from the room, and only when she had gone did Mr Paget say, 'Miriam, it's me, Alec,' taking her hand in his. He could feel a faint pulse like a memory gone out of reach, not able to be reclaimed. He stroked the fingers. He was overwhelmed by the familiar hopelessness. What was the use? Would she not be better dead than lying silent, unknowing in a world where he could not reach her?

The nurse came back. She put the berries on the window sill, where they made a splash of colour. The slim skeleton-shaped leaves soared, like spears, against the glass.

'With winter coming and the leaves turning, there'll soon be only the late berries.'

'Yes,' Mr Paget said.

The nurse looked at him, answering his unspoken question, her face warm with sympathy. 'There's been no change, Mr Paget. But she's not suffering at all.'

'No,' Mr Paget said.

He waited for the nurse to say what everyone was saying to him now, beating the words about his ears until he wanted to cry out for mercy, 'It will be a happy release for her when it comes.'

The nurse did not say it and he was glad. She smiled and left the room, and he sat watching the narrow ribbon of afternoon light that had bound itself across the window pane and the sill and the berries, surging in their glass like tiny bubbles of blood. Mr Paget shivered. He began to feel afraid. What will it be like, he wondered, when death comes and I am with her?

He looked again at his wife's hand, at the wrinkled soft skin; new skin. He stroked her fingers and his heart quickened and a warmth of joy spread through him as he realised her skin was new; and of course her fingernails had been cut; and if they had been cut they had also been growing; her hair, too. Her hair had been cut. Quickly he leaned to touch her damp mouse-coloured hair. It had grown and been cut. They had cut her hair! Then the wild joy began to ebb as he remembered that even after death the hair and fingernails may grow and need to be cut. Was this growth then more a sign of death than of life?

'Oh no, oh no,' Mr Paget said aloud.

For while his wife lay in a coma, again and again they would need to cut her fingernails and hair, to bathe her, to take from her each day the waste of the food they had given her, and each day was different, had been different all the weeks she had been ill; and he had not dreamed, they had not told him, he thought bitterly. They had said, 'No change, no change,' when each day one speck more or less of dust had to be washed away, one ounce more or less of food was stored, rejected; and one day the wide blade of sunlight pressed burning and sharp upon her face while another day she lay in cool dark shade. She was alive, in the light. In the grave there was no sun, no shadow, touching of hands, washing of body.

When Mr Paget smiled happily as he said goodbye to his wife, the nurse looked startled. Poor Mr Paget, she said to herself.

That evening, Mr Paget took special care in trimming the hedge, stepping back to admire its evenness, putting the clippings into a neat pile. He felt quite frivolous as he ran the old-fashioned mower over the lawn; chatter-chatter it gossiped throatily, spewing out the green minus-marks of grass. Then, before he went inside to phone the hospital and watch television, in a spurt of extravagant joy he picked two clusters of rowan berries, and as he was springing back the branch a neighbour passed on her way home.

She saw Mr Paget. Her face assumed the appropriate expression of sympathy. 'And how is Mrs Paget?'

Mr Paget's accustomed answer flowed from him. 'There's been no change.'

He heard the despair in his voice as he spoke. Then, sympathetically, he asked, 'And how's Mr Bambury?'

The neighbour's husband had been ill. She released her news. 'They're stripping his arteries tomorrow.'

There was a jubilant consciousness of action in Mrs Bambury's voice. Mr Paget groped from a dark void of envy to his new joy: no change, no change indeed!

He smiled at Mrs Bambury. He wanted to comfort her about her husband and his arteries but he knew nothing about the stripping of a person's arteries: the resulting nakedness seemed merciless; he was grateful that his wife lay enclosed in sleep, her arteries secret and unyielding.

'I hope everything will be all right with Mr Bambury,' he said at last.

'Oh, there's a risk but a very strong chance of recovery. I do hope there'll be a change in Mrs Paget's condition.'

'Thank you,' Mr Paget said humbly, playing the game. 'So far there has been no change.'

'No change?'

'No change.'

They said goodbye. On his way to the house he stopped to scan the garden. He looked tenderly at the pile of grass and hedge clippings and the succulent golden hedge with the dark pointed roof-shadow eating into it.

Mrs Paget died in late autumn. It is winter now. The berries are gone from the rowan tree, some eaten by birds, some picked by the wind, others scattered by the small boys switching the overhanging branches up and down as they pass in the street. In a luxury of possession rather than deprivation, Mr Bambury, his arteries successfully stripped, rests in a chair on the front porch of his home, looking across the street at Mr Paget in his garden. Mr Bambury and his wife say to each other, 'Mr Paget is tied to his garden.'

Others notice it, too, for Mr Paget seems now to spend all his waking time in the garden. 'Since his wife's death, he's never out of the garden,' they say. 'Why? Nothing grows now but a few late berries. Nothing grows in the garden in winter.'

They wonder why Mr Paget stands for so long looking at the dead twigs, the leafless shrubs, the vacant flower beds set like dark eyes in the middle of the lawn, why he potters about day after day in the dead world where nothing seems to change. And sometimes they think perhaps he is going mad when they see him kneel down and put his cheek against the skin of the earth.

You Are Now Entering the Human Heart

I looked at the notice. I wondered if I had time before my train left Philadelphia for Baltimore in one hour. The heart, ceiling-high, occupied one corner of the large exhibition hall, and from wherever you stood in the hall you could hear its beating, *thum-thump-thum-thump*. It was a popular exhibit, and sometimes, when there were too many children about, the entrance had to be roped off, as the children loved to race up and down the blood vessels and match their cries to the heart's beating. I could see that the heart had already been punished for the day — the floor of the blood vessel was worn and dusty, the chamber walls were covered with marks, and the notice 'You Are Now Taking the Path of a Blood Cell Through the Human Heart', hung askew. I wanted to see more of the Franklin Institute and the Natural Science Museum across the street, but a journey through the human heart would be fascinating. Did I have time?

Later. First, I would go across the street to the Hall of North America, among the bear and the bison, and catch up on American flora and fauna.

I made my way to the Hall. More children, sitting in rows on canvas chairs. An elementary class from a city school, under the control of an elderly teacher. A museum attendant holding a basket, and all eyes gazing at the basket.

'Oh,' I said. 'Is this a private lesson? Is it all right for me to be here?'

The attendant was brisk. 'Surely. We're having a lesson in snake-handling,' he said. 'It's something new. Get the children young and teach them that every snake they meet is not to be killed. People seem to think that every snake has to be knocked on the head. So we're getting them young and teaching them.'

'May I watch?' I said.

'Surely. This is a common grass snake. No harm, no harm at all. Teach the children to learn the feel of them, to lose their fear.'

He turned to the teacher. 'Now, Miss — Mrs —' he said.

'Miss Aitcheson.'

He lowered his voice. 'The best way to get through to the children is to start with teacher,' he said to Miss Aitcheson. 'If they see you're not afraid, then they won't be.'

She must be near retiring age, I thought. A city woman. Never handled a snake in her life. Her face was pale. She just managed to drag the fear from her eyes to some place in their depths, where it lurked like a dark stain. Surely the attendant and the children noticed?

'It's harmless,' the attendant said. He'd been working with snakes for years.

Miss Aitcheson, I thought again. A city woman born and bred. All snakes were creatures to kill, to be protected from, alike the rattler, the copperhead, king snake, grass snake — venom and victims. Were there not places in the South where you couldn't go into the streets for fear of the rattlesnakes?

Her eyes faced the lighted exit. I saw her fear. The exit light blinked, hooded. The children, none of whom had ever touched a live snake, were sitting hushed, waiting for the drama to begin; one or two looked afraid as the attendant withdrew a green snake about three feet long from the basket and with a swift movement, before the teacher could protest, draped it around her neck and stepped back, admiring and satisfied.

'There,' he said to the class. 'Your teacher has a snake around her neck and she's not afraid.'

Miss Aitcheson stood rigid; she seemed to be holding her breath. 'Teacher's not afraid, are you?' the attendant persisted. He leaned forward, pronouncing judgement on her, while she suddenly jerked her head and lifted her hands in panic to get rid of the snake. Then, seeing the children watching her, she whispered, 'No, I'm not afraid. Of course not.' She looked around her.

'Of course not,' she repeated sharply.

I could see her defeat and helplessness. The attendant seemed unaware, as if his perception had grown a reptilian covering. What did she care for the campaign for the preservation and welfare of copperheads and rattlers and common grass snakes? What did she care about someday walking through the woods or the desert and deciding between killing a snake and setting it free, as if there would be time to decide, when her journey to and from school in downtown Philadelphia held enough danger to occupy her? In two years or so, she'd retire and be in that apartment by herself and no doorman, and everyone knew what happened then, and how she'd be afraid to answer the door and to walk after dark and carry her pocketbook in the street. There was enough to think about without learning to handle and love the snakes, harmless and otherwise, by having them draped around her neck for everyone, including the children — most of all the children — to witness the outbreak of her fear.

'See, Miss Aitcheson's touching the snake. She's not afraid of it at all.'

As everyone watched, she touched the snake. Her fingers recoiled. She touched it again.

'See, she's not afraid. Miss Aitcheson can stand there with a beautiful snake around her neck and touch it and stroke it and not be afraid.'

The faces of the children were full of admiration for the teacher's bravery, and yet there was a cruelly persistent tension; they were waiting, waiting.

'We have to learn to love snakes,' the attendant said. 'Would someone like to come out and stroke teacher's snake?'

Silence.

One shamefaced boy came forward. He stood petrified in front of the teacher.

'Touch it,' the attendant urged. 'It's a friendly snake. Teacher's wearing it around her neck and she's not afraid.'

The boy darted his hand forward, rested it lightly on the snake, and immediately withdrew his hand. Then he ran back to his seat. The children shrieked with glee.

'He's afraid,' someone said. 'He's afraid of the snake.'

The attendant soothed. 'We have to get used to them, you know. Grownups are not afraid of them, but we can understand that when you're small you might be afraid, and that's why we want you to learn to love them. Isn't that right, Miss Aitcheson? Isn't that right? Now who else is going to be brave enough to touch teacher's snake?'

Two girls came out. They stood hand in hand side by side and stared at the snake and then at Miss Aitcheson.

I wondered when the torture would end. The two little girls did not touch the snake, but they smiled at it and spoke to it and Miss Aitcheson smiled at them and whispered how brave they were.

'Just a minute,' the attendant said. 'There's really no need to be brave. It's not a question of bravery. The snake is harmless, absolutely *harmless*. Where's the bravery when the snake is harmless?'

Suddenly the snake moved around to face Miss Aitcheson and thrust its flat head towards her cheek. She gave a scream, flung up her hands, and tore the snake from her throat and threw it on the floor, and, rushing across the room, she collapsed into a small canvas chair beside the Bear Cabinet and started to cry.

I didn't feel I should watch any longer. Some of the children began to laugh, some to cry. The attendant picked up the snake and nursed it. Miss Aitcheson, recovering, sat helplessly exposed by the small piece of useless torture. It was not her fault she was city-bred, her eyes tried to tell us. She looked at the children, trying in some way to force their admiration and respect; they were shut against her. She was evicted from them and from herself and even from her own fear-infested tomorrow, because she could not promise to love and preserve what she feared. She had nowhere, at that moment, but the small canvas chair by the Bear Cabinet of the Natural Science Museum.

I looked at my watch. If I hurried, I would catch the train from Thirtieth Street. There would be no time to make the journey through the human heart. I hurried out of the museum. It was freezing cold. The icebreakers would be at work on the Delaware and the Susquehanna; the mist would have risen by the time I arrived home. Yes, I would just catch the train from Thirtieth Street. The journey through the human heart would have to wait until some other time.

Insulation

In the summer days when the lizards come out and the old ewes, a rare generation, a gift of the sun, gloat at us from the television screen, and the country, skull in hand, recites To kill or not to kill, and tomatoes and grapes ripen in places unused to such lingering light and warmth, then the people of Stratford, unlike the 'too happy happy tree' of the poem, do remember the 'drear-nighted' winter. They order coal and firewood, they mend leaks in the spouting and roof, they plant winter savoys, swedes, a last row of parsnips.

The country is not as rich as it used to be. The furniture in the furniture store spills out on the footpath and stays unsold. The seven varieties of curtain rail with their seven matching fittings stay on display, useless extras in the new education of discernment and necessity. The dazzling bathroom ware, the chrome and fur and imitation marble are no longer coveted and bought. For some, though, the time is not just a denial of gluttony, of the filling of that worthy space in the heart and the imagination with assorted satisfied cravings. Some have lost their jobs, their life-work, a process described by one factory-manager as 'shedding'.

'Yes, we have been shedding some of our workers.'

'Too happy happy tree'?

The leaves fall as if from other places, only they fall here. They are brittle in the sun. Shedding, severing, pruning. God's country, the garden of Eden and the conscientious gardeners.

Some find work again. Some who have never had

work advertise in the local newspaper. There was that advertisement which appeared every day for two weeks, full of the hope of youth, sweet and sad with unreal assumptions about the world.

'Sixteen year old girl with one thousand hours training at hairdressing College seeks work.' The *one thousand hours* was in big dark print. It made the reader gasp as if with a sudden visitation of years so numerous they could scarcely be imagined, as if the young girl had undergone, like an operation, a temporal insertion which made her in some way older and more experienced than anyone else. And there was the air of pride with which she flaunted her thousand hours. She was pleading, using her richness of time as her bargain. In another age she might have recorded such time in her Book of Hours.

And then there was the boy, just left school. 'Boy, sixteen, would like to join pop group as vocalist fulltime' — the guileless advertisement of a dream. Did anyone answer either advertisement? Sometimes I imagine they did (I too have unreal assumptions about the world), that the young girl has found a place in the local Salon Paris, next to the Manhattan Takeaway, where she is looked at with admiration and awe (one thousand hours!) and I think that somewhere, maybe, say, in Hamilton (which is to other cities what round numbers are to numbers burdened by decimal points), there's a pop group with a new young vocalist fulltime, appearing, perhaps, on *Opportunity Knocks*, the group playing their instruments, the young man running up and down the stairs, being sexy with his microphone and singing in the agony style.

But my real story is just an incident, a passing glance at insulation and one of those who were pruned, shed, severed, and in the curious mixture of political metaphor, irrationally rationalised, with a sinking lid fitted over his sinking heart. I don't know his name. I only know he lost his job and he couldn't get other work and he was a man used to working with never a thought of finding himself jobless. Like the others he had ambled among the seven varieties of curtain rail and matching fittings, and the fancy suites with showwood arms and turned legs, and the second circular saw. He was into wrought iron, too, and there was a wishing well in his garden and his wife had leaflets about a swimming-pool. And somewhere, at the back of his mind, he had an internal stairway to the basement rumpus. Then one day, suddenly, although there had been rumours, he was pruned from the dollar-flowering tree.

He tried to get other work but there was nothing. Then he thought of spending his remaining money on a franchise to sell insulation. It was a promising district with the winters wet and cold and frosty. The price of electricity had gone up, the government was giving interest-free loans — why, everyone would be insulating. At first, having had a number of leaflets printed, he was content to distribute them in letter boxes, his two school-age children helping. His friends were sympathetic and optimistic. They too said, Everyone will be wanting insulation. And after this drought you can bet on a cold winter. Another thing, there was snow on Egmont at Christmas, and that's a sign.

He sat at home waiting for the orders to come in. None came. He tried random telephoning, still with no success. Finally, he decided to sell from door to door.

'I'm going from door to door,' he told his wife.

She was young and able. She had lost her job in the local clothing factory, and was thinking of buying a knitting-machine and taking orders. On TV when they demonstrated knitting-machines the knitter (it was always a she, with the he demonstrating) simply moved her hands to and fro as if casting a magic spell and the machine did the rest. To and fro, to and fro, a fair-isle sweater knitted in five hours, and fair-isle was coming back, people said. Many of her friends had knitting-machines, in the front room, near the window, to catch the light, where, in her mother's day, the piano always stood, and when she walked by her friends' houses she could see them sitting in the light moving their hands magically to and fro, making fair-isle and bulky knit, intently reading the pattern.

'Yes, door to door.'

The words horrified her. Not in her family, surely! Not door to door. Her father, a builder, had once said that if a man had to go door to door to advertise his work there was something wrong with it.

'If you're reputable,' he said, 'you don't advertise. People just come to you through word of mouth, through your own work standing up to the test.' Well, it wasn't like that now, she knew. Even Smart and Rogers had a full-page advertisement in the latest edition of the local paper. All the same, door to door!

'Oh no,' she said plaintively.

'It can't be helped. I have to look for custom.'

He put on his work clothes, a red checkered shirt, jeans, and he carried a bundle of leaflets, and even before he had finished both sides of one street he was tired and he had begun to look worried and shabby.

This is how I perceived him when he came to my door. I saw a man in his thirties wearing a work-used shirt and jeans yet himself looking the picture of disuse, that is, severed, shed, rationalised, with a great lid sinking over his life, putting out the flame.

'I thought you might like to insulate your house,' he said, thrusting a leaflet into my hand.

I was angry. Interrupted in my work, brought to the door for nothing! Why, the electrician had said my house was well insulated with its double ceilings. Besides, I'd had experience of that stuff they blow into the ceiling and every time there's a wind it all comes out making snowfall in the garden, drifting over to the neighbours too.

'No, I'm not interested,' I said. 'I tried that loose-fill stuff once and it snowed everywhere, every time the wind blew.'

'There's a government loan, you know.'

'I'm really not interested,' I said.

'But it's new. New. Improved.'

'Can't afford it, anyway.'

'Read about it, then, and let me know.'

'Sorry,' I said.

My voice was brisk and dismissing. He looked as if he were about to plead with me, then he changed his mind. He pointed to the red print stamped on the leaflet. There was pride in his pointing, like that of the girl with the thousand hours.

'That's my name and phone number, if you change your mind.'

'Thank you, but I don't think I will.'

He walked away and I shut the door quickly. Insulation, I said to myself with no special meaning or tone. How lovely the summer is, how cosy this house is. The people here before me had carpets that will last for ever, the ceiling is double, there are no cracks in the corners, that is, unless the place decides to shift again on its shaky foundations. How well insulated I am! How solid the resistance of this house against the searching penetrating winds of Stratford. The hunted safe from the hunter, the fleeing from the pursuer, the harmed from the harmer.

'How well insulated I am!'

That night I had a curious ridiculous dream. I dreamed of a land like a vast forest 'in green felicity' where the leaves had started to fall, not by nature, for the forest was evergreen, but under the influence of a season that came to the land from within it and had scarcely been recognised, and certainly not ruled against. Now how could that have been? At first I thought I was trapped in a legend of far away and long ago, for the characters of long ago were there. I could see a beggar walking among the fallen leaves. He was the beggar of other times and other countries, and yet he was not, he was new, and he was ashamed. I saw a cottage in the forest and a young woman at the window combing her hair and — a young man with a — lute? No, a guitar — surely that was the prince? — and with the guitar plugged in to nowhere he began to play and sing and as he sang he sparkled — why, it was Doug Dazzle — and he was singing,

> One thousand hours of cut and set
> my showwood arms will hold you yet
> baby baby insulate,
> apprentice and certificate,
> God of nations at thy feet
> in our bonus bonds we meet
> lest we forget lest we forget
> one thousand hours of cut and set . . .

The girl at the window listened and smiled and then she turned to the knitting-machine by the window and began to play it as if from a 90 per cent worsted, 10 per cent acrylic score. I could see the light falling on her hands as they moved to and fro, to and fro in a leisurely saraband of fair-isle. Then the beggar appeared. He was carrying a sack that had torn and was leaking insulation, faster and faster, until it became a blizzard, vermiculite falling like snow, endlessly, burying everything, the trees and their shed leaves, the cottage, the beggar, the prince, and the princess of the thousand hours.

The next morning I found the leaflet and telephoned the number on it.

'I'd like to be insulated,' I said.

The man was clearly delighted.

'I'll come at once and measure.'

We both knew we were playing a game, he trying to sell what he didn't possess, and I imagining I could ever install it, to deaden the world. All the same, he measured the house and he put in the loose-fill insulation, and following the Stratford custom, although it was summer, I ordered my firewood against that other 'drear-nighted' winter.

Uncollected Stories

Lolly-Legs

Lemmy Wheen lived mostly in two places, the railway station and the wharf, and nearly every day he could be seen going from one place to the other, sometimes walking slowly with his head down and his hands clasped behind his back; other times with his head out like a duck and his hands flapping, racing against the train while all the little boys on the street cried out, 'Go it Lemmy! Go it Lemmy!' Yet no matter how hard Lemmy went it the train always won. But why should he race the train? Why should he do anything? What did he think about? No one really knew for Lemmy could not speak. He made strange noises that were not speech, only a kind of singing cry. He was not all there, folks said, his mouth was made funny, he could hear all right, and at times he knew what you said to him, but he wasn't all there, and that was why he lived on a pension already, a boy of twenty-five who would never come out as anything, only hang around the railway station watching the train and picking up the empty bottles; or on the wharf lording it like an admiral whenever the dirty orange and black wheat boats were docked in.

Lemmy's third place to live was his Aunt Cora's house, two-storied, with venetian blinds. Lemmy's bed was there and his toy ships and trains in his bedroom. And every morning his plain, wholesome breakfast, at midday his lunch, and evening his dinner. And there was Aunt Cora, fading and restless, her hair covered with a bright flowery scarf to hide the curling pins. 'For people will look over the gate, Lemmy, and see me and think I'm an old hag who curls her hair. And I'm not, am I?'

Lemmy wouldn't answer, of course. Sometimes he would smile as if he understood, a big wide grin that his deformed mouth changed to a sneer one moment later. His mouth would not keep still, but twitched in a continual torment of near-speech.

And Aunt Cora would continue her favourite topic of Aunt Cora. 'Let the people look over the gate. I've a home of my own, two-storied. I've a radio of my own, carpets, all paid for. I've a wicker rocking chair, too, and although wicker rocking chairs are out of date they're nice to rock in. And I've given shelter to a homeless child. Lemmy, people keep talking about your going on the station and the wharf all the time, be a good boy and stay with your toy trains and boats at home.'

And Lemmy would listen with his fingers pressed against his lips and his eyes staring in a vacant way. Then he would laugh and give a wailing kind of cry like the cry a swamp hen makes out of the mist in the early morning; and then he would be off down to the station for the train.

'The train will depart in two minutes' time. All seated, please!' It is no use to grab a black shining monster and hold on to it. The people kiss and wave and climb in and the train is gone. Then begins Lemmy's real work. A moment ago the train had blocked sight of the sea. Now in the foreground there is a glittering blue and green strip of sea like light on a screen. And the seagulls have come to play at being people. They swoop noisy and querulous to the platform where the broken and sodden bits of fruit cake lie half sunken in muddy yellow saucer lakes of tea. They pick eagerly at odd floating peninsulas of crust attached to a mainland of ham or egg sandwich. Lemmy's as busy as the gulls. He grabs the necks of lemonade and ginger ale bottles and rushes to the refreshment room for threepence a bottle. He gathers the cups for the waitress, who gives him in return a plate of left-over sandwiches. Lemmy's as busy as a clock and then suddenly everything's over and there's nothing to be on the station for and the seagulls fly back to the beach. The keeper of the sandwiches seems tired and irritable. She slops up wet tea from one of the clean tablecloths and tells Lemmy Wheen to clear off in the name of heaven and stop being a nuisance. She signals with her hands. Lemmy understands but cannot speak his understanding. He sets out for the wharf. There is no train to race, so he wanders along blinking at the sun and the cars and the few people. He's like a ship that has called at a port to load cargo and finding the wrong cargo or the port closed must journey elsewhere, perhaps miles and miles, to a new place, the wharf and the sea. But all things are journeys, some that never finish, like Lemmy's beginning to speak and saying no words.

It was the not speaking that worried Aunt Cora so much that she resolved one day to do something about it. The not speaking and the wandering around the station and the wharf, why, anything could happen to the boy. After all, she thought, he'll just go on and on, and I'll just go on and on and never have a real life of my own. It's time I had a life of my own. With her home and radio and carpets Aunt Cora had gained practice in ease of possession. Now she had an unshakable though perhaps unwarrantable faith in an easy life of her own, nothing to pay, either, no weekly instalments and forms to sign. Each night now Aunt Cora would look across the table at Lemmy and wonder. Lemmy was so much like his father, Captain Lemmy, who had been drowned at sea. His father was always journeying somewhere back and forth; no wonder the poor lad was fond of trains and boats. But he wasn't right in the head, the poor lad. There's a place for those folk, thought Aunt Cora. They're nice places. He'll learn to be useful and weave and do woodwork. Some of them make baskets. And I certainly must have a life of my own.

So Aunt Cora made arrangements for everything, and one day when Lemmy came from the railway station to home, a port of call before going on to the wharf, he found a tasty lunch on the table. There was a big bun like a wheel snowed under with coconut right in the middle of the table between him and Aunt Cora. With the coconut bun and the teapot and speech separating them Aunt Cora told Lemmy about the new place where he would be going. Why had she worried? Lemmy grinned and made his peculiar bird-like cry, then he reached for a segment of the monstrous circular bun and stuffed it in his mouth. And then calm as noon he ambled to the bedroom while Aunt Cora showed him the new suitcase she had bought for him. She lifted the lid from the deep red emptiness. Sometimes when Lemmy was younger she used to cook something nice and show it to him cooking. She would lift the lid of the saucepan. Lemmy would lick his lips and peep in on something, there was always something there. But the suitcase held nothing and smelt of nothing and there was Aunt Cora standing with her hand on the lid and smoothing proudly and possessively over the soft leather that held nothing to be tasted or taken hold of or looked at. Lemmy turned and picked up the black beret one of the wharfies had given him and Aunt Cora knew he was going to the wharf. How could she stop him? He could look after himself in the traffic or he seemed to be able to, but it was all a terrible tie. But tomorrow by the third bus, no, the eleven-thirty would be better . . .

Aunt Cora went to the wardrobe and prepared to pack

Lemmy's clothes. Everything was ready, really. Let the poor boy have a last look around the wharf.

When Lemmy arrived at the wharf he always hurried first to the edge to look at the sea and the waves that elbowed each other in their continual journeying. The sea departed always, not just in two or three minutes' time. It came in always beating against the kauri piles and then later, quiet and remorseful, licking the deep cracks that gaped like wounds in the side of the aged kauri logs. And then it would break on the rocks at the other side of the wharf, and although the rocks stood up jagged and fierce the salt water did not tear or bleed but stayed whole and shining.

Who knew what Lemmy Wheen thought or dreamed as he watched the sea? He was standing there staring this afternoon when the wharfies passed. There was the captain of the boat, too, in gold braid. 'Hy-ya, Lemmy,' the wharfies cried, 'Hy-ya, Lemmy.'

Lemmy's bird cry broke from him and the captain turned to look. He called one of the wharfies over and questioned him. They stood beside Lemmy and Lemmy listened. Who knows what he heard or understood?

'By jove, that's Lemmy Wheen's son. I sailed with Lemmy Wheen. You couldn't beat Captain Wheen. We used to call him Lolly-Legs. I heard somewhere about his son.'

The wharfie turned to get on with his work but the captain continued talking. The wharfie lit a cigarette. After all, on a day like this, and there's always overtime.

'Yes, we called him Lolly-Legs.' The captain's voice rolled from side to side as if it were on board ship and trying to keep balance. 'He broke his leg once and while it was still in plaster he used to get around with a piece of red stuff tied around it. He looked like one of the peppermint walking sticks you buy.'

He fished in his pocket and held up a peppermint stick. 'I always have one somewhere. Sticky, but it's a quirk of mine to remember Lemmy. If ever a man was a born sailor it was Captain Wheen. Lolly-Legs. But I'd better be off. Don't you believe it, but the cook gets better pay than I do.'

The captain strolled away and the wharfie stubbed out his cigarette and made for the cranes and tarpaulin-covered trucks. Lemmy still looked at the sea. The sky was blue and the water shimmered. There would be dogfish down in the water, little apologies for sharks, and then later at teatime the red cod when the fishing boats snuffed and chugged home around the breakwater. And then the one winking eye of the harbour light would shine.

Lemmy didn't stay to help around that day. He picked up a handful of wheat and stuffed it in his pocket, then dawdled along past the boat, across the railway line. He was going home. There was a wooden ship in his bedroom. He would sail in it. He would sail in it on every sea in the world.

He passed the shop at the corner and looked in the window. There was a fly sitting on a piece of cardboard and beside the cardboard there was a peppermint stick red and white, the sort that the captain had held up to show the wharfie. Lemmy went into the shop and pointed to the stick in the showcase.

The shop girl put down her knitting and came over. She stared at Lemmy.

'Well?'

Lemmy still pointed to the peppermint stick. Then he put on the counter the threepence he had been given for a bottle. He didn't ever go shopping, but he knew the little silver money that could be put down on the counter in exchange for things. The shop girl shook her head. 'It's

not enough. They've gone up,' she said abruptly. 'Anything else you fancy?'

Lemmy let out his strange cry, his mouth twitched and he left the shop and walked slowly up the street. The wheat kept dropping from his pocket until there was a thin gold trail behind him, like the trail of crumbs the story character left so as to find the way back. But in the story the birds flew down and ate the crumbs and there was no way back.

Face Downwards in the Grass

He had not thought about it at all; he had made no preparations. It came to him suddenly as the ten of them walked along the path from the recreation hall. They were tired because it had been a good game of bowls, with a bit of gambling on the sly; and tense because they were going back and it was all over, for one more afternoon anyway, this bowling and knocking upon a stretch of green felt laid out like a false lawn across the floor of the hall, over the white badminton lines and the basketball circle. But this was what the prisoners needed, the authorities said. This was recreation, rehabilitation, and in ten or fifteen years' time when they were free, why they could walk down Queen Street like any honest citizen and no one would guess; they would be accepted into the community — even the killers, like Ivan. He had killed seven years ago, when he was twenty. Even on these outings they watched him carefully, particularly Melville who was his special guard, walking beside him, shouting back some kind of conversation to one of the other guards — Lane. And Ivan, as he walked, had made no preparations at all. They were all walking back quietly.

'Hey, I didn't get what you said,' Lane called out to Melville. Melville glanced at Ivan and slipped to the rear to repeat his words to Lane. He shouted. He was used to shouting. Ivan could hear him.

'I said, don't forget to come. Everyone's expecting you. Everyone. Remember, it's a date.'

Then it came suddenly to Ivan, it came in a flash, the idea of an escape — no, not really an escape, just a run and run and run to a place where everyone would be expecting him, and the doors open, inviting, and people saying, 'Come in, come right in, we're all expecting you.' Melville's words, like a secret message in Ivan's brain, told him to leap from the path into the bushes, and run, and keep on running, not looking back. So he leapt and ran, but softly, and sneaked and could scarcely breathe all the time he struggled through the bushes at the back of the hall. He sobbed as he ran, not the sobbing of grief — it was just the way his imprisoned breath kept bursting from his body, to get free in case the body itself were caught. He heard a shout, and bent low in the bushes. Somebody passed by, running heavily, with no secrecy or delicacy, like a charging pig. But Ivan stepped now, like a deer, very softly and preciously; except for the sobs of breathing; until he stopped, exhausted. He did not know where he was — it must have been in a park or reserve, for there was a lawn and a statue spitting water into a fountain. He crouched in the shrubbery. His bladder emptied itself involuntarily. He breathed more slowly, but he was shaking and the sweat was making his fine civilian clothes stick to his body, and smell; and his sleeve was torn, and his trouser-leg. He sucked the blood from a scratched hand, and blew his nose on his shirt sleeve; and his clothes weren't fine and civilian any more. They were prison clothes, killer clothes. And the words were going over and over in his head: 'Don't forget, everyone's expecting you. You're invited. Everyone's expecting you.'

Then he laughed. He had escaped. Pity on old Melville. And ahaha, three pounds tucked in the toe of his shoe. Even a lifer has to bet and win sometimes, even — what did they call him at the trial — a brutal sex-killer. And too bad for his bowling partner, some scraggy little printer's assistant who didn't even know which way to put the bias.

'Everyone's expecting you.'

He tried to plan; he didn't know the area. Where would he get food, where would he sleep? He was hungry now; he wanted a drink too. How long was it since he had been in a pub, cheese on toast, sausages, fish balls — what was the song:

> The waiter bellowed down the hall
> crying One fish one fish one fish ball;
> The waiter bellowed down the hall
> crying One fish one fish ball.

Christ! He burst into obscene laughter and emptied his bladder once more. He was cooler now, almost shivering with cold. With his torn clothes and bloody hand and frightened eyes, how could he cross a road in front of people, looking careless, self-assured? How did people walk along the street after seven years in prison? What sort of stride did they take? He felt lonely suddenly for the rest of the gang. Walking all together on their outings they would joke and have fun about themselves and not care a fig about the outside world and the snobs in their flash cars. But now it was different. He was alone. Did people smile at each other in the streets now, as they had done seven years ago when he was twenty and the war had not long finished, and the soldiers back and everyone mad and in love and whistling, wolf-calling on every pretty girl, and night after night in the southern city — oh boy! What did people do now? What were people like, ordinary people? Sometimes in his cell at night he would try to remember perhaps the small part of the street he had passed through on a bowls or a table tennis outing; but the memory would not come — the people refused to walk in the street; they stood stiff and stern like the pop-up pictures Melville had shown him. Pity on old Melville. A man needs a hard heart — not a kid's heart. And the dream-street stayed empty always save for the line of prisoners with Melville, Lane and the rest, trudging along, happy, sure, after the sweet little game of bowls with a scraggy Bible class or Temperance Union.

Ivan looked out from his hiding place to see the street. Across the road was a milk bar, then a grocer's shop. It must be a small suburb. He must have run miles. He would buy groceries, and something to drink, before the alarm was all over the city and his picture in the papers, and the john-hops out with revolvers. So he watched the people walking. They just walked ordinarily. Did his eyes look too frightened? What about his torn clothes? He must remember to be casual, even to stop, blow his nose or scratch himself; not to look over his shoulder; take possession of the street.

'Come on, you're welcome. Everyone's expecting you.'

He walked across the road. Not so stiffly, he told himself. Smile. he smiled at the air. He scratched his head, the natural touch.

He walked into the grocer's shop. He gazed at the glittering food and tried to select something with body in it, but he couldn't think. Pickles, ah pickles, frozen strawberries. He was the only man customer. The swarming women turned to stare at him. Aha, he thought to himself, when a man's wife (*what wife*) is away at the maternity home he has to do a bit of shopping, gardening, get grubby, hasn't he?

It was a long time to wait before he was served. He tried to keep calm. More women came into the shop. At last he was confronted by the grocer.

'A pound of ham, please.'

'Lean or medium?'

'Lean — no, medium. A loaf of bread.'

'Wholemeal, bermaline, or the special rye and barley.

Then we have the wrapped bread, a penny dearer.'

'Oh, ordinary bread. White.'

'Very well, sir. Anything else?'

He knew he would have to go. They were staring at him, at the blood on his hand. But what about a drink?

'Oh, a drink, a large bottle of orange — the kiddies you know. Open it please and stick the top on.'

The grocer's manner changed. This young chap was a family man. Kiddies and their orange drink. The grocer's own wife was expecting her third child any time now, and he prayed heaven she would not be overdue. What husbands had to go through! Last time . . .

The grocer smiled at Ivan. It was the first real civilian smile for a long time. He did not say, 'Come on over, everyone's expecting you,' but he found a small bag and dropped two sweets into it, one shaped like a toy aeroplane and the other like a pig; and he twisted the frail white bag and gave it to Ivan.

'For the kids,' he said.

He was a family grocer, not yet of the food-market kind with their silver rail to keep grocer and customer apart. Ivan paid for the food and received his parcels. The women glanced at him as he went out. He looks thin, they thought protectively. Thin and over-anxious, and dark circles under his eyes.

By now he had grown confident. He would get on a bus and go towards the bush area on the outskirts of the city. It was the only place he knew. So he climbed on a bus — just a family man taking home the groceries — and left it at the end of a street, just before the track to the bush. There he saw the evening paper stacked outside a milk bar. A photo of him already. How did they do it? He saw the words: Killer, sex-crazed killer. He ran then. The visit to the grocer's was a dream he had walked in, but woken with food in his hand

and a bottle of drink. The orange slopped over as he ran. He put it to his lips and drank some, but his breath choked. He coughed. The fear was there all over again, and the dream gone, and he must run. So he ran and struggled and crawled on and on through the bush, and did not stop till he heard nothing about him but silence and a small creek trickling. He drank from it. And lay down in the fern. And he slept, even without eating his food, and the orange drink spilled and soaked, *Bottled Sunlight*, over his shirt. And he dreamed it was morning and he was back there, sitting in his cell, scooping his porridge into his mouth. He was happy. The day was planned. There was no need to hide. But the porridge bowl was a strange shape, like a heart, and it glittered with little blue stones — they might have been sapphires, set about the edges; and red ones, like rubies, in between, and all like the brooch the woman had worn on her left breast, seven years ago. So he cried and threw the bowl from him, and the porridge spilled, but the bowl did not break. And his cell became a cage with great orange bars bent about it, like ribs, and the bowl dancing up and down glittering against the bars of the cage, but not breaking. Then Melville was there, and the dream finished, and Ivan woke shivering, his heart beating fast. It was dark and cold. The orange drink was all spilled. He chewed at the ham and bread and swallowed the little pig and aeroplane. Then he slept again and did not dream, and woke suddenly to daylight and the sound of voices and shouts. They were after him.

'You are invited, everyone's expecting you.'

And the next day and all the next night and the day and the night after were spent scrambling though bushes and hedges and hiding in grass, and not once a drink of tea, and the food all finished. He knew he would have to face people again and buy food with the money he had left. Funny, he had not thought of stealing it — he who was a thief. And, he smiled bitterly to himself, he had not even killed anyone. A killer at large. He was so tired and hungry and sleepy; but sleep would be dangerous, like lying in a bed of snow. So the morning of the third day, with the words still in his ears —

'Come on over. Everyone's expecting you' — What strange words, how could he ever walk up the path to all those houses and face the door, and knock, and have the door spring open to receive him, and be face to face with people and the world again? It was all a mad dream.

So the morning of the third day, exhausted, he crept through the grass on the side of the road. A little girl passed him. He stood up.

'Good morning,' he said. 'How are you today?'

She did not speak. She looked afraid. Her mother had warned her about a convict, a killer man with a knife in his hand. He watched the little girl going on her way to school. He felt numb and sick. There was still money left. He would go across the road and buy something to eat and drink. He began walking when he saw them approaching. Someone had spied him. Someone had peeped from behind the venetian blinds and fawn looped curtains of their home, and seen him, and not opened the door, but hurried to the telephone and phoned the police; and then dialled a neighbour to talk about it.

'And it's him, I know it's him. I've phoned the police. He looks just as they say he is, a vicious sex-killer. Heaven knows what he's done while he's been at large. The prison authorities will get the rap for this. Bowls indeed. But it's him. Thank God we can breathe again. The police are on their way now.'

The police came. They were armed. They flourished revolvers and batons. Ivan looked over at the house with the shut door, and sank down in the grass. They found him, unresisting, lying face downwards in the grass.

A Boy's Will

All the wild summer holidays Peter was angry. The rain came down heavily almost every day but it was not the rain that angered, it was people — family, visitors, neighbours — who moved judging, complaining in their subtropical sweat and steam with their damp skin clinging to the new plastic-covered chairs in the sitting room and their voices tired and their eyes puzzled when they looked at him, as if they did not understand; and then he grew puzzled too for he did not know what they were trying to understand.

He wanted to be left alone. His fourteen years belonged to him like trophies. He sensed that this, his fifteenth year, would be so much prized by himself and others that he would need to fight to preserve it for himself. Everyone had suddenly become intensely interested, seeming to want to share him and explore him. In the first week of the holidays when in answer to his mother's question, 'Where have you been?' he said,
    'Nowhere,'
    his Aunt Lily who had come to stay began to chant with an inexplicable triumph in her thick country throat,

> Where have you been?
> *Nowhere.*
> What did you do?
> *Nothing.*

'It's begun, Cara,' she said softly. She was standing by

the telephone pressing her hand gently upon the cradle, circling her index finger on the black polished curves.

'It's begun, Cara.'

Her hand quivered as she spoke.

What did she mean by her chant? 'Nowhere, nothing, no one'?

Why did everyone know so much about him? About his future too, what he would become, where he would live, how he would feel in his most secret self?

His aunt had said,

'In a few years Cara, he'll want to break away. You can see the signs already.'

His mother replied,

'As I've told you, Lily, it's a scientific career for him. With his IQ.'

His IQ was high. He'd heard them say it was so high it couldn't be marked. His mother had said in tones of awe as if she had been describing an elusive beast instead of his intelligence, that it was so high it had 'gone off the page', while Aunt Lily had replied in a sour dry voice,

'These tests are not as reliable as they were once thought to be.'

Then his Aunt Lily sighed as if she wanted something that would never be given to her and though he possessed skates, a transistor, a half-share with his brother Paul in a dinghy and there were few things he wanted desperately, he identified the feeling Aunt Lily had and he felt sorry for her with her hairy chin and her footballer's legs. When she came to stay everyone always told her, 'You're one of the family, Lil, you're one of the family,' but it was said so often that nobody seemed to believe it any more and she was really not one of the family, she laughed too loudly and her clothes were funny and she was just a woman living by herself in a room, in Wellington: in a room, not even in a house. It was when she came to stay that Peter's mother talked about him and Paul and their young sister Emily, describing what they had said or done, how from the every first he'd shown signs of exceptional intelligence, how he'd skipped classes at school, had learned to play the piano and was now on to Chopin Waltzes and Beethoven's Moonlight Sonata.

When Aunt Lily arrived Peter had to play all his music to her.

'Play the Beethoven,' his mother said, closing her eyes and humming, De-De-De, De-De-De, De-De-De . . .

'Now the Minute Waltz again, Peter. (He does this well because it ties in with his mathematics.)'

Peter felt his fingers moving stiffly. He'd been shirking his practice. His aunt murmured in her sour dry voice,

'He's good technically but he thumps.'

He heard his mother's quick intake of breath and her protective,

'He hasn't always thumped. He hasn't been practising. You should have heard him —'

and his aunt's cold reply,

'Anyone really interested in music practises all the time.'

His mother sighed then.

'There are so many demands placed on him, with his intelligence . . .'

He played his pieces too, when a family friend arrived by plane from America, and though the friend had been flying all night and his eyes were dark with wanting to sleep he sat on one of the new plastic-covered chairs listening to the messy blurr of notes made by Peter's unpractised fingers.

The expression masked on his face he said calmly,

'That's all right.'

Peter saw his mother frown, searching the remark for the comforting word 'brilliant'. Not finding it, she looked lonely and Peter, turning and seeing her face and knowing what she wanted, felt miserable. He finished in a hurried swallow of notes banging the final chords down like a window sash and taking the kid's toy, an American police car the visitor had given him, he escaped through the kitchen and downstairs to the garage where, his misery giving way to anger, he leapt up and down on the lid of an apple box until it snapped beneath him, sharply, satisfyingly.

Auckland this summer was a factory of storms. Lightning, thunder, rain swept from West to East, Tasman to Pacific, rolling big smoke-white clouds like a bushfire in the sky with tongues of lightning darting and stabbing and the thunder exploding and more rain like sheets of aluminium falling. Peter dealt with each storm by recording it, calculating, experimenting. He collected and measured the rain in his rain-gauge, he read his barometer, his maximum and minimum thermometer, and then after such close disciplined reading he spent hours reading the sky, in agreeable free translation. His teacher had written on his School Report, 'What has happened to Peter's reading? Must read more.' Peter had not explained that he suddenly found clouds more interesting than words. Clouds, light, heat, sound. On their Christmas trip around the East Coast in the family car he carried his barometer like a book on his lap, reading it.

'He'll be a meteorologist,' his mother said, almost destroying his new passion with the weight of her tomorrow.

He made a sundial too and set it on one of the fence

posts but there had been so much rain and so little sun that its apple-box surface was sodden. Only once or twice at the beginning of the holidays he had been able to read the time by the shadow but now, when the holidays were nearly over, that time seemed so long ago, a time when he had not been angry, when his anger did not seize him so completely that he threw things or slapped his young sister, prompting his mother's cry,

'Peter, stop bullying. Remember your fourteen to her eleven. Be your age.'

His brother Paul, two years older, had a job for the holidays and would let no one forget that he earned five pounds a week and was grown up. He was studying photography, too, and spent his spare time shut in the downstairs bathroom with a sheet of cardboard over the window and the slit under the door sealed with newspaper, developing and enlarging films. With his savings and his earnings he'd bought himself an enlarger, all the James Bond paperbacks, two books of science fiction, a bottle of Cedar Wood pre-electric shave lotion, and he'd had his trousers tapered. One Saturday early in the holidays he'd gone with Peter for a train ride to Swanson where they sat in the Domain sheltering under the macrocarpa trees, licking ice-creams, jelly-tipped on sticks, and reading comics bought at the railway book stall. It rained, they came home early, and on the way home Paul made it clear that he hadn't gone out with Peter for the day, that he'd *taken* Peter, and as they loitered up the drive, preparing answers to embarrassing questions they might be asked, Paul said, 'I'll never go anywhere with you again. You act like a kid.'

Now, in the weekends, Paul went to the pictures with a girlfriend and Peter saw little of him except when they watched television.

There had been a fuss about that too. His Aunt Lily nearly died when she saw the new television set. She had cried out as if she were in danger.

'What about the children? For their sake . . .'

Peter's mother flushed.

'Ted and I made the decision. It's easy for you as you've no children —'

Aunt Lily nodded meekly.

'I just hoped,' she said quietly, 'that it wouldn't draw the children too much.'

Draw? Once when he had a boil on his neck his mother had put a poultice on it, as she said, to 'draw' it. She had burned the poultice in the oil drum at the back of the section.

Certainly they watched television at first. They enjoyed the easy programmes, those with the laughs, and escaped when the serious news appeared showing jungle warfare, poverty, disease, famine. But that, too, had been at the beginning of the holidays before Peter began to get angry. Now he seldom watched except for the programme starring the cowboy who gambled. Peter knew all the poker terms. 'I'll raise you,' he'd say coolly to an imaginary opponent. He'd seen a programme, too, about the chances of a fly settling on a certain lump of sugar and he'd worked out the probability and had even snared Paul's interest in this, though what was the use when all their windows and doors had insect screens and flies never landed on the sugar?

It was just before he began to make his kite that he heard his mother saying to Aunt Lily,

'Do you notice how impatient he's getting? His intelligence will be no use if he has no patience. Paul is the one who perseveres. Paul will go far.'

'You mean he's the plodding type?'

Peter saw his mother's shocked face as she absorbed all that plodding implied. Oh, no, her children were bright, quick, surely they would never plod.

'I think *persevere* is the word. Peter will find life hard if he has no patience. He's grown so quick-tempered!'

Peter pulled a face to himself. Who did they think they were to try to live his life for him?

'This interest in the weather. It could be permanent. I rang up the Department —'

He heard his aunt's manuka-stick voice,

'The experts now say . . .'

He did not wait to hear what the experts now said. He escaped from the top of the stairs down to the garage and ten minutes later Emily came upstairs crying.

'Peter thumped me!'

Peter sat on an upturned apple box in the garage. He could imagine his mother's exclamation,

'Thumped you!'

And her tender admonition afterwards,

'Peter you must be kind to your little sister. Boys must be gentle with girls.'

How could he explain that the thumping had been Emily's fault? They'd all watched a programme on television the night before where there was an old woman, so old and tired that she had to be moved from her little house to be put among the old people, and the film showed her arriving with the few belongings she'd been allowed to bring with her, and one was a photograph of herself as a young girl, and just when she was deciding where to hang it in her new bedroom, a big nurse in a white fly-away hat had rushed into the room, admired the photograph, said the woman had not grown a day older, then she'd seized the photograph and the old woman stood looking unhappy and lonely with her arms dangling and her hands empty. But that had been last night on television. Now, this morning, Emily had taken an open page of Peter's *Boy's Book of Outdoor Hobbies* and drawn a picture of the old woman clinging to her treasure while the nurse tried to take it from her. Peter had no quarrel with Emily's drawing. The programme had frightened him, too, for old age was part of tomorrow and tomorrow was like one of those tools that clamped down and screwed tight, permanently fixing everything beneath it. But Emily had drawn the picture where she shouldn't have, over the diagram of the kite that Peter planned to make, and surely a thump was small punishment for such a crime?

The *Boy's Book of Outdoor Hobbies* was one of the few consolations Peter had during the holidays. He had worked carefully through it, making the sundial, the wind gauge, other interesting items not connected with the weather. He had skipped the chapter on Photography and Radio for these were Paul's interests and it was better, at this stage, to know nothing about them than to try to compete with Paul's accurate detailed knowledge. With an elder brother in the family it was a case of the younger taking the leftovers or perishing in the comparisons that would follow.

'When Paul takes photographs he —'

'Paul knows how to fix the TV when it breaks down —'

Peter had decided, therefore, as his next project, to make a box kite.

He rubbed angrily at the pencilled lines of the old woman and the photograph and the wicked nurse. Emily ought to have known better. The figures quite covered his diagram and measurements. And even if he managed to decipher them and make his kite would the weather be clear for kite-flying? Rain steamed in the sky, the leaves of the big subtropical flowers grew glossy, their stems grew tall, the bush on the hills had a milky green appearance as if rain and milk had fallen together from the sky.

Peter found paste, bamboo sticks, string, a roll of blue and white crepe paper left over from someone's attempt at fancy dress, and forgetting about Emily and the old woman and thumping and the weather and his future he began to make his kite.

Just then he heard his mother and aunt coming downstairs.

'In this gap between showers I'll show you the passion fruit growing by Emily's playhouse.'

His mother looked into the garage.

'What are you doing, Peter? Oh, making a kite.'

She turned apologetically to Aunt Lily.

'I suppose it's a childish thing for him to make. For all his intelligence he's young for his age.'

'All normal boys like kites,' Aunt Lily said smoothly.

They crossed the lawn to the playhouse where Emily, with the innocent gaze of one who has been thumped and avenged, peeped out at them.

'Aren't they big? It will be ages before they ripen. I've always wanted to grow passion fruit.'

'I love passion fruit.'

They were coming back across the lawn. Peter's mother seized the opportunity to scold him for his treatment of Emily.

'We can't have these rages, Peter.'

He heard her saying with sadness in her voice as they climbed the stairs,

'Though he has always played the piano best when he's been angry. I'm sorry he's giving it up. Ted's sorry too. I don't know what's come over the boy these holidays. There was a drop in his schoolwork, too, at the end of last year. The teacher remarked on it. He doesn't seem to have the patience.'

'You have to have patience,' Aunt Lily said, snapping shut the insect-screen door.

It took Peter several hours to make his kite. He knew he was perhaps the only boy in the street making a kite; he knew also that as soon as it was launched everyone would be flying kites and no doubt some would break the rules, flying theirs in forbidden places like the street where entanglement in the wires would cause electrocution and death. Peter had been warned. There was not much his mother and his father and his teachers had not warned him about. When he thought of his kite as an instrument of death he began to breathe quickly and his hands grew cold and he could not believe that anything so beautiful could help to destroy. It was a box kite, blue and white, as light as a bird's wing on bamboo-stick bones. None of the other boys in the street would make a box kite; theirs would be the usual kind, flat, a skeleton cross of sticks fleshed with brown paper or plastic with a sharp nose and tail and though it would fly the flight would be a plunging swooping movement as if it were not at home in the sky and longed to descend to earth whereas the box kite, Peter knew, would float and drift without panic or restlessness, like a cloud. To Peter, the clouds that passed overhead during all the wild stormy rainy holidays had been unlike any others he had known; or perhaps his feeling for them had changed. In a mysterious way they seemed to contain promises of a wall or a window opening beyond into the light. Sometimes in the evening the sun setting in secret appeared to grow so full of light that it could not contain itself and burst through, suddenly, thrusting like a shaft through the big soft clouds down, down into the earth. Watching, Peter knew a feeling of strength, of himself powered by light, of a discovery that he could not understand or control. He felt after closely reading, translating the sky day after day night after night (the 'holiday reading' *Under The Greenwood Tree*, *Great Expectations*, lay unopened on his bookshelf) that the clouds in their lightness would offer no resistance when the time came for the moment, *his* moment, to burst through. Without being able to articulate his dream he thought that the moment might come when he flew his blue and white box kite.

When that evening he drew aside the curtains in the sitting room he could not suppress his joy when he saw the clear bright sky.

'Ooh Mum, it'll be fine tomorrow. Isn't the sky lovely?' he called. He frowned when he heard her comment.

'Come and look at the sky everyone. Peter says come and look at the sky.'

And her loudly whispered aside to his father.

'It's the poet in him, Ted. Peter's discovered the wonders of Nature.'

Peter felt the rage growing in him. It was *his* sky, *his* sky, *his* light, *his* clouds. He had impulsively let others intrude to claim them.

Before the whole family could surge about the drawn curtain he swung it back across the window.

'It's gone now,' he said sullenly.

'Will you fly your new kite tomorrow?' his mother asked, and turning to his father said proudly,

'Peter made such a beautiful kite today. Not the ordinary sort of kite, either.'

And then turning to Aunt Lily,

'He's clever with his hands as well.'

Peter decided then that he would not make an event of the flight. If the next day were fine he would sneak out, launch the kite, fly it to his satisfaction, then come home without any of the family knowing what had happened. At the back of the house there was a playground as big as two paddocks where the Catholic children played games and where during the holidays the grass had grown as tall as wheat and had browned without sun as everyone's skin, too, had turned brown in the humid sunless weather. Day by day the rain lashed the grass and the strong winds rippled it and the cloud-shapes twisted across it in plaited shadows. It was an ideal place to fly a kite. Peter dreamed of it as he lay in bed. He would run through the grass with his kite flying behind and above him. He would not feel any more the irritating rage and impatience that kept overwhelming him for there would be nothing to rage over, then, flying his kite, with his face looking up at the clouds and the sky that swung like a vast ship's deck under the surge of the sky's waves. He could almost feel that he might be standing in the sky, sailing through it, steering his path on a voyage of discovery.

The day was fine, the sky clear except for cottontails of cloud and rather more wind than Peter had hoped for. He did not hurry to get up. He sneaked a plate of Weet-Bix from the kitchen to his bedroom, ate most of it, then lay waiting for Paul and his father to go to work and for Emily to go about her recent domestic craze of making clothes for her teenage doll. Then, when Peter was sure the coast was clear he made ready his kite, but his plans for secrecy were destroyed when he met his mother by the kitchen door. She was standing, waiting, while the washing eddied in its white machine. Did all mothers know how to destroy in such subtle ways? Surely she too had not been thinking all night of whether today would be fine for kite-flying? Surely mothers had other things to think of besides their children and their abilities, their intelligence, and what the future held for them in such proud frightening store?

'A nice day to fly your kite, Peter.'

He grunted. Then remembering his manners, he said,

'I think I'll try it in the Catholic playground.'

'Good!' His mother said, seeming to think, but not saying, that once he had flown his kite he might go on to activities more suited to his intelligence. Her eyes as she looked at him were heavy as if his future lay inside them like a dark stone.

He climbed through the fence and ran into the playground. The kite obeyed at a touch, stumbled in a jaggling way, at first, over the long grass until it caught and was caught by the passing wind when it began to float like a feather then to turn and swim lightly like a fish in buoyant air, while Peter ran, his feet and legs soaked in the long wet grass, the grass-seeds like clusters of shot stinging his knees; feeling the kitestring as if, tied to himself, it were part of his own body. He knew a pleasurable feeling at once of lightness and of anchorage, as if his fast-running legs were tangled forever in the twisted stems of grass while another part of himself was floating lightly up near the shredded white clouds; then suddenly he found himself out of breath, with running and flying, and he was sobbing with his eyes full of stinging tears, and he stopped running and stood still while the kite jerked and laboured above him, no longer flying with freedom and grace. He felt the tears falling down his face. He was aghast at his weeping but he could not stop it, and all the while he clung fast to the kitestring feeling the weight like that of a restless wing upon his arm. It was then that a stronger gust of wind came buffeting, gashing the fragile blue and white crepe paper body, and as the kite drifted down the blue and white paper trailed behind it like shreds of skin. It fell a few yards from where Peter was standing. For a moment he stood still. Then slowly he wound the string and calmly picked up the broken kite. He felt no rage at its breaking. He carried it over the playground, through the gap in the back fence and was crossing the lawn when his mother, hanging out the washing, saw him and cried out, her face full of sympathy,

'Oh Peter, your lovely kite! What happened to it?'

'The wind was too strong.'

'What a shame!'

His mother spoke into the white flapping sheets. He knew that when she went upstairs she would say to Aunt Lily who would be reading her share of the morning paper,

'Peter's kite is broken, his lovely kite!'

Perhaps she might also say,

'More tantrums, I suppose. That boy. For all his intelligence, that boy . . .'

That boy. He was that boy. He was intelligent. He had been in the Silver class at Intermediate and his brother, for all his photography and repairing of radios, had been in the Bronze, and his sister — well, sisters were not the same.

That boy.

Immune, he went to the garage. He understood now what the television preachers meant when they insisted the skies had opened. He believed them. He saw his mother with a stone in her eyes and a bone in her throat. Stone and bone were his future and she could never remove them nor perhaps would he want her to. He did not want her to grow old, to go to an institution and have her treasure snatched from her. He felt suddenly protective towards her. He looked at her standing passively on the lawn while the flying sheets and towels slapped at her face and he felt a surge inside him as if he still anchored the blue and white kite and the kite itself flew on towards the hidden sun.

'Now keep your temper, Peter. Just because your kite's broken don't go throwing things around or interfering with Emily's playhouse!'

Shrugging his shoulders as he'd seen his father do, Peter laid the kite gently on the garage floor. Then taking the remaining whole pieces of crepe paper he began patiently to renew and repair the broken body.

They Never Looked Back

When Tom and Deanna had been living together for three years, people said of them as they say of those with problems solved, illness cured, 'They've never looked back.'

They said the same a few years later when Tom and Deanna, believing neither in marriage nor in work for gain, were married in a friend's herb garden, and went up north to work on a small farm they'd once seen and remembered. They found the farm had been demolished, the land cut up in ten-acre sections, but there was another where they did find work, Tom as rouseabout, Deanna as cook, and where their eighty-year-old farm cottage was the joy and envy of their city friends who dropped in exclaiming with delight at the coal range complete with flue and damper and polished brass clothes rack, the water pumped from an unpolluted deep well, the old wash-house with its copper and copper fire and the antique washboard on which Deanna used to rub the nappies and towels. She even draped the sheets over the manuka bushes. The word 'pioneer', having been in their childhood a dirty word, had become clean and fashionable once again. Tom and Deanna used it often to describe their way of life.

They were happy up north. They made their own clothes and furnishings, grew and ate their own vegetables and fruit. It was only when Deanna was expecting their second baby that they thought it would be better to move to the city to be near the National Women's Hospital. Back in Auckland once more, in Ponsonby (room, kitchen, share bath), Tom found a job making sandwiches and filling rolls in a downtown coffee bar. With his hands busy, he thought, his mind would be freed to work on the television play he almost had in mind. Unfortunately as the soft filling seeped into the sandwiches, so the work seeped into the part of Tom's mind which should have been impermeable, and the nascent television play was suffocated, while others, conceived, lost the health of a whole dream and fell apart.

Life was tough that year. The rent was more than they could afford. Although Imogen was born whole and perfect, little Cordelia developed a stomach upset which, the doctor hinted, might be caused by a congenital malformation of the intestine. This was too terrible to think about. Tom and Deanna blamed the city life, the rat race, the everlasting fumes. They heard of a bach for sale, cheap, by the sea, and a lawn mowing round, also cheap, in the neighbourhood, and drawing all their savings from the bank where they had pretended to themselves they had nothing, as they didn't believe in bank accounts, they went up north again, by the sea, to a three-roomed fibrolite bach that had kick holes in the walls and paspalum tide-marks along the side where the garden had been, and pieces of rusty iron, and old motor tyres lying in the clusters of purple-headed silky grass that grew in deeper depth and greener green over the burying places of the old dunny. Scraggy mynahs, curious, perched on the dunny and cried Whaa Whaa Whaa; and huge black-backed gulls tramped about like workmen on the roof.
'Just the place for us,' Tom said.
Deanna agreed.
They never looked back.
Most of their new neighbours were retired, spending the days that at last belonged exclusively to them, trying to improve the appearance and comfort of their house and land, adding a terrace here, a flamingo there, a rose-arch,

an orchid house, a new fence, new furniture, new rooms. Carriers and concrete contractors with their revolving grey-bellied mixers were forever arriving, unloading, turning awkwardly half on the road, half on the footpath; sometimes a small heap of concrete blocks would appear overnight as if a new kind of mammoth had passed by; or a bulldozer would be discovered in a den in a clump of manuka, or parked in a driveway lying in wait for the performance of a new trick of landscaping. How busy the people were, who had said goodbye to work!

'It's not our way of life,' Tom and Deanna said. 'But they ARE human.' And when one of the neighbours brought them hot lentil soup the week of their arrival they said, how kind, how human.

'This is the place to be. I can feel it,' Tom said.

'I can feel it too.'

'And we've never lived by the sea before. We can get to know it.' They could see it from their living room, and on stormy nights they could hear the waves seeming to lap against the walls of the house.

'I can take the children on the beach. I can tell them about the sea,' Deanna said.

What fulfilment and riches their new life promised! Even the depressing thought and the frustrating actuality of the lawn mowing round were vanquished by the old optimistic knowledge that nothing from without could destroy the inner resources.

'I still have my mind,' Tom said. 'And I'm my own boss. After all, Jim Baxter once worked as a postman.'

'Yes, I believe he did.'

'Look at the work he managed to do! Traipsing up and down half the day, dogs at his ankles. And look at the poems he wrote. If Jim Baxter could do it, I can.'

They were talking together, as they often did of an

evening, when the children were in bed and the future invited itself to share the hearth that was symbolic only, as the bach had been a summer place, without fires. Tom's remark about Jim Baxter had the effect of silencing them. Tom felt ashamed of his boldness. But did he not have talent? Did not Deanna, and many of their friends, have faith in his talent? He'd read almost every worthwhile modern book, poetry and prose and many of the classics, and he could talk literature with anyone, he could quote, name names, criticise intelligently. Surely, now they were here by the sea, he had his chance!

'Yes, if Jim Baxter could do it, I can.'

Deanna frowned.

'It's good we have a hero, don't you think, in our own country? That our generation are proud to claim possession of a person rather than a thing? Everybody owns Jim Baxter. Everybody has a story about him — you know — he said this to me, to me alone, he said that, he read this poem, that poem, I was the first person to hear it. If you were in his company you had to breathe and he had to breathe and he breathed poetry.'

'They say.' Tom felt a little as if he were being robbed. After all, they were talking about HIM, THEM, their future.

'It is good,' Deanna said, 'that we have someone to admire. I think my mother was taken over by Hollywood. I know that my grandmother had Aunt Daisy for a heroine. "Christmas cake (Doctor's wife)." And Mabel Howard with her bloomers (XXOS).'

'And what about you?' Tom asked.

'Oh, I have you.'

So it was all right then.

How happy they were in the bach. Once more they grew and ate their own vegetables and fruit, and Deanna knitted for the children and sewed dresses on an antique sewing machine, and the children learned to love the sea, and Deanna told them of its treasures, and the fish. And insect-time came, and the manuka scrub was thick with praying mantises and crickets and grasshoppers and cicada; and stick insects walked up and down the fibrolite walls of the bach, and the wetas came inside after the subtropical downpours — the world was full of life, and noise, with the busily retired people hammering and sawing and clipping back the alarming growth of their gardens; and the newly married couples in their newly built homes on their newly bought sections, they too hammering and sawing and mowing; and the summer sun like a golden fog stifling the breath; and the seasons passing; and winter, with a velvet light filling the royal purple sky.

One day a neighbour phoned.

'We've caught so many fish. Would you like some?'

How kind, how human, Deanna thought.

They'd had fish before from the same neighbour. Snapper or trevalli so neatly prepared, wrapped in waxed paper, on a pretty blue plate which Deanna immediately washed and returned, Oh you must have it back at once, it's so pretty.

'I'll leave them in the box at the gate,' the neighbour said.

Later when Deanna went to the gate she found in the milk box two gaping-eyed dead fish, curled to fit into the box; like corpses. She shuddered. Then plucking up courage she took them against her breast, cradling them, as this was the only way of carrying them, and when she reached the kitchen she dropped them on the sink bench, shuddered again, and set to work to clean them. In no time, she told herself, she'd have fish fillets ready for cooking.

She'd forgotten however, that fish had blood. She'd had a vague idea that 'cold-blooded' meant having no blood.

'Only whales and porpoises, the warm-blooded mammals, suckle their young.' The sentence came, half remembered, to her, out of a natural history book she had bought for the children: Fish and the Sea: Man and his first home.

It seemed that the blood escaped almost before she touched the fish. Swiftly she sawed off the head as she could not bear the gaping eyes, and now finding she had nowhere to grasp the fish she pegged them with a clothes peg to the rim of the plastic basin, and trying to remember and copy the calm action of her father who always cleaned fish so neatly and swiftly, she began to slit the belly, first of one, then of the other, and the red and blue and black curds of guts spilled out into the basin and with them (giggles, they used to call the guts) came the fish smell that bore no relation to the white-salt deodorising sea. The smell filled the small kitchen, the big brown blowflies that haunted the septic tank outside began to drone at the back door, knocking on the thin hardboard panels, their bodies sounding heavy, insistent. Deanna felt sick. A feeling of panic came over her. Her hands were bloodied, the guts stuck to her skin, the scales too, like those flat white seeds of the plant honesty that she and her friends used in 'dried arrangements'; and the more she tried to get rid of the scales and the smell the more the presence of the fish invaded her and the room. A blowfly, surging in through a gap in one of the louvre windows, knocked against her check. She gave a small scream. Cordelia, playing in the sitting room, cried out, Mummy, Mummy. She had been nervous lately. Her stomach. They would have to take her to the specialist in Auckland. Perhaps they'd have to move back to Auckland. What if there was really something wrong, a congenital malformation? There couldn't be, and yet if there was, they'd have to face it. People faced things like that every day. Yet it seemed not to have any relation to their life, the stone-ground flour and the 'oven-baked' bread, the natural wool cardigans, the television plays that Tom would be writing soon, the sea and its wonders so close to them. Deanna thought, had she and Tom tried too hard just to LIVE? Should they have let their life flow over them, like the tide? The way they lived was the only way they felt they could be happy, yet why did they feel, at the same time, as if they were being watched over, judged, that they had to be strictly against or for? Their world was full of domestic enemies (I'm against white flour, she had found herself saying one day, with rage in her voice). Yet one had to declare oneself, to take a stand. Yet a stand meant boundaries, and they were against boundaries.

Cordelia's crying became louder.

'It's all right,' Deanna called. 'Mummy's here.'

Having finally managed to sculp a reasonable likeness to fish fillets from the almost intractable bulk of blood and slime, Deanna gathered the remains in a bucket and quickly went outside and emptied them on the compost heap. I'll bury them later, she thought.

Cordelia was still crying.

Deanna hastily washed her hands and went to the living room. Imogen was awake now, and also crying. She lifted Imogen from her crib. She had a sick feeling of failure and shallowness that she could not explain and longed to be rid of. She gave the now hysterical Cordelia a sharp slap, and at once felt remorse, and tears came to her eyes. She felt that she hated herself and the children and Tom with his lawn mowing round and the television plays he dreamed of writing because the NZBC were 'crying out for television plays'; and the way their life seemed to belong to other people rather than to themselves — yet how could that be? It's that stupid fish, Deanna thought. Why didn't the neighbours prepare it? They've always cleaned it before now. The milk box will smell, too. They just dumped the fish there as if they were getting rid of bodies.

By evening all was well again. Deanna had bathed herself and the children, and had changed to a special screen-printed dress that she knew Tom admired. The evening was calm, the tide was in, right up over the mudflats and the sand, and the sea was scarcely moving, with only a lapping of waves at the rim of the shore and elsewhere still, in a grey-green film over itself. There was a faint sweet smell of salt and manuka flowers and honeysuckle from the last bach but one, near the water.

Tom, tired and hungry, noticed Deanna's dress.

'You're wearing your screen-printed.'

'Yes,' Deanna said, as if she herself were surprised to be wearing it. 'I've almost made the tea.'

She went to the kitchen where two pieces of fish were set on a large plate above a saucepan of already boiling water. Hastily she turned the pages of *Aunt Daisy's Cookery Book*, stopping at the page headed, 'Invalid Cookery'. 'Steamed Fish. Scale, clean and bone. Set between two buttered plates . . .'

The instructions were soothing. Carefully Deanna buttered another plate and set it above the first, then she went to the living room to talk to Tom about his work and his day and her day and their proposed new life in Auckland. For Cordelia's sake. In no time they'd be back up north again. By the sea. Or on a farm. They were young, they had inner resources. They talked until midnight while their future, always the invited but invisible guest, sat with them, and such was their excitement at the prospect of it that they would never have noticed if, wanting to satisfy its hunger, it helped itself to the remains of the fish fillets lying on the plate in the kitchen.

Two Widowers

'I'm making the trip,' he said, 'because my wife died three months ago and they advised me to get away for a change, to go to the Old Country. But I wish I'd never left Australia. As soon as the ship docks at Southampton I'm coming home.'

He talked to me every morning. He talked about his wife and the leg operation that had killed her.

'It was successful yet three weeks later she was dead.'

'King George the Sixth had the same trouble,' I said.

'Fancy your knowing that! My doctor told me about it. He said, King George the Sixth had the same trouble and not even the best surgeons could save him. That helped, you know. Having something in common with the King. My doctor knew it would. But she was so well, and then one morning there she was, unconscious.'

'Perhaps,' I murmured, choosing from the array of commonplaces, 'perhaps it's better that she died.'

'Yes. She might have been crippled for life. A blood clot. Only three years ago she had the first illness of her life. *Literally*. A stomach operation.'

Lifting the flap of his shirt and baring his stomach he drew his straightened finger, like a knife, across his skin.

'Twenty-four inches of good stomach cut open.'

His voice became loud, protesting: 'Twenty-four inches of good stomach!'

I could see that his love for his wife had been mixed with practical economy and a hint of animal husbandry.

Then he spoke quietly, confidentially, leaning towards me: 'I'll never marry again. Some do. My friends said:

"Marry again." But I'll never marry again. Smoking and drinking is all the women do these days. My wife looked after me. Chose everything. Had taste. Chose this shirt I'm wearing. See?'

He pinched at the sleeve and held it for me to examine.

'Just my colour.'

I agreed.

'Knew what colours to choose.'

He had dispensed with the personal pronoun and was speaking telegraphically. 'Was a business woman, too. Had a little dress shop. Knew how to manage money.'

I thought he seemed as if he were making or measuring a new distance which ordinary leisurely sentences could not traverse and which, indeed, would soon be beyond the reach even of telegrams.

'I'm well off, you know. I don't spend my time in the bar drinking and smoking. My home's a nice little flat. I haven't sold up everything like some of these.'

He looked around the empty deck imagining it, I suppose, as it would be later in the morning, crowded with the emigrant families whose torment was known to everyone. They had sold everything. They were returning to Europe. They were restless, apprehensive, the young uprooted from their adopted country and the only language they knew, the old, with no home anywhere apart from a desperate tonguehold in the native language that not even their children understood.

'Yes, "sell out", they said to me, "Go and live away from the memories. Start a new life." My son wanted me to live with him and his family in Brisbane. But why should I? I've got everything at home. Hi-fi, too. And a second TV in the bedroom. If I were home now I'd make my tea — scrambled egg — none of your wine for me, then I'd go to bed and watch a programme. Educational. Great company. My wife had nothing against it. She was getting on so well. They said there was a risk with the operation but until three years ago she'd never had a day's illness. *Literally.'*

Having telegraphed his bereavement to wherever it might be received he had returned briefly to speaking in the third person. My wife. She.

As more people came on deck for the day his emotional focus widened and I could hear him, from time to time, explaining himself to others: 'I'm a widower you know. My wife has been dead three months. They said it was a good idea to go on a sea voyage, visit the Old Country.'

He was pale. He had lost weight or acquired an inner formlessness which made his clothes hang loosely on his body and which, for all his professed pride in his appearance, gave him the general untidiness of someone depressed and, for the time being, not quite at home with himself or those around him. Day after day, I, and others, were embarrassed to hear the 'twenty-four inches of good stomach' protest voiced in anger at the wastefulness of good material misused and at the revealed imperfections of his wife and her final unforgivable imperfection of dying. He acted like a man who had been cheated, and I saw him in the coffee shop carefully counting his change and inspecting his coffee for faults.

He behaved also like someone who had been in great danger and must in future exercise caution, so that once he had found himself a routine on board ship he made it his ally, a kind of extra force with a hint of superstition, to control and shape the dishevelled elsewheres of his day.

Everyone knew about his daily goal of a required number of turns of the deck. He was not alone in this. Others for various reasons were trapped in the compulsion, for after all when the ground has given way to water beneath your feet you have to find some framework. He was determinedly honest in his walking. He never skirted the part by the stairs but walked right up to the bulkhead and even touched it to make sure.

When he'd completed his number of turns he came to talk to me, always beginning with: 'How are you today?' And when I smiled my seasick smile he would give me his advice.

'Get up and walk around the deck. It's the answer, you know.' He was offering me advice, the medicine which others had offered him as being 'the answer' and which he was finding unpalatable.

'Yes, take a walk on deck. There are games you can play, too. I wouldn't go near the bar. They're rotten in there. That was one thing about my wife. She neither smoked nor drank. Yet we enjoyed ourselves. She was always full of surprises. Liked to surprise me. Would have a present tucked away as if it were my birthday. Liked to go away on her own, too. Liked to visit her mother and our son.'

He was sending further telegrams from the supply he had inherited on his wife's death. Some day, I thought, he would find there were no more telegrams and then he would come back into the personally pronounced world.

Now there was another passenger, an elderly man, who appeared to be alone. He too was untidy and as he did not mention a wife (on board ship where almost everyone's tongue behaved like the ocean in constant ebb and flow) it was assumed that he, too, was a widower. The rumour that his wife was ill, confined to their cabin was belied by his apparent aloneness and air of loss.

On his third day at sea he bought two modern marvels — a watch, waterproof, shockproof, antimagnetic, etc; and one of those transistor radios the size of a small suitcase with all possible wave-bands, a slot for cassettes, a portable microphone, playback at several speeds, impressive dials, indicators, aerials that could be telescoped and twirled. The watch and the radio became the old man's constant companions. He took them everywhere, he showed them to everyone, and one morning when he was leaning over the ship's rail trying to get decent reception on his radio, away from what people called 'the ship's interference', and the Australian was making his required number of rounds of the deck, the two met.

Together they tried to listen to the radio. Together they walked the deck. Later, they sat side by side in their deck chairs drinking their beef tea and talking. Two widowers. The two were so obviously untidy and depressed and bereaved, so much that they embarrassed, with the fraying edges of their lives, many of the oh so neatly hemmed passengers, and there was general relief when the two found each other. Their common ground or wave was their widowerhood.

Some said the old man was a distinguished scholar, that he could speak several languages and he read foreign books from the library. The Australian, they said, was a retired electrician, which fact caused some surprise, for in the sweeping stereotype of international waters, Australians are thought to be 'rangy cattlemen or sheep farmers'.

For the rest of the journey across the Pacific the two were inseparable. The tale of the twenty-four inches of stomach was no longer given public recital. The Australian gradually lost his air of dishevelment while the old man no longer slept half the day with his mouth open and his belly poking out between his shirt and shorts and his arm cradling the transistor radio. Both acquired the grooming of friendship, for, make no mistake, when people feel themselves to be within the human race they have a way of grooming one another invisibly, as birds do visibly, and animals, lions in their pride.

And now when the ship stopped at a way port the two went ashore, tourists together, and returned with their new T-shirts and Panama hats and sandals. They began to take part in the ship's games: quoits, shuffleboard, deck tennis. Soon the new tide of belonging closed over them, submerging, merging them with the other passengers, and their status as 'the two widowers' was seemingly forgotten.

Then one day when the ship was about to dock at Ponta Del Garda I saw the old man standing by the purser's desk checking a number of suitcases. He turned to speak to a tall pale woman whom I'd not seen before. They linked arms.

He saw me and beckoned. 'This is my wife, Ella. She's been ill, confined to the cabin.'

'Oh,' I said, 'I'm sorry. Are you disembarking here?'

'Yes. About time too,' the old man said. 'We grew very tired of that long journey across the Pacific, didn't we dear?'

I hoped that I wasn't staring too closely at them. He no longer appeared widowed. There was no sign of his cherished watch and radio, still less of his Australian companion. Perhaps his widowed state had been an effect of the voyage, for after all, if the sea can work miracles of cure can it not also work miracles of kill? I wondered.

And then I saw the Australian coming up to the desk. He stopped abruptly, seeing the two. I saw him glance once, then again, and a third time, as if to make sure that it was indeed his friend of so many days, his Pacific friend — the Pacific Ocean had driven many of the passengers to a kind of madness — then he looked again at his friend's wife. Surely, I thought, he must have known she existed. I saw the familiar, prim, 'neither smoked nor drank' expression come on his face, transparently over a fleeting hurt and betrayal. He stared again at the two and did not speak. I saw him turn and walk up the stairs, holding fast to the stair-rail.

The next morning when we were once again full steam ahead and the Australian had completed his turns of the deck, he sat down beside me.

'You know,' he said, 'I think I'll make a go of the Old Country after all. An awful waste of money to go straight home again. I've joined this club, I joined it this morning. They take you to your hotel in London, they look after you.

'Might go to the Continent in the Spring. Might even see the Swiss Alps. Be glad to get home though.'

He was sending telegrams to himself now, about himself. Then, having proclaimed the urgency of his own life, he returned to ordinary speech, setting his dead wife at last beyond the reach of the carefully measured distance of dream-telegram.

'My wife would want it this way,' he said. 'My wife would want me to enjoy myself.'

Janet Frame was born in Dunedin in 1924. She was the author of twelve novels, four collections of stories, two volumes of poetry, a children's book and a three-volumed autobiography. She was a Burns Scholar, a Katherine Mansfield Fellow, a Sargeson Fellow, and won numerous awards, including the Commonwealth Writers' Prize for Best Book, the Hubert Church Award for Prose, the New Zealand Book Awards for both fiction and non-fiction (each one twice) and two Wattie Book of the Year awards. She was made a CBE in 1983 for services to literature, awarded an honorary doctorate of literature from The University of Otago in 1978, and one from The University of Waikato in 1992. Additionally, she was an honorary foreign member of the American Academy of Arts and Letters. She received New Zealand's highest civil honour in 1990 when she was made a Member of the Order of New Zealand. In 2003 she was among inaugural recipients of a Prime Minister's Award for Literary Achievement and was named an Arts Foundation of New Zealand Icon Artist. Janet Frame died in January 2004.